BRENT J. LUDWIG

THOSE WHO WOULD BE KING

THE
PEOPLE'S PRINCE

RIVER GROVE
BOOKS

Published by River Grove Books
Austin, TX
www.rivergrovebooks.com

Distributed by River Grove Books

Design and composition by Greenleaf Book Group
Cover design by Greenleaf Book Group
Cover images used under licence from Shutterstock.com

Publisher's Cataloging-in-Publication data is available.

Paperback ISBN: 978-1-966629-72-6

Hardcover ISBN: 979-8-88645-063-7

eBook ISBN: 979-8-88645-064-4

First Edition

PROLOGUE

Maleziland, Central Africa, May 1990

The condensation from the doctor's fifth double scotch on the rocks formed intersecting circles on the polished mahogany bar. Though many aficionados would disdain the use of ice in so fine a liquor, the doctor didn't need to add to the already turgid heat and humidity with the fire of the rare beverage. Ice moderated the burn and made his objective of rapidly ingesting copious amounts that much more attainable. The middle-aged man's tolerance for drink was slight. He hadn't consumed more than one alcoholic beverage in a sitting in over a dozen years. But this day in the life of Dr. Nkota Kabanga was far from normal. The gods had signed his death warrant.

A lustrous, high-gloss, long-case grandfather clock, said to have been made by the ancient British timepiece master Francis Perigal, stood stoically on watch from the corner of the lounge. No one remembered when it last worked, not even Freddie, who, since getting the bartending job as a boy thirty-five years ago, had not missed so much as an hour's work, though he did take a half day off for his maman's funeral. Whether the clock no longer functioned, or whether it simply had not been wound, the fact that it did not keep time seemed appropriate in a locale where people's daily lives were only loosely structured upon the earth's rotations as it trekked around the sun.

Other than Freddie, the doctor was the only Black man in the bar. Typically, the sole patrons of so lofty an establishment, located in the finest hotel in the country, the venerable Marlowe, were White tourists. Their currencies, rocks of stability when compared to an average daily 100 percent inflation, stretched a long, long way. Dr. Kabanga didn't consider himself a run-of-the-mill doctor, though, in a land where physicians fared little better than their patients, economically. King Mabanda appointed Dr. Kabanga as the royal physician ten years ago, and the good doctor had served this role faithfully and diligently until this very day.

Dr. Kabanga slumped as he swirled the remaining liquid in his glass. Although his professional life was outwardly a resounding success, his personal life was roiling in turmoil. Most of his every waking hour was given to the service of his master, King Mabanda, now benevolent life leader of all Maleziland. The good doctor had long put second his family, friends, and all personal pleasures and pursuits to the service of his king. Initially, it had been easy. As the king's personal physician, Nkota enjoyed wealth, comfort, and respect beyond the wildest dreams of ordinary Malezilanders. His family had grown and prospered under the regime whose health he so carefully oversaw. He adored his son and daughter, aged seven and nine, as he did his newest family addition—a bit of a surprise—a little girl who was nearing nine months of age.

But today, thoughts of the family he loved were blurred as the effects of the alcohol set in. Nkota was getting drunk. Shitfaced. Blotto. He drank with purpose. His objective was rapidly being achieved, and only now, on double scotch number six, did the tension begin to ease from the furrowed brows and rigid jaw muscles that, just one hour ago, had felt etched into his face like chisel marks on Mount Rushmore.

He felt his pager vibrate furiously, but Dr. Kabanga, on call 24/7/365, refused to be roused from his scotch-hazed trance by its urgent pulse.

His head resting on the glass-like wooden bar top, Dr. Kabanga foggily reminisced about the beginnings of the regime he now so faithfully served.

Colonial Central Africa. 1966. Long, long before the loyal doctor's service for the regime. The colonial oppressors, the French, had finally succumbed to "natural evolution," the rallying cry of the downtrodden, and begrudgingly granted independence to the country of Maleziland. The word *natural* was a nod to Black men like Nkota who had ruled their own domain for fifteen thousand plus years. *Evolution?* The doctor thought perhaps it should have been "devolution." However, "evolution" was chosen to represent the return of equality, enfranchisement, and freedom to the land's original peoples.

Nkota remembered the feeling of excitement during those heady, idealistic days. The country's first free election—and its last—was held, ironically, on July 4, 1966. The victor was mostly self-declared, as the democratically elected house had thirteen parties, of which the largest party, the Pan-African Peoples' Front, held but nine seats. The leader of the party was none other than Aseyo Mabanda, the father of the current king of Maleziland.

Hundreds of thousands of countrymen had donned their finest garb in a spontaneous street celebration that stretched election "day" from twenty-four to forty-eight hours. Young Nkota had never witnessed a more vibrant, joyous sight, as his countrymen and women, reveling in the streets, donned their finest clothing in honor of the great event. Love, passion, excitement, and joy resounded through Maleziland for the days and weeks and months that followed.

If only his people had the ability to see into the future, even a few short years, to understand the course of action upon which they were setting their little country. Once elected, Aseyo Mabanda never relinquished power. Now his son and heir lived on as the omnipotent ruler of Maleziland.

Yet the king's servant Nkota would surely die. He knew this full well.

As a doctor, Nkota had watched AIDS transform from an affliction of only men who had sex with other men to the scourge of modern-day Africa. It was surely a bigger threat to the survival of her peoples than any man-made or god-made threat or pestilence in history. Over the years, he'd seen patients affected by the ticking Time Bomb of Death that now lurked potentially behind every coquettish glance and betwixt the legs of every lover, male or female.

Dr. Kabanga didn't know how he himself had contracted the disease. It didn't much matter now.

His pager continued to pulse. Nkota's thoughts, typically focused solely upon serving the king, blurrily drifted elsewhere.

CHAPTER 1

Maleziland, South Central Africa, Winter 2004

The dining hall was exponentially larger than any room Mateyo had ever seen before, yet it was by no means the largest room in the royal palace. He was sitting at one end of a table almost as long as a football field. An ornate, gold bohemian crystal chandelier, fully six meters tall and six meters wide, hung from the ceiling over the center of the table. As he sat, bewildered, a team of palace servants began removing each piece of crystal, cleaning it to a clear and dust-free luster.

Although Mateyo had been waiting for twenty-five minutes, he was hardly alone; no fewer than four servants were there to tend to his needs. He had no idea why so many were required, nor was he used to being waited upon. He sat silently, trying his best to take in his surroundings without his quest being discovered by the staff.

A lanky wisp of a man wearing a black suit and spotless white gloves strode to the far end of the hall, whereupon he opened wide double doors that Mateyo guessed were over seven meters tall and made of solid ebony. The king loomed malevolently in the doorway.

The cavernous entry should have dwarfed King Mabanda, as he was rather short and unimpressive physically; however, his presence was larger than life to every soul in Maleziland, godlike in both power and authority.

Mateyo tried to repress a quiver and failed. The king took his seat at the far end of the table without saying a word, but not unassisted. All four servants had vanished from Mateyo's side and had, apparition-like, reappeared next to the king, where one was holding back his chair as a second placed a huge, pristine white linen napkin on his lap.

The silence in the room remained unbroken as two full teams of waitstaff appeared, resplendent in black uniforms and crisp, heavily starched white shirts. One team attended to the king, while the other focused on Mateyo. They carried enormous silver trays with a half-dozen silver domes upon them. Mateyo had never seen anything like them before. A tiny, balding man of seemingly advanced age silently and efficiently placed a dome on the table in front of Mateyo. With practiced but unspoken coordination, each of the domes was simultaneously removed with a flourish.

Mateyo's eyes widened as he stared at the plate upon which a mountain of snails awaited their gastronomic fate. He managed to control his instinctive impulse to swat the mollusks off the fine, almost translucent plate in front of him, but he wasn't successfully able to mask his revulsion. When he realized that the escargots were intended for his stomach, the already roiling bile began to rise to meet its snaily challenge. No, they would have to shoot him first, which they might, but that end was preferable to Death by Snails. At the other end of the table, the king grunted with pleasure as he loudly slurped down the nasty little creatures.

Mateyo stared blankly downward at his offensive plate. Only four short hours ago, he had been playing Bwana, a checkers-like game using dried beans, squatting on the dusty and filth-ridden street in front of his home, when a motorcade roared up, sending both villagers and beans scattering. Much to Mateyo's utter shock, the two jeeps and a polished, large black Range Rover stopped in front of Mateyo's dilapidated shanty. Mateyo knew this meant trouble, as only powerful, dangerous men traveled in this fashion. Mateyo rose and squinted into the dark-tinted rear window as a silhouetted man pointed at him. Immediately, armed military men leapt from the jeeps and surrounded Mateyo, yet none laid a finger upon him.

The largest man in the detail boomed out an order to Mateyo. "Come," he'd simply said.

Even though no weapons had yet been drawn, Mateyo and the small-but-growing crowd of onlookers knew the soldiers wouldn't hesitate to draw and fire their semiautomatic Glock 43s with only the slightest provocation. Mateyo nodded and started toward the back of one of the jeeps but was gruffly redirected toward the rear seat of the Range Rover, whose open door awaited them. He had scarcely recovered from that shock when he noticed his elder brother, Shigeku, sitting in the roomy, plush cabin of the car. A guard sat beside him with a loaded Glock pointed at his brother's head. Mateyo hadn't seen his brother for over half a year; clearly, though, Shigeku had sold him out.

For the entire journey, Mateyo tried to meet his brother's eyes, but Shigeku stared straight ahead, his escort's firearm continuously trained between his eyes. Perhaps the guards did not view him as a threat, thought Mateyo, as no weapon was pointed at his own forehead. Mateyo cringed at every bump, jump, and lurch along the road. Not a word was spoken between the brothers. Shigeku had betrayed him, dooming Mateyo to certain death. Yet what value did his life or death possibly have to these men?

The Range Rover finally stopped in an alleyway. Mateyo was led from the car and through a large wrought iron gate in an impossibly high wall. He didn't resist, but he almost needed to be dragged, as he felt drained of all strength and ability to propel himself of his own accord. He wondered where his brother was being taken as the Range Rover roared away. In pitch-black darkness, the men hauled him into what appeared to be an enormous edifice and down narrow, dark corridors, barely wide enough for one man to travel. They exited the corridor into blindingly brilliant lights only briefly, and finally led him through a grand doorway and deposited him onto the floor of the most amazing room Mateyo had ever seen.

Every square centimeter of the floor was covered in a cream-colored stone, smoother and more polished than anything Mateyo had ever known. He had never even eaten off anything so shiny and so clean, let alone walked on anything like it, and of doing that he was afraid lest he should soil it. But he got to his feet and took a few steps, noting the furs and skins of the rarest and most protected of Africa's great beasts—lion, giraffe, leopard—adorning a sitting area at the far end of the room, defined by towering, perfectly clear, unblemished glass windows.

In the center of the room rested the largest bed imaginable to young Mateyo, with each of its four posts looking as if it had been hewn from one of the Maleziland's greatest trees, each hand-carved to replicate the stalk of a baobab.

Mateyo hadn't even noticed the solemn, silent man—dressed in a black uniform with a gleaming white shirt—quietly standing beside the doorway through which he had come. Much to his surprise, this man began to strip him of his soiled and disheveled clothing. Again he did not protest. Mateyo was led, naked, through a doorway to the right of the grand bed. It took him the better part of a minute to realize that the room into which he had been led was an ornate washing room of sorts. He was then directed to enter some sort of stall and told to clean himself. Looking around, he saw water taps but no spout. He frowned and twisted both knobs aggressively. Water immediately burst from an aperture in the ceiling, and Mateyo jumped backward like a springbok avoiding the jaws of a crocodile at a watering hole, slamming into the hard, slippery wall.

Mateyo was even more confounded when, after a few short seconds, the water became warm. Mateyo had heard of taps and running water. He had even seen a few such devices, but heated running water? *This is crazy!* He fiddled with the taps until the water ran cold, and his stress level subsided as he enjoyed the water cascading down over his body. He stayed in there for a good forty-five minutes, primarily because he was afraid of what was going to happen to him next.

When he stepped out of the stall, a young woman, again dressed in black and white and not much older than him, handed him pure white, thick towels. Mateyo had never seen anything like them before. When the servant girl started to rub him with the plush fabric from head to toe, silently and oblivious to his nakedness, he again didn't object.

Mateyo's bathroom attendant instructed him to follow into a changing room filled with hundreds of bare wooden hangers and myriad empty shelves and drawers. A single colorful robe of the finest material hung on its own. Without looking up at him, the servant girl whispered, "Put this on."

Mateyo gasped as he recognized the red, green, and black pattern of the royal family of Maleziland. It was absolutely forbidden for anybody else to wear it. Surely this was part of his death sentence, and he would be mocked, tried, and convicted for daring to don the ornate garment. Trembling, he went along with the ruse and placed his arms in the sleeves of the robe.

The girl didn't leave his side until he was dressed, and she then led him back into the bedroom. No words were spoken. *How appropriate for a condemned man.* The girl motioned for him to sit, and he did in the middle of the floor, cross-legged, as far away as possible from any bed, furniture, or fur.

Left alone in the colossal room, Mateyo wondered why Shigeku had sold him out, to whom, and for what price. And why on earth, if Shigeku had sold him out to the royal family, did the guards have a gun pointed to his head? Mateyo had long known of Shigeku's intense hatred of Maleziland's ruling family. Mateyo also suspected that his brother had crossed the border to the neighboring country of Zambwana, whose regime longed to overthrow the Malezi royal family. All Malezis knew of the Zambwanan plan to "liberate and unite" the two countries whose tribal people had spanned both sides of their common border since the end of the Second World War.

After minutes—or perhaps hours—the same older gentlemen had opened the bedroom's massive door and gestured for Mateyo to follow, and he'd been led through dark, narrow corridors to where he now sat.

"You have the right to know why you have been brought here," boomed the king in his unmistakable and mellifluous voice from the opposite end of the table.

Mateyo jerked his head up from his reverie.

"Were you an ordinary street dog, you would have no such right to know anything about your king's affairs. But, it appears, you are not a street dog. You are the crown prince of Maleziland . . . my son."

At that, Mateyo's vision went dark.

CHAPTER 2

Maleziland, Central Africa, May 1990

"My son." Shigeku's mother, Shileza, forced the words between heavy, breath-laden moans. "I need your help if I am to live."

Shigeku knew Maman was getting older, by Maleziland's standards—at the age of thirty-four, she was soon to birth her fifth child—but he, of course, didn't think she was going to die.

The eleven-year-old boy had never known his mother to experience any difficulty in childbirth before now, including with a set of twins. In fact, he knew that all but one of his siblings had arrived at home or in the fields, and his brother, who had indeed been born in a hospital, had only been afforded that rare privilege because the babe decided to enter the great big world while Shileza was delivering produce on the stoop of the hospital's commissary.

Shigeku knew that his family was poor, but the villages in which much of Maleziland's population lived, not more than slums by Western standards, were all he had ever known. Fresh water was drawn from a well that had been hewn from the mud and rock years ago by some charitable relief agency, though the water it produced was murky and brown.

His home was made from red mud bricks, with a grass thatch roof that was mostly leakproof. Nevertheless, Shigeku loved his home and was, in fact, very proud of it. It afforded basic protection from sun and rain, but it had no sewage, electrical, or wireless service. Each such home in his village was similarly constructed, as wood was a scarcity in a country with so little forest. Shigeku and other villagers relied on wood and charcoal to cook and provide warmth. The fact that Shigeku could discern no true roadways seemed normal to him. Shigeku knew of only a handful of shanties wherein fewer than ten souls resided.

Shigeku recognized a different sort of pain in his mother's eyes. Not the "ordinary" pain of childbirth, which he had seen many times before, and from which she had nothing to fear. He could sense there was something mortally wrong within the deep recesses of her womb.

Maman lifted her head weakly from the bare straw mattress on which she was lying prostrate and in obvious agony. "Shigeku, I need to speak with you," she stated, her voice barely a whisper.

He nodded and leaned near her. Obedience came naturally to the children. Obedience was, in fact, a base survival instinct, for in a large family with no protector and no principal earner, life itself depended on working together, caring for the young ones, and quickly and cohesively moving as one out of harm's way.

"I am soon to leave this world," said Maman.

Shigeku nodded slightly, awaiting his mother's next instructions.

"As you know, when a mother dies in childbirth, her soul passes to her newborn child; it does not matter what the sex of the child might be. As your maman, I have always tried to do my best for you and your brothers and sisters. I need you to make this promise to me. Promise me that you'll always look after this soon-to-be-born child. Treat it as if it were your own child. Do for it what you don't think is possible. Sacrifice of yourself whatever you must for this child, for in so doing you're giving back of yourself to me."

Wide-eyed, Shigeku nodded almost imperceptibly, then ran from the shanty out into the streets.

Shigeku's mind raced, far faster than he could run. He was absolutely terrified of death, and the thought of the burden being thrust upon him by his maman made him break into a cold sweat. He knew that the only way he could avoid this oath was to save his maman's life.

He swiftly sprinted one thousand meters down the road to Kamazo's hut, praying that his friend with the rickshaw was there and that the transportation device was in working order. Shigeku knew that "broken" was not an unusual state of repair for the rickshaw, his friend's sole source of income and most prized possession. Kamazo was resting languidly on his doorstep but snapped to high alert on seeing Shigeku running urgently at full speed toward him.

"Kamazo, we must run with your rickshaw back to my shanty," Shigeku yelled. "Maman must go to the missionary hospital! She is in terrible pain—the baby is coming—and she thinks she is dying!"

Kamazo followed Shigeku, the rickshaw careening emptily behind them, with both of them spanning the distance at a pace that taxed but did not overcome their fragile physiques. They passed by roadside piles of tomatoes, collard greens, stacks of wood, and live chickens strung up by their necks—the "shops" of the shantytown. People who would have ordinarily crowded the road gave way, sensing the urgency behind the pace of the boys.

Maman was unconscious and breathing shallowly. It seemed that blood was everywhere, even caking up as it flowed from between Maman's legs and poured from the mattress onto the dirt mud floor. Neither Shigeku nor Kamazo had ever seen so much blood before, which was quite interesting considering that death and injury were not uncommon. Maman was a large woman, and they used every ounce and fiber of strength to drag her, as best they could, from the mattress, across the blood-addled dirt floor, out the doorless entryway, and onto the rickshaw, which groaned audibly as they hoisted first one, then the other leg onto its carrying platform. With a perfectly timed heave, they loaded her onto the crude wagon.

Shigeku struggled mightily in his frantic effort to share the burden that his friend more easily hauled. The paths they traveled between the shanties did not make for easy progress, and even once they made it to the main road, they were slowed by enormous upward and downward heaves in the dirt thoroughfare. Livestock—primarily goats and chickens—darted in front of them. Shigeku was quite certain that at least one smallish goat got caught betwixt the wheels of their careening cart, but neither boy slowed their pace in the slightest. The owner would come to them later to collect a debt owed if indeed the goat had been killed.

When they dropped the bars of the rickshaw to the ground with an exhausted thud in front of the hospital steps, Shigeku leaned his head upon his maman's chest, which no longer rose with each breath. She was gone.

Despite Maman's considerable girth, her stomach heaved and pitched, and Shigeku knew that the baby was still alive, as its life-and-death struggle manifested before the boys' eyes. Two nuns emerged from the hospital and ran down the crude front steps. Shigeku watched their faces grow sullen with grave concern, and they quickly barked out orders in perfect French. Almost immediately, two huge orderlies appeared, whereupon they quickly hoisted Maman's cadaver onto an emergency trolley bed and whisked her into the hospital. Shigeku quietly slipped into the hospital behind them, unnoticed. He held out little hope for the entombed babe. He quickly bade his dead mother farewell and quietly turned to leave.

⚬ ◆ ⚬

King Mabanda thought his third wife, Carolanda, was by far the most beautiful of his current five, even in the final throes of her first maternity cycle. Tall, fair-skinned, and fine featured, rumor was that she was forged of mixed blood; however, the king had convinced himself this wasn't true, as he would never have deigned to marry the progeny of their long-banished former overlords. Mabanda paced back and forth nervously. He felt deep in his dark soul that this childbirth was more important to him than the first six of his children. Of course, none of Mabanda's wives had ever knowingly dared deny him anything, but unfortunately for each of them and for Mabanda himself, none had ever borne him an heir—a male heir. Mabanda was acutely aware that only a male heir could inherit his line and eventually become king.

His first wife had proved eager to bear him the desired male heir but had been barren, and his second birthed only females. *Useless.* His third wife, Carolanda, had promised him a boy and had even offered to take her own life by suicide if she should fail. The king thought this a reasonable bargain. To see her writhing now, the king indeed believed the good Lord would deliver on that promise and that it was indeed a boy fighting its way into the world through her yet untested birth canal.

"Makiko, you useless dung beetle," shouted the king at his trembling chief of staff. "Where in the name of God is that other piece of excrement, Kabanga?"

Makiko's repeated attempts to raise the doctor had proved futile.

Mabanda glared toward his chief of staff, cowering in the corner of the room. *Pathetic piece of shit.* A dung beetle, in fact, had more utility on the planet. King Mabanda's father, Aseyo, had taught him carefully and well how to hold on to the reins of power. Show no mercy, let none survive in exile, tolerate no interference. Demonstrate to all that you are *dangerous.*

Mabanda paced back and forth, scowling malevolently and audibly muttering obscene curses as he waited for the royal physician to respond. He somehow *knew*, deep within the recesses of his dark heart, that an heir to his throne resided within Carolanda's womb, and he needed this child to survive. Of course, the royal surgical suite had modern ultrasound technology to determine the child's gender in advance of its birth, but Mabanda knew that using such modern means could anger the gods and thwart his dreams of having an heir.

Every other palace attendant, save Makiko—and Mabanda insisted that there were forty of them on duty at any given point in time, day or night, seven days a week—had long since disappeared from the room. His foul mood must have driven the fools away. His negative energy, though invisible, was unmistakably deadly.

Mabanda watched intently as Makiko frantically continued to try to raise Dr. Kabanga. *Idiot!* thought Mabanda. He was tempted to put a bullet between Makiko's eyes, a fitting reward for his ineptitude, but he did not want attempts to raise Dr. Kabanga to abate even for a second. With a barely suppressed chortle, he pleasantly recalled at least half a dozen staffers whose existence he snuffed out this year, often for less heinous ineptitude than Makiko was demonstrating. It did make him smile to himself to be above the law—indeed to *be* the law.

Mabanda narrowed his eyes and pointed at the trembling Makiko. He knew that Chief of Staff Makiko was a nervous man by nature, and in this circumstance, it was obvious to the king that Makiko feared he had little chance to escape the strongman's wrath to prolong his life. Makiko cringed and visibly shook at the knees when he heard his name bellowed from across the room.

"If you cannot procure that gutter dog who thinks he's a doctor within five minutes, I'll cut off both of your cocks and have them rammed up each other's assholes before you bleed to death."

The king stopped pacing. Perhaps it wouldn't be so bad. He didn't really care if Queen Carolanda died or not, though he would miss her unusual beauty and her seemingly insatiable zeal for wild, physical sex. But even that particularly strong quality could be otherwise bought or replaced.

"Your Exalted Highness," Makiko blurted nervously, using one of the contracted but formal forms of Mabanda's official title.

The king would rather everyone refer to him fully as the "Exalted, Most Noble, and Honorable God-Anointed Highness King Mabanda," but he let the annoyance go.

"It is my belief as your chief of staff that delaying your departure for the missionary hospital will gravely jeopardize the life of your wife and that of the child that she bears. We must plug our noses, stifle our senses of smell, and cast aside our mistrust of the foreign institution and head there at once. The hospital may be our only chance. Sire, forgive my brash insolence, but if we delay further, the future of your lineage may be at risk."

King Mabanda snapped out of his furious rage long enough to understand that Makiko spoke the truth. They would have to depart for the hospital immediately. It was the only way to save his heir.

"Make it so," he barked.

Instantaneously, bodies mobilized throughout the palace. Valets rushed into the king's dressing room, bodyguards with heavy armament stationed themselves outside to the vehicles in the escort detail, and drivers started their vehicles to ensure that the AC had sufficiently cooled them to make them drivable. Within minutes, the king, Queen Carolanda, and Makiko were all loaded into the royal limousine, one of a dozen such vehicles. Despite the real urgency of this particular mission, the king suppressed a smile at the power he wielded. He always traveled in this style, and the general populace would know no difference, as the royal motorcades screamed through the countryside with the same urgency each and every time they hit the streets.

King Mabanda *hated* the missionary hospital. Of course, missionary hospitals had existed in Africa for hundreds of years, doling out medical aid with heaping doses of religion. There was little he could do to control them or shut them down, and he knew—but hardly cared—that they provided a valuable philanthropic service to his subjects. It bothered him deeply to think that his heir was about to be born in a hospital that was, by Western standards, little more than a triage station on a battlefield.

The king's motorcade careened to a halt in front of the hospital. The king could see no emergency entrance, nor was there a formal admitting process. Nevertheless, the crowds properly parted before the king, giving way without question or protest. The autocratically enforced "natural order" meant that everyone knew their place, especially in the path of their king and his chosen ones. The chaos within the center was evident to the king, and it further heightened his angst.

"Fucking overeducated lab rats, get your asses over here NOW!" boomed the king as he strode out of the limo, forgetting to assist his heavily breathing wife as she exited the vehicle. The doctors, all Western-trained and properly accredited, left the patients they were tending to and rushed immediately to the assistance of Queen Carolanda. Hippocratic Oath notwithstanding, there were pragmatic realities associated with the "privilege" of being permitted to practice their profession and save lives and souls in the heart of Africa.

Despite the king's sense of nervousness, it turned out that Queen Carolanda's birthing process was advanced but far from mortal. The doctors assured Mabanda that she was young and strong, and she had led a life of relative health, prosperity, and privilege. Her labor was not unlike several thousand witnessed by the hospital in the decades before. Having been assured by the team that there would be no complications, the king exhaled and relaxed, quite oblivious to Carolanda's mounting screams of pain and birth-related terror. A snap of a finger directed toward one of his impeccably dressed attendants brought a solid gold, perfectly chilled flask of thirty-year-old Highland Park single malt scotch. The king eased into a comfortable lounging chair that somehow had been procured for him and watched contentedly as Carolanda sired a healthy baby boy. The king sprung from his chair as the babe was appropriately delivered. *Fucking disgusting*, he thought, fully revolted by the vernix-covered, squirming child.

"Take my son, you fools, and clean him up so I can hold your future king!" Mabanda barked. He watched and grinned as two of the doctors scurried away like dung beetles. The good doctors seemed quite thankful for the opportunity to get out of his line of fire. And this pleased Mabanda greatly.

Shigeku shook in the corner of the hospital room as he watched the doctors slice open Maman's stomach. It was obvious to Shigeku that the medical staff had no concern for anything other than cutting the baby from its life-suffocating host. Shigeku knew Maman was dead. This thought did not cause him fear. What terrified him was the burden that had been foisted upon him by Maman. He prayed softly that the baby wouldn't live, and then prayed that he wouldn't go straight to hell for uttering such a thing.

Shigeku simply couldn't bear the thought of the obligation Maman had placed upon him. Life and survival in the streets were horrifically difficult already. Shigeku had no idea how he could possibly help his poor little sibling, if it lived. He had nothing . . . he had less than nothing . . . to give. He barely kept himself alive. Yet he could not, and would not, forsake a death oath, even though it had been thrust upon him rather than proffered.

It sounded like dozens of people were all yelling simultaneously, and the activity level was chaotically frenetic, but above the din, Shigeku heard a faint, weak squeal, unmistakably that of a newborn. Seconds later, a tired-looking middle-aged doctor who looked like he hadn't shaved in five days turned to him and presented him with his baby brother.

They, of course, had no one else to hand the babe to. Shigeku, though conscious, lost track of what happened next, as his racing mind was completely overwhelmed by it all.

Shigeku woke up from a trancelike daze when the two doctors entered the room where he had been sitting cross-legged on the cold linoleum floor. The medical men began frantically ransacking the cupboards, presumably seeking towels and soap. His own baby brother lay in a tiny crib beside him, a bottle of formula with a nipple on it beside his head. The newborn was sleeping peacefully; Shigeku knew that he was looking at the soul of his maman, and once again the burden of his oath bore down upon him like the weight of the world.

Across the room, two doctors continued to search shelves while the screeches of another newborn echoed from the hall. Over the pandemonium, Shigeku heard the unmistakable baritone of King Mabanda, roaring orders to all who were within earshot. The entire country knew that Queen Carolanda was about to give birth. However, Shigeku absolutely couldn't fathom why they were at the missionary hospital with the common folk. In that instant, he formed his plan. Growing up in the gutters, Shigeku had honed many talents to the level of instinct, for without these, survival was impossible. Lightning quickness, the ability to create diversion, and the cunning to pilfer were all necessary to eat and live, and Shigeku took pride in his cunning.

By this time, the doctors had managed to clean and swaddle the royal babe and were about to depart the room in order to present the newborn to the king. Shigeku needed to quickly figure out a diversion, even if but for a moment. He darted to a wastebasket as he pulled out his most valuable personal possession—a butane lighter. Like most kids his age, he bummed cigarettes, smoked discarded butts, and acted as tough as an eleven-year-old boy could. With a quick flick, the wastebasket was afire.

Almost instantly the flames roared to half a meter's height. Shigeku shrieked in order to draw the attention of the doctors, who were already en route back to Mabanda with the swaddled babe. Reacting instinctively, the doctors quickly set the royal babe down into an adjacent but empty receiving crib and ran to find fire extinguishers. Shigeku made the switch, baby for baby.

Shigeku exhaled and smiled broadly. His promise to Maman had been fulfilled.

CHAPTER 3

Summer 2004

Crown Prince Mandebala kicked angrily at nothing in particular on the gleaming white marble floor of his magnificent bedroom. With frustration manifest on his increasingly purple-hued face, he raged internally. The prince was well aware of his status and power—at age fourteen, he was indisputably the second most powerful, and arguably the most ruthless man in all Maleziland. Yet why was it so difficult for his tailors to make garments for him that made him look other than short and squat? Clearly, he was taller and slimmer than these *rags* made him look. He bellowed, in a barely post-pubescent voice, for his aide.

Mandebala knew that his father, King Mabanda, loved him blindly, with all his heart and soul. In his father's eyes, he could do no wrong. On multiple occasions, Mandebala had witnessed his father fly into an astonishingly cruel and lethal blood rage, even over the tiniest perceived transgression. Indeed, Prince Mandebala knew that there was no small injustice done to him that would not meet with the full fury and force of the state and legal apparatus that were simply tools for King Mabanda to play with. Mandebala was tired of looking half as wide as he was tall. His tailor would have to pay the price for making him look this way.

One of Mandebala's aides broke through his dark train of thought. The butler, whose name completely escaped Mandebala's mind—to him it was largely irrelevant—appeared through the large doorway to Mandebala's room.

"How may I be of service, Prince Mandebala? And might I add that you look very handsome in your black silk robe this afternoon," said the butler. Mandebala was positive that he recognized a tiny glint of mockery in his eyes, and this particular perfidy only enraged Mandebala further— it seemed that every servant always attempted to convince him that his clothing made him look slimmer, or taller, or *both*—and on this partic- ular day he was having none of it! His own father, King Mabanda, had taught him the lessons of *power,* and what good was power if one didn't use it? Indeed, Mandebala was well aware that in the eyes of many citi- zens, Mabanda was indeed malevolent. Woe betide all subjects, friends, and acquaintances who fell, often inadvertently, on the wrong side of Mabanda's favor. Nevertheless, Mandebala's good father had shown him how much of Maleziland's populace believed that the country needed a strong man to guide her. They supported Mabanda irrespective of his brutality and seeming indifference to the lot of the common folk.

Mandebala had grown up the same as any other multibillionaire's child whose father was a king. He ate nothing but the best food, had nothing but the best tutors, and indeed had the best instructor in his own father on how to act imperiously and without remorse, especially when it came to eliminating threats to one's life of privilege and power.

Prince Mandebala quickly learned that if he did not get his way with anyone or anything, that person or thing or obstruction could simply be removed. Servants, tutors, and even friends could be made to disappear at the nod of his head, never to return. In fact, Mandebala knew that several former playmates—boys and girls his age—had been tortured and executed for incurring his wrath, often over the most trifling of incidents. As a consequence, putative friends and even tutors became few, and Mandebala was lonely.

Only two individuals in the land were insulated, metaphorically, from his wrath. King Mabanda, of course, had nothing to fear from the lad, as his father was the omnipotent ultimate ruler of all Maleziland. And although her life could have been snuffed out with a single breath whispered from his lips, his mother, Queen Carolanda, had nothing to fear from Mandebala either.

Mandebala's mother, Carolanda, could say anything, offend in any way, or trespass in any manner, and in Crown Prince Mandebala's eyes, she could do no wrong. Oedipus himself knew no stronger bond; Mandebala often found himself ashamed, confused, aroused, and embarrassed by his dreams, asleep and awake, of his mother. Upon having his first wet dreams as he approached manhood, the event having been dutifully reported by the servant staff to King Mabanda, he was congratulated by his father. Mandebala certainly did not, however, confide his incestuous thoughts to King Mabanda.

Mandebala often spent his lazy days in the royal den, smoking fine Havanese Cohibas while nestled among exotic furs, opulent Renaissance masters' artwork, and rare first editions of literary masterpieces. The bookshelves in the high-ceilinged room were so tall that a ladder on tracks had to be rolled into place to permit access to the uppermost shelves, though Mandebala had never so much as set a single foot upon one of its rungs.

On one nameless day subsequent to Mandebala hitting puberty, King Mabanda strode into the den. "Son," he said, "it is time for you to learn the power of your royal scepter."

King Mabanda and Mandebala settled into huge water-buffalo-hide wingback chairs, both of which faced an ornate crystal-and-gold coffee table. No ashtray was visibly present for their cigars, both of which had been expertly clipped and lit by servants. When needed, servants dutifully tipped and removed the ashes from their Cohibas.

Prince Mandebala felt pure elation at the prospect of this conversation, yet he knew better than to speak until after his father had. It seemed to take absolutely forever for his father to take two arduously long hauls on his torpedo-tipped, sixty-two-gauge cigar and callously down a full glass of Remy Martin Louis XIII cognac, expelling a resonant, smoke-flavored belch before he spoke. Mandebala made a mental note to step up his own servants' performance, as he noticed the king's glass was refilled before he could set it down.

With its deep resonance and musical lilts, one might easily have mistaken King Mabanda's voice for one filled with compassion and kindness, and indeed Mandebala often thought of it in that exact way.

Mandebala felt close to his father. Some of Mandebala's first memories were of King Mabanda spending countless hours teaching him about power—how to wield it, but more importantly, how to maintain power. The king lectured for hours on the royal family's divine right to rule and how God Himself had made Mabanda an instrument of His will. He also spent hours and days lecturing Mandebala on the natural order and how the people of Maleziland needed and wanted a strong leader.

"Son," he began that day in his deep serious-lecture voice, "the people of this world are like stray dogs. On their own, they are just mangy mutts, capable of little. But with a strong pack leader, these scrawny pups become a coordinated, powerful team, capable of taking down the largest of beasts. People need a strong leader. They need and want to know their place in the pack. They want and need the safety and security provided by their good king, who then benevolently provides for their needs and looks after their security and shelter. Elections and democracy mean nothing here, as God Himself chose me, Mabanda, to be His right arm on this earth, and to deny God's will by allowing elections would lead to His disfavor and wrath. Our people *know* this. And the people do not need, or want, the uncertainty and chaos that changing leaders brings. This is the way it has been in all of Africa from the first memories of time. This is God's will; we shall not deny our God."

Mandebala was bemused the first time he heard this speech, and today, it seemed like his father spoke with heightened fervor and sincerity. Even if Mandebala had the temerity to question it—and he did not—Mandebala had no doubt that his father had spoken these words often enough to believe each and every syllable of his own gospel. Mandebala was well aware that they were more than just words to his father—in two decades, the good king had ruthlessly and bloodthirstily suppressed and eliminated thousands of men who opposed or so much as questioned his rule. Indeed, it was said that "the crocodiles feed at night," leaving no traces to be found. Mabanda had indeed come to believe that he was doing the Lord's own work each and every time that he watched the life flicker from the eyes of yet another tortured, beaten, and maimed detractor.

But today, after three-quarters of a three-hour cigar had been inhaled, and after at least five crystal tumblers of the outrageously expensive cognac, the good king broached a new subject.

"Mandebala, you have spilled your first seed; you are now a man," his father said, without explaining how he knew this fact. The king continued, "Any woman in this country that you desire is yours for the taking—you need only let your intentions be known. If any woman should fail to give herself to your royal scepter, then of course she must be punished to the full extent of God's own law—*our law*—for it is only natural that God's own seed be spilled wherever *we* desire. This is, of course, God's will and way, practiced by the kings of Europe for centuries, and it is well known that it pleases our God. Let no woman ever deny your—and God's—will. So fuck whatever you fancy and punish harshly those that refuse your—and God's—blessings."

Mandebala smiled, but his reverie was fleeting, as he suddenly grew cold and began to shake when thoughts of forcing himself upon Queen Carolanda burst into his head.

CHAPTER 4

May 1990

Only a few short seconds after engineering the switch at the hospital, Shigeku realized the flaw in his plan. For his ruse to work, and continue to work, he could never, ever tell anybody what he'd done. If discovered, the king would switch the babies back, his brother's lot in life would not improve, and he would fail to honor his maman's death oath. He shuddered visibly, as a death oath was sworn at the peril of one's own mortal soul. No, Shigeku had to continue the deception forever, and the burden from which he initially thought he had been discharged remained.

Shigeku named the baby Mateyo, as he could come up with nothing beyond the first name that struck his mind. To the shock of all, especially Shigeku, baby Mateyo somehow managed to gasp out an existence and live. Perhaps, thought Shigeku, it was because Maman had been such a good, kind, and caring member of their decrepit little community; perhaps it was because the villagers always looked out for one another, a way of life and survival learned over thousands of years. When he arrived back in his village, Shigeku made the rounds throughout the shantytown, begging for a spare breast on which to latch his little charge. He knew that there was no shortage of lactating breasts to be found, as at any time at least half of the women over the age of twelve had a baby on the hips or on their teats; that said, finding a breast not thoroughly drained by a ravenous baby demanding more than its mother could produce on meager caloric intake proved difficult. Mindful of his ruse, Shigeku made his baby-feeding rounds regularly, collectively sating the young Mateyo's hunger with rich, cream-laden after-milk from multiple sources. Mateyo thrived.

Shigeku thought he knew well how excruciatingly difficult the struggles of life had been, but he had no idea of how harsh his daily life could be without Maman. Although he wasn't unfamiliar with helping Maman care for and nurture his brothers and sisters, Shigeku had little concept of how much she had done for their family. His six other siblings, including one set of identical twins, all pitched in to one extent or another, but primary care responsibility now fell squarely upon Shigeku's slight shoulders. An already impossible existence was made doubly impossible, and yet somehow the young family would survive—they had no other choice. Shigeku's already difficult world began with hours upon hours of toiling in the fields in order to bring home a few cups of dried maize for his family. His younger siblings would have the fire started and water boiling so that their staple starch—patties fashioned from crushed, ground, and sieved maize—could be fashioned, some days with side servings of greens, chicken, or other proteins or critters that could be harvested or scrounged from the streets.

Long days were met by sleepless nights, and Shigeku grew increasingly tired. And after weeks of sleep deprivation and never-ending caregiving, Shigeku's mind felt as though it were blanketed in a perpetual fog. On one such night, after a particularly long, murderously hot day, when the family had even less food to eat than usual, the shrieks of his newborn baby brother pierced his foggy brain. *What now?* thought Shigeku. This had to be the fourth time Mateyo had bellowed out that night. Shigeku very much resented how his life had become so difficult, and the first tiny crystals of resentment began to form in his mind, slowly but surely creating jagged, long, and lethally sharp shards of vitriolic anger toward his ward, the former crown prince of Maleziland.

The next day, as if Shigeku's neighbors could sense that his little family unit was at a breaking point, the village rallied around them and saved the family. A pot of gruel was left in the doorway that morning. Further such offerings ensued and included the occasional goat meat stew, and jugs of milk kept Shigeku and his siblings alive. Somehow, and in some way, the little family got by.

Although it made his task of looking after Mateyo and his entire family as the eldest child easier, the kindness of his shantytown neighbors somewhat irked young Shigeku. It felt like the women of the village doted on young Mateyo, spoiling him to the extent that pangs of hunger were not felt by the young babe. Shigeku jealously noticed how quickly his charge grew longer and chubbier. When Mateyo was but a few months old, one of Shigeku's neighbors remarked on the young babe's obvious size, strength, and development. And still, it was obvious that Mateyo had become the entire slum's own pet child, claiming the care, affection, and protection of all. And right before Shigeku's eyes, it felt like overnight he grew from baby to toddler, wobbling his way from hut to hut. Indeed, Shigeku often watched his little brother make his rounds, accepting little snacks and tidbits of food from each home before moving on to his next benefactor. There was no doubt whatsoever that Mateyo was by far the best fed member of his family, and yet he was spared the hard manual labor that Shigeku engaged in on a daily basis. Shigeku saw how quickly Mateyo became a gregarious, social, and friendly little child, even before he knew how to speak. His happy smile, his chortling noises, and the sparkle in his bright young eyes were thanks enough for all, and it began to drive Shigeku mad. Everyone was Mateyo's benefactor; everyone was his friend. Shigeku watched enviously as the world's poorest people somehow spared from their own to look after the boy on a daily basis and how Mateyo's happy-go-lucky, friendly personality made him a very popular and welcome young boy among his people.

Winter 1994

On his regular milk runs with Mateyo as an infant, Shigeku knew to skip past Miss Kalibwa's shanty, as she had nothing to offer from her breasts. Yet one day, years after Shigeku and Mateyo had first begun their feeding rounds, Shigeku was following his little brother, who was happily making his way down the dusty street. Ever the curious child, Mateyo often interrupted their rounds for one inquisitive reason or another. This time, however, young Mateyo decided to stroll into Miss Kalibwa's abode, and Shigeku followed. Miss Kalibwa was one of the very few Black teachers at the local British boarding school, the Rhodes Academy, and Shigeku knew her to be kind. With no children of her own, she doted on her students. Shigeku ran to catch up with his stray brother.

Miss Kalibwa's mouth opened when Mateyo bounded into her home, but her face warmed the instant she saw Mateyo. The teacher nodded at Shigeku, who returned the welcome. Shigeku was surprised by how clean and orderly this nice-looking lady's home was. There were pictures on the walls and even flowers in a vase. Miss K herself was dressed equally neatly in an impossibly white and perfectly pressed high-collared cotton blouse; a sensible black skirt, cut just below the knee; and equally functional but polished black shoes. Her hair was pulled upward into a tight bun, and she wore moderately stylish, black-rimmed glasses.

Shigeku's little brother stuck out his hand to Miss K. "Hello! My name is MATEYO—you spell that M-A-T-E-Y-O. What's *your* name?" he asked, as if the words he uttered were the most important things ever communicated.

"Well, hello, Mr. M-A-T-E-Y-O. How are you today?" she asked with a grin.

"I'm good," said Mateyo. Clearly remembering his manners, he added, "How are you?"

"I am very well, Mr. Mateyo. It is an absolute pleasure to meet you," she said. "My name is Miss Kalibwa, but you can call me Miss K if you'd like. May I ask how old you are? I'm going to guess that you're six or seven, based upon how big and smart you appear to be. Am I right?" She bent down to her knees and squinted at him.

"No way!" said Mateyo, his eyes widening. "I'm four! Four is less than seven."

"Well, thank you for the mathematics lesson, young man! I'm an English teacher, so I can always use a little math refresher."

Mateyo grinned. "I can come back anytime you'd like another lesson!"

"Perhaps if you help me with my math, I can help you to learn to read and write. Would that be okay with you?" asked the schoolteacher.

Before Mateyo could answer, Shigeku grabbed his wrist and yanked hard. "I'm sorry. We must leave," he said.

Most people in Maleziland didn't know how to read or write, and Shigeku saw little value in visiting the schoolteacher, kind or not. Education was not a priority for those struggling with life and death on a daily basis. Shigeku himself could not read or write, and few of the village's denizens had any formal education at all—despite literally hundreds of millions of dollars of foreign aid earmarked annually for childhood education. Yet Mateyo began visiting the teacher every day when school let out, and Shigeku began to see that Miss K loved Mateyo very much, and Mateyo eagerly lapped up every bit of knowledge she cared to impart.

At first, Shigeku didn't mind Mateyo's daily visits with Miss K. In fact, he was quite pleased to have Mateyo occupied and cared for by yet another villager. One day, however, Shigeku saw Mateyo with a book, and it startled him. Mateyo was reading, or at least appeared to be reading, for Shigeku couldn't tell. "Mateyo," asked Shigeku, "are you actually reading?" Mateyo nodded, his eyes wide, and Shigeku demanded, "Show me!"

Mateyo held the book so that his biggest brother could see it and traced his finger across markings on the page while saying words. Shigeku was keenly aware of the pedantic way in which his youngest brother, at the age of five, was showing him up. He swatted the book out of Mateyo's hands harshly and strode out of their shanty.

The world around him fascinated Mateyo. As he walked down the streets of the slums, he barely heard a passerby holler, "What are you looking at this time, Mateyo?" It was a phrase so oft-repeated that he rarely, if ever, paid heed. At that particular moment, he was sitting by the roadside watching a huge ant colony. The ants' complex social structure and intricate, thoughtful engineering works captured his mind and his mind's eye for days on end. On another day, watching birds building nests or staring into the clear blue sky in order to observe clouds form, darken, and unleash their life-giving precipitate—basically watching anything that emanated from nature and God's own hand—captured his attention endlessly as a young lad.

One day, while wandering through the outskirts of town, Mateyo stumbled upon a juvenile wild piglet hiding in the low-lying, almost barren shrubbery filling the ditch along the principal road into the town. The piglet squealed anxiously once it realized that Mateyo had discovered its hiding spot, but made no attempt to run. *That's odd,* thought Mateyo, wondering why the pig held fast in its position. As he got closer, Mateyo could see quite clearly that the little swine's back right leg had been snapped in two, just above its ankle. Finding and catching a wild piglet was truly a fortunate event; the protein and essential fats from such a beast—even a juvenile—could feed his family for days. Such thoughts did not, however, cross his mind. All Mateyo could think about was caring for the little piggy, which, although nervous and anxious as Mateyo initially picked him up, quickly calmed with the soothing voice of his rescuer. "Come, little piggy, I am going to bring you home. We'll tie a stick onto your leg, and in a couple of weeks' time, you'll be as good as new!" said Mateyo in his most soothing voice.

None of Mateyo's siblings were at all surprised when Mateyo walked into their shanty with a maimed pig under his arm. He left the pig in his elder sister's care while he went outside to procure twine and two short, straight, flat sticks to use as a splint. Having successfully found some twine and some wood that would suffice, he made his way back home, excited to be able to help the piggy. Just before he entered the shack, he heard an ethereal squeal from within it. *No!* he thought. As he burst into his home, Shigeku looked up at him, grinning from ear to ear. Shigeku was kneeling on the floor holding the lifeless carcass of the piggy by its hind hooves, allowing the blood to run from an enormous and deep gash in its throat. The blood poured into a well-worn metal bowl, and the sound of it plinking as it hit the vessel made Mateyo nauseous. Mateyo did not speak to his brother for weeks and refused to eat any part of his former charge.

As Mateyo sat on the stoop of his family shanty, a scrap of newspaper blew past his feet. He stomped on the tumbling paper with his foot and was pleased to learn that it was the cover page of the *Johannesburg Times,* the leading newspaper in all of Africa. Mateyo excitedly delved into it, keen to read every word about a global scourge called AIDS that had become a full-blown pandemic in his country, and indeed in most of sub-Saharan Africa.

Shigeku was sitting by the roadside one day idly kicking dirt into a pile when the unmistakable roar of a motorcade came within earshot. He looked up out of curiosity, and as the motorcade passed by at near-to-perilous speed, he briefly laid eyes upon his true brother for the first time in nine years since he was cut from Maman's belly at the missionary hospital. His brother, known as Crown Prince Mandebala, was peering through the windows of the black luxury Range Rover sedan, and Shigeku was positive that their eyes met. Mandebala had a rotund face, as wide as it was long.

Shigeku seethed. *Why should I have to struggle when that fat little bastard lives like a king?* But again the terror associated with breaking his death oath flooded into his mind, making him shudder from a cold chill running down his spine. His childhood had died on the day he'd made that death oath to Maman.

Mabanda could see that his son, Crown Prince Mandebala, was shorter and heavier boned than his tall and willowy mother, Queen Carolanda, and that he had grown pleasingly plump on the rich royal diet. Despite his mother's beauty, Mandebala grew up as an odd-looking royal. His physical looks were extremely different than those of Queen Carolanda's; however, the king thought nothing of it, as he himself was short, heavyset, and moderately rotund. In fact, the king was pleased with the little "mini-me" in his household and couldn't help but think that the boy was a particularly handsome little fellow. Clearly, God saw fit to create His son in His own image, mused Mabanda, never differentiating in his own mind whether the pronoun referred to the God in heaven or the God of Maleziland, King Mabanda Himself.

Mabanda often watched his boy from the sidelines, looking for opportunities upon which to seize in order that he might impart some teaching to his son. He observed one day when his son, at the age of eight, was much affronted by a young child who had refused his demand to give Mandebala a toy. Clearly, the only reason that Mandebala coveted the toy was simply, as is the way with children, because the other boy had the toy, not because Mandebala actually wanted it. King Mabanda smiled gleefully as a physical skirmish over the toy ensued, and Mandebala bit the ear off of his playmate without hesitation, first chewing on it for several seconds before spitting it on the floor at the feet of the child's horrified mother. The king was quite pleased.

King Mabanda had little or no regard for the value of human life and wanted to ensure that his son was of similar mind. Though well and expensively educated, the king chose Mandebala's tutors and texts carefully, restricting their lessons and content, lest enlightened concepts of enfranchisement and democracy dared take purchase in Mandebala's dark, round little head. And Mandebala's chief instructor, Mabanda himself, took every opportunity to personally lead by example. The king made sure that Mandebala was well aware that only three lives on the face of the earth had any value: his, his father's, and his mother's.

Mabanda strolled through the east palace garden. He was feeling quite pleased with himself. The World Bank for Reconstruction and Development had just transferred $2.1 billion into Maleziland's Disaster Relief Account, but of course the second the money hit the account, it was rerouted to a Swiss account in the king's personal name. Indeed, African strongmen across the continent all knew which bank manager at the First Swiss International could handle sensitive transfers. It made said manager wealthy by Western standards but paled in comparison to the hundreds of billions of dollars his institution held on behalf of many of Africa's ruling overlords, whether elected democratically or otherwise.

Mabanda was nigh giddy. He had staged the crisis perfectly. Maleziland's primary water source, Lake Malezi, was on the brink of catastrophic failure, caused by years of mismanagement, overuse, and toxic runoff. Or at least that was what the international media had reported, and it did not take much to get that fictional ball rolling. Celebrities rallied to the cause, responding instinctively and predictably to the release of regular media updates staged by his team of photographers and videographers, and foreign countries lined up to bankroll the solution. His engineers had worked up plans for almost two hundred deep aquifer wells to be drilled to once and for all secure a safe drinking water source for his people. Of course, other than a staged event for the media showing the first well being drilled—and Mabanda would absolutely not even waste the money to complete that well—nary an actual well would ever be completed.

In fact, King Mabanda loved his people. God had chosen him to be their leader. He knew, as they knew, that death was part of life, and equally well that they were there to support and worship their king and God. Mabanda's mind continued to wander. It wasn't as though he went about murdering his subjects on a daily basis, though he certainly *did* on occasion. Although occasional Western media reports tried to claim that he was directly accountable for the premature deaths of thousands of his subjects every year through policies that encouraged famine, lack of education, and little spending in infrastructure or other economic measures to improve the lot of his citizens, he knew better. It was simply the will of God.

The king was well aware of the external world's views on Maleziland. News agencies and journalists called it a "blight on the global landscape." As a nation, they reported, it had one of the lowest life expectancies on the planet, a direct function of its also lowest GDP per capita. They were highly critical of its abysmal healthcare system and almost total lack of infrastructure—a function of absolutely nil government spending on such necessities since the transfer of power from the French colonials in 1966. By virtually every international statistic used to measure quality of life—infant mortality, maternal childbirth deaths, literacy rates, and education rates—Maleziland was an economic and social disaster. Yet all this data meant nothing to Mabanda. His people were content. They loved him. They were pleased with their lot in life and of course, most important of all, were exceedingly happy to see their beloved king treated as God Himself should be treated.

The king was deep in thought as he strolled out of the palace and into a lush, immaculately manicured garden. In fact, the view of the royal palace was particularly spectacular from the east garden, as its architectural lines and tall, gleaming white marble pillars were unobstructed from the king's perspective. The palace currently had 185 rooms—and counting, as at any given point in time, there were a number of additions under construction. It seemed natural to the king, of course, as only God personified in the king could live in such an abode. Perhaps some additional solid gold water features could now be commissioned for the gardens, mused Mabanda. That would be pleasing to him.

Summer 2004

Prince Mandebala watched as his tall and elegant mother, Queen Carolanda, strolled past him in the garden. The queen was ridiculously tall—she towered over Mandebala by at least a full head. When she walked, she flowed with a grace and composure that was incomprehensible to Mandebala's mind, especially as compared to his brusque and staccato pace. Today she was wearing a tan-colored sundress that went beautifully with her light brown, smooth skin, but no matter the color, she always looked as though she were otherworldly. The form of her body beneath her white and nearly translucent dress drove Mandebala nearly mad. It irritated him to no end to know that she would never speak to him unless he first engaged her. Apart from his mother, only the king could be so rude to him.

"Queen Carolanda," he said and beckoned her over. He never called her "Mother."

"Yes, Mandebala," she replied quietly as she glided over toward him.

"D-did you see the sunrise this morning?" he asked, suddenly unable to think of anything to say in her presence.

"Of course I did, Mandebala. You know I watch the sun rise and set every day, as I give thanks to God for His gifts at those times." Her eyes seemed devoid of emotion, and her voice held no intonation or timbre.

"Th-that's . . . nice," said Mandebala.

"Will that be all?" Carolanda asked, with a slight bow of her head.

Still at a loss for words, Mandebala nodded vigorously. Quickly and silently, Queen Carolanda disappeared into the depths of the garden's luscious foliage.

Fuck! Why does that ALWAYS happen to me when I speak to that bitch? It made no sense to him at all, but he could not think straight or even speak properly in her presence. His pants had grown tight at his groin. *Fuck, fuck, fuck.* He called an attendant, who appeared like a ghost from behind a carefully tailored bush.

"Boy," he said to the white-uniformed servant, "bring me that slut from town from last week—the tall one with light skin. NOW!"

The servant scurried away, and Mandebala grinned sadistically as he headed inside the palace to his bedroom.

CHAPTER 5

Spring 2004

The day had finally arrived for Shigeku. The fourteenth anniversary of his maman's death. Fourteen years since his utterance of the death oath that had spelled ruin for his life. This day would also mark the fourteenth birthday of Crown Prince Mandebala.

With every passing motorcade, with every royal event (and there were shockingly many), and with every whispered rumor of the life of royal privilege, Shigeku's blood seethed and boiled. And this day was a particularly monumental celebration for the royal family, as this year was Mandebala's royal birthday and the prince's official welcome into manhood—his "Manhood Day." All young men in Maleziland celebrated this day when they turned fourteen, but the king had proclaimed the crown prince's Manhood Day a national holiday, which rubbed poignantly acrid acid in Shigeku's mental wounds.

Shigeku was brooding to himself while exercising in the shade of a large tree near the creek that flowed through their shantytown. *At least the king gives us special food on this day,* Shigeku thought, interrupting his tenth set of fifty push-ups to queue for some beef stew. He had no idea what all was in it, but to his poor palate, its rich, flavorful protein tasted amazing. For no reason that he had ever formulated in his head, when he wasn't working or otherwise trying to eke out an existence for his family, Shigeku was constantly training and had been doing so for years. It was, of course, a poor man's training regime: push-ups, sit-ups, chin-ups, and long-distance running. The physical exercise was often the only thing that enabled him to find peace enough to sleep at night.

As Shigeku savored his meal, Mateyo sauntered into the shanty, an extra happy spring to his step.

"Brother!" he said, his face lighting up, "do you know what today is?"

Shigeku rolled his eyes.

"It's my Manhood Day!" said Mateyo.

"And how are you going to celebrate it, brother?" asked Shigeku in a deadpan tone.

"Oh, I'm just going to visit with all of our friends here in town and let them know how much I appreciate them all," said Mateyo, nodding.

Shigeku silenced a curse and walked away. *Fucking idiot belongs in the royal palace, living like a king. He lives here in a shanty, barely scraping out an existence, yet he is happy beyond all reason!*

Shigeku trained with increased fervor on the day that followed Mandebala's manhood celebration, fueled equally by the prior day's food and by the acerbic wound reopened yet again. As he finished a set of sit-ups on the shanty's front steps, a military jeep pulled in front of his home for the third time this year.

"Shigeku," called out the Malezi army captain from the front of the jeep, "have you got a minute?"

Shigeku nodded but didn't interrupt his subsequent set. "No, Jomoyo," he said to the captain, "my mind has not changed. I am not suddenly overwhelmed with either patriotic fervor or incredible gratitude after yesterday's celebration."

Most Malezis would have jumped at Captain Jomoyo's continuous attempts at recruitment. As captain in Maleziland's most elite fighting force, Jomoyo knew well of Shigeku's superior strength and endurance *and* of his short temper, often channeled into successful bouts of street fighting.

Shigeku could simply not, however, bring himself to serve as the strong arm of the man who was the notional father to his true baby brother, and who was most clearly shaping his brother in his own image. Jomoyo drove away, shaking his head.

Several days after Mandebala's big day, Shigeku settled on a plan. *It was time to get even*—or perhaps die trying. Maleziland's hostile neighboring country, Zambwana, had ten times the land mass and five times the population of Maleziland. And Shigeku had heard rumblings that they were not-so-secretly raising an army with the express objective of invading Maleziland and adding her territory and peoples to her own. *I will cross the border and find this army to fight my true enemy.*

Of course, he reasoned, the Zambwanans had always maintained—and they were in fact correct—that they were tribal brothers of all Malezilanders. The oral history that Shigeku knew told of how their land was arbitrarily divided by European powers long ago—so long ago that storytellers had lost track of which European skirmish had drawn a line on the map between her people, though the map of Africa drawn up at the end of World War II had reaffirmed it. The Zambwanan ruler, President Kureba, had been brought to power years ago in an election in which he ran upon a platform promising to unite his tribal brethren in Maleziland.

Shigeku was quite certain that it had been at least a decade since Kureba had been elected—no subsequent elections had ever been held—and her people were apparently clambering for war. All Maleziland had heard that President Kureba intended to invade, and indeed that all who wished to serve the cause of reuniting her peoples, from either side of the border, would be welcome to join his crusade.

Shigeku made his decision. He arranged to meet with a man known to be a Zambwanan sympathizer who was rumored to have helped several men and boys from the shantytown find their way across the border. As Shigeku strode toward the man sitting in the shade of a massive tree, his skin deeply tanned by many days of sun exposure, the man barely looked up and said, "We leave at 4:30 a.m. tomorrow. Make sure you bring your fee." Shigeku packed a light bag that night. He did not bother to say so much as "farewell" to any of his brothers and sisters. At 4:25 a.m., when his alarm rang, he shut it off before anybody else in their shanty awakened. His guide was outside the hut when Shigeku emerged, and nodding slightly, turned and left. Shigeku was barely able to see the back side of his guide, who was barely over one and a half meters tall and now dressed in camouflage. He headed down the road leading out of the village, eastward toward the border. Shigeku followed silently. After fifteen minutes at a brisk pace, the small man suddenly darted through the thick, dense underbrush with nary a swing of his machete. Shigeku was forced to constantly swing and flail his own blade to make sufficient room to pass. The border was approximately fifteen kilometers from where they entered the jungle, and he knew it was going to be a taxing journey. Although the dense foliage intermittently gave way to a more clear, less dense underbrush, and even to the occasional game trail, Shigeku knew that their progress was slow.

There! Finally! The Malezi River demarcated the border, and after a shallow ford, Shigeku knew that they were finally in Zambwana; however, they continued walking until his guide announced, "We are here." Shigeku looked around at the dense jungle surrounding them. *Where the fuck is here?* When he turned around, the little man was gone. *Where on earth did that little man go?* Shigeku hadn't noticed any trail or path upon which they'd been traveling, nor could he see any path upon which he could continue his course. With a sigh, Shigeku kept slogging forward in the same general direction. With luck, he would find people. Without it, he would perish. *For fuck's sake!* This wasn't good.

The jungle that straddled the Zambwanan side of the border was impossibly thick. A treetop-high canopy of vegetation blocked out 85 percent of the sun's light, and what little filtered down to the jungle floor was thin and vapid. Vines hung everywhere, and thick, dense undergrowth made progress extremely slow and difficult. A machete proved an able tool for clearing a path, but forward advancement was even slower and more painfully physical. Border guards were hardly necessary, thought Shigeku, when the vegetation itself stood *en garde* for each side.

Shigeku froze in his tracks when he heard the loud *click* of an AK-47 safety being disengaged. He didn't need formal military training to recognize the noise right next to his left ear.

He smiled calmly despite the mortal threat pressed against his pulsing temple. Raising his arms slowly, he called out to his unseen would-be assailants, "I am unarmed. I come as a brother to help the rightful President Kureba of Zambwana to unite his people with Maleziland and throw out the dog Mabanda."

"Big talk for a lost pup in the jungle," said a resonant but clearly dangerous voice from somewhere behind him, just as Shigeku felt the butt of the AK-47 crash into the side of his skull.

⸺ ◆ ⸺

As he lay back on his luxurious bed, Crown Prince Mandebala exhaled audibly. He was very much enjoying his newfound status as a man, less than a week after his official celebration. No longer a boy, at the exalted age of fourteen, he could now enjoy the newfound pleasures of being the royal male heir.

Mandebala had soon found that his thirst for sex was positively unslakable, and his father was more than willing to supply objects with which he could try to quench that craving, if only temporarily. Women of every age had been brought to him, including no fewer than five virgins. The first time Mandebala had seen the blood of a young girl's maidenhood, he'd been quite disgusted, yet the fear on a virgin's face was worth the temporary mess.

This evening's poor girl seemed younger than the prince and had been dressed in an ill-fitting, see-through white garment. She was waifish and small, with two barely visible breasts, and that turned on Mandebala even more. A servant had thrust her through the prince's bedroom doorway, and she stood frozen where she had been presented, cowering, a look fashioned by pure fear and hatred on her young, unblemished face.

I cannot wait to make her bleed.

Mandebala grabbed the girl by her long braid and threw her onto the bed. Seizing an enormous half-meter blade, its hilt encrusted with jewels, from his bedside table, he held it beside her neck. The poor girl was entirely immobilized with fear as Mandebala used the hunting knife to slice her garment.

When he had thoroughly ravaged her to his liking, he rolled off of her and fell fast asleep after a servant whisked the sobbing girl away.

The very next morning, he had his servant bring another, slightly older female participant to his bed. He was feeling particularly virile that morning after the young girl from the previous evening. Upon entering her, the royal prince looked down between the girl's legs. *Nothing.* His royal member shriveled even as his blood boiled.

"Did you lie to my servants, you little whore?" Mandebala roared. "Did you tell them that your flower was intact?"

"Come to me," cooed the smooth-skinned girl, "and learn the pleasures of sleeping with a woman who knows how to please Your Royal Highness."

Mandebala spit in the woman's face. *Trash.* He again grabbed the razor-sharp hunting knife and slit her from her sullied opening to her navel. Her eyes widened and she gasped slightly before quietly and politely bleeding to death on the royal bed.

The teenaged prince smiled as his manhood was restored to its former glory. His prideful moment was fleeting, though, as he quickly realized that he had entirely cut apart the object of his desire.

"Butler!" he bellowed. "Get me another girl! And don't you dare bring me an old, worn-out whore, or it will be you bleeding to death next time!"

The prince would decide later whether the aide who had procured the corpse now sullying his linens would be lucky enough to escape with his life.

⁂

Shigeku's head felt like it had been cleaved in two. He wished, at that very moment, that it had, but soon banished the thought. He was able to focus, just barely, on the sounds of voices and clicking metallic parts. Footsteps, machinery. He couldn't see, but what he thought was a blindfold proved to be bandages wrapped around his head and eyes. His wound had been expertly bandaged by someone who knew what he was doing . . . He had to be in a military camp!

He called out, "Brothers! Unbind me! Please take off these bandages! I come as your ally, your friend, your brother, to help unite our people once again and to cast off the wretched Mabanda."

Hands fumbled to remove the bandages, and Shigeku's eyes began to regain their ability to focus. He looked around to survey his surroundings. He had been right. It was a military camp, and a very large one at that. The men who had unbound him stood around him in a circle, weapons drawn. Although they all sported consistently patterned camouflage overalls, they were otherwise a motley crew of varying heights, weights, skin tones, and builds. The weapons that they had trained upon him were equally varied, from handguns to AK-47s. Shigeku smiled, thinking how silly it was for them to be positioned as such, as surely most if not all would catch bullets from one another if he decided to make a break for it. As Shigeku peered in every direction, he could see tattered but well-organized rows of faded beige canvas tents. Men in similar camouflage combat fatigues—not of Malezi issue—swarmed about everywhere, at a pace and with a sense of purpose that underlined a sense of urgency, thought Shigeku. No one seemed to be in a rush to interrogate him, and there was no form of questioning whatsoever. The group of men stood silently outside the row of tents.

After at least half an hour, a very large, menacing-looking man barked out, "Fall in line!" The men holstered and slung their weapons as Shigeku and the others joined several dozen men following their apparent leader. As they marched deeper and deeper into the camp, Shigeku was able to see that hundreds—perhaps *thousands*—of similar deserters had spirited themselves across the border, lured by the promise of a better life under a different ruler and the equally attractive promise of three square meals a day as combat soldiers.

Shigeku was then brusquely guided toward a collapsible wooden table with rusted metal legs where he gave his name and age and was in turn given numbered dog tags. Shigeku and the men were then made to queue up at various supply tents over and over again. First, boots—reasonably impressive and well made. Second, fatigues—loose fitting and identical to what everyone they could see was wearing. Third, bedding—consisting of impossibly thin sheets and a well-worn nearly opaque blanket. And finally, the armory.

Shigeku and a random group of similar men were then led to what appeared to be the edge of the encampment, though dozens more tents were being hastily erected beyond their locale. They were assigned to specific tents and ordered to unpack, rest, and await orders. The men complied.

Shigeku's tent had six sets of bunk beds in it, and he scurried quickly to claim a lower bunk. He did not think he could possibly sleep suspended that high in the air, and the thought of falling out of bed in the middle of the night and breaking his neck sent a shiver down his spine. Eleven other souls quickly claimed bunks and associated trunks for storage, and when an enormous man lumbered onto the bunk above him, and Shigeku saw the cheaply made, rusty springs stretch and groan beneath his bulk, he began to wonder if he was in even greater peril down below. The men rested silently, each processing myriad thoughts.

Although Shigeku was quite pleased to be in the Zambwanan army on his path to exact revenge, he tried his best to dismiss his thoughts about the historic reality of war in Africa. On the African continent, war was a zero-sum game—either you were on the winning side, or you died. Neither side would be taking prisoners.

King Mabanda was in a foul, dark mood. Mandebala had seen his father stomping around the castle, throwing precious *objets d'art* crashing into walls and through windows, berating staff members, and other-wise sharing his mood with staff and visitors alike. Everyone within the administration and the entire royal palace staff, and even his son, knew to be particularly wary of him at these times. But Mandebala sought his father out anyway, finding him in the library, nestled into his favorite wingback chair, smoking a half-consumed, now unlit cigar and drinking scotch.

Mandebala walked up to the king and swallowed his fear. "Father, what's troubling you? You've seemed a bit disturbed over the last few days."

"It is nothing at all, my son," said King Mabanda, only slightly too quickly. Mandebala frowned, and the king sighed. "Oh, it's the Zambwanan cur, Kureba. My sources tell me that he's marshalling an invasion army at our border and that he is finally going to act upon his boastful threats of the past years. As sure as God favors our people, we are going to be invaded."

Why would the king be worried about the imminent attack? Mandebala wondered. All his life, the prince had been told of the superiority of Maleziland's fighting forces and of their God-favored and God-given invincibility. Mandebala had heard this repeated with such frequency that he believed every word of it to be beyond reproach, and, to a great extent, it was true. Better trained and armed than any other professional fighting force on the continent, Maleziland's army had developed, over the decades, a reputation for just that—invincibility.

"Father," Mandebala blurted, the uneasy realization of vulnerability settling and weighing on him for the first time in his life, "you don't think that the Zambwanan scum can defeat our forces, do you?"

"Of course not, son. But it is an unfortunate event. Wars are costly, and our country's foreign benefactors have been less than forthcoming of late with funding for our latest infrastructure projects. They continue to prattle on about accountability and a global economic crisis. I'm afraid that some of the additions to the royal palace might have to be delayed for a few months."

"That's ridiculous!" said Mandebala, almost shouting. "We must have the new swimming pool completed before the next dry season. The old one simply isn't big enough, and the chlorine is intolerable!"

The king smiled. "All in due time, son."

⚬ ◈ ⚬

Each night in his tent, alone with his thoughts but far from alone in reality, Shigeku grew more impatient. The stench of sweat and male hormones was enough to make most people's eyes water—pungent in a way that only a dozen unbathed men per tent could emit. Personal hygiene was not a priority. Training, and then sleeping when not training, was of paramount import. Shigeku didn't mind the physicality of army life. His wiry frame packed strength disproportionate to its mass. No, he was simply impatient to get on with the task.

He wasn't alone in his anxiety. He knew the great majority of the new conscripts shared his eagerness, as well as his overriding fear that the putative war might only be yet another war of words between the two countries. Other than minor border skirmishes, the last time the two states had been embroiled in actual conflict stretched back at least two decades and had otherwise simply been an epic battle of rhetoric. Despite reassurances from their commanding officers, the eager men were apprehensive about whether an actual offensive would indeed be mounted, and their apprehension would only be assuaged by armed combat and the spilling of blood.

Shigeku woke up to the now-familiar clanging of beds with wooden sticks at 4:30 a.m. sharp—again. Within five minutes of having their cages rattled, all troops had to be in formation, fully outfitted, backpacks loaded, for their morning double-time run. Ten kilometers later, with a healthy measure of reprimanding push-ups having been meted out to laggards along the way, Shigeku and the other men wolfed down a meal of hot maize gruel, augmented in caloric content by rendered pork fat.

Unbelievable how good this tastes when you're so hungry, thought Shigeku rather absentmindedly.

After breakfast, Shigeku and the troops went back to their tents for a fifteen-minute break. To a man, each flopped on his cot to maximize their rest opportunity. After only a few moments, Shigeku was brusquely awakened by two men in his tent yelling loudly at each other. Shigeku and his troopmates watched wide-eyed, content to let the men work out their issues on their own. Shigeku smiled somewhat bemusedly as the two men began physically slamming each other with their chests. But when the slighter of the two men, feeling physically overwhelmed by the larger, suddenly whipped out a combat knife, before Shigeku or anyone else could intervene, the head count in their tent had been reduced to eleven. The men quickly cleaned up the spilled blood and disposed of the body, forgoing the balance of their rest break.

Although at the start of their training, few words were spoken and Shigeku had made no friends, as they chatted among themselves about that morning's dramatic event, the first bonds of friendship began to form among the men. Shigeku and a handful of other Malezi defectors formed a loose group of sorts—united, it would appear, by a common dialect and fierce hatred for King Mabanda. They were indeed a motley crew: a tall, lanky, dark-skinned fellow from the north named Mobuto; a quick-witted, sharp-tongued, spry youngster of about fifteen years old (though certainly a "man" for armed services purposes in Africa) named Chala; a quiet, heavyset fellow from the capital city of Lalonga named Zansha; and an enormous, powerfully built man from the south named Moto. Over the days and weeks, the sub-troop developed a comfortable rapport that could almost be called friendship.

"Shigeku, you skinny litter runt, help me load this jeep," said the giant of a man Moto with a broad, toothy grin.

"If I'm such a skinny runt," replied Shigeku, "why would a strong, big dog like you have to ask for my help?" He smiled back at his friend.

Shigeku one day watched open-mouthed as Moto squatted and bear-hugged a full barrel of fuel. He then stood up straight-backed with the barrel, his powerful legs straining at his pants, and walked it twenty meters to hoist it onto the back of a truck.

"Incredible, my friend!" Shigeku cried out.

Moto turned back and gave him a thumbs-up.

Of the men in Shigeku's combat group, the Malezis were the stand-outs, obviously overall the most highly motivated among their peers.

Zambwana's top military commander, General Zumba, stood over-seeing the military combat training early one morning. As Shigeku and his crew advanced past the command observation post, yelling and encouraging one another forward in the face of enemy fire, screaming, "Death to Mabanda" and "Kill the Malezi scum," Shigeku was close enough to overhear the general declare to his subordinate officers, "Those Malezis are going to kill a lot of Royalist pigs."

Shigeku smiled and picked up his pace.

One of the king's transplanted men stepped into the deep jungle seconds after the command to move out was issued. The latest military satellite phone technology, thought to be possessed only by the fighting men of the United States of America, was dramatically smaller and more portable than anything ever seen in the public sphere. He ducked into the obsidian darkness to transmit an urgent message back to his king. "We are moving" was his simple three-word transmission.

A highly trained officer in Maleziland's standing army, the traitor was well motivated to do whatever he could to undermine the Zambwanan effort. He held the Malezi rank of lieutenant, but if his efforts contributed to a Zambwanan military failure, the king had promised him a promotion of multiple ranks into his country's military ruling elite of generals.

The transmission to his king accomplished, the Malezi loyalist quickly and quietly fell back into his squadron, unseen and unnoticed.

Shigeku and the entire cadre of Zambwanan troops proceeded to form up and begin their march toward the west.

"Time to hunt some Malezi dog," Moto said to Shigeku, "and perhaps fuck some of their women along the way." Moto chuckled.

Shigeku gave a broad smile, his usual response to such crudity. Chala looked concerned and said nothing, while Zansha and Mobuto whooped with excitement. Though he wasn't overly interested in the latter of Moto's objectives, Shigeku was more than ready to do his share of killing. His bloodlust, and that of all his adrenaline-charged corpsmen, was by now off the charts.

After a pause, Shigeku turned to Moto. "Yes," he said, flashing brilliantly white but jagged teeth, "the time has come."

Several hours of double-time marching through deep jungle later, the Zambwanans were halted on the edge of what Shigeku was sure must have been the border—a cleared cutline that demarcated the edge of Malezi territory. By mutual agreement, on this part of the border where there was no river, each of the countries had taken turns clearing the border twice annually, lest a person on either side should accidentally stumble into enemy territory.

The troops stopped under a cover of trees and waited, less so to preserve an element of surprise, which was deemed impossible, and more so to avoid the radiant and strengthening heat of the newly risen sun, already inflicting its own form of violence.

Shigeku's heart raced as the ground beneath his feet began to tremble violently. *Had they angered God? An earthquake?* He looked around at the troops, who fell to the ground. Moto placed a hand on his arm and uttered a single word: "Tanks."

Shigeku's mind was racing, and his friend's words did not register.

"Tanks always lead," Moto continued. "They can provide a very quick penetrating strike, but as effective as they may be, only troops can consolidate and hold ground. They will lead, and we will follow. But typical armies have few tanks. They are expensive. We humans are not." Moto issued a half grimace, half grin.

Shigeku's troop scattered just as the tanks burst through the dense foliage and into the border cutline. Several hundred Zambwanan troops barely escaped becoming casualties before the first shots were fired under colossal, heavy metal tracks. Shigeku stared, his coursing pulse making his helmet feel unusually tight and his brain becoming engorged with adrenaline-filled blood.

The tanks turned left and then right, heading down the border cutline, until fully fifty tanks had fanned out along the border. Shigeku watched as the tanks, without pausing, all spun ninety degrees and surged into enemy territory. The men on the ground braced for the return fire of the Malezi armed forces. None came. Seconds later, General Zumba's voice screamed through their radios. "ATTACK!" Immediately, sixty thousand troops loyal to Zambwanan president Kureba flooded onto Malezi soil.

The battle had begun.

Shigeku's troop was used to advancing at a fast pace; however, with the tanks rumbling ahead of the men at a furious clip and belching foul, unfiltered diesel fumes in their wake, the men struggled to follow apace. Mercifully, thought Shigeku, at least the tanks cleared well-defined paths for the men to follow—without their spoor, the task of following would have been slow and arduous. After about half an hour, the only evidence left of the tanks was their destructive, cleared wake. The machines were long out of range of sight, sound, and smell. Their commanders urged them forward relentlessly hour after hour.

Shigeku glanced around nervously while advancing, a shockingly cold sweat pouring down his brow. *Surely it can't be this easy!* They had to be at least thirty kilometers into Malezi territory, and nary a bullet had been fired. He continued to strain his senses for the sure-to-come resistance. None materialized.

By the end of the first day in enemy territory, Shigeku and the others heard reports that fully 40 percent of the tank cavalry had been laid waste by mechanical failure, without a single shot yet being fired.

CHAPTER 6

The "Situation Room" in the royal palace was unlike any other room Mandebala had ever seen. It was one of very few rooms he had been expressly forbidden to enter—or suffer the wrath and reprisals of his father. As a small child, he had once been brought in the room by the king, but from what he could remember, the entire room had changed. A massive wall of flat-screen TVs—easily more than a hundred—were joined together to form one continuous, gigantic panel. Although it could be separated into different feeds, it currently displayed a camera view from the helmet of an aide to the king's top five-star general, Jibwa, with such clarity that Mandebala was astonished. The aide must have been very close to Jibwa, and as he looked toward the general, the image he was projecting onto the panel of TVs was both enormous and menacing. The king and his four generals sat U-shaped around a clear glass table suitable for seating twenty, all of them focused on General Jibwa.

Mandebala was nervous—*extremely* nervous—for perhaps the first time in his life. He could not understand why, or how, his father could remain so outwardly calm in the face of the attack by the dramatically larger Zambwanan force. He tried to project calmness, but try as best he could, the right side of his face twitched violently every five seconds or so.

King Mabanda spoke. "Generals, if I am expressly not to be on the battlefield, I want to go over our battle plans *again!*" Mandebala fleetingly questioned in his own mind whether his father seriously would ever put himself that close to harm, but then refocused on the plans.

"King Mabanda, sir," stated a four-star general whose name Mandebala did not know, "your armed forces are extremely well trained and well disciplined. I daresay that there is not a better armed force on the continent. Further," he said, sounding somewhat exasperated at having to repeat the plan yet again, "we have debated, anticipated, and trained for this very attack for twenty years. For such a magnificent fighting force, reacting will seem like little more than a drill when the time comes to fire real bullets rather than blanks. Indeed, your men will do so without thinking, and without an even slightly elevated pulse."

The men pored over maps and arrows upon maps for hours, and yet for all the discussion and debate, Mandebala thought the defensive plan was both simple and working to perfection.

"So *you* are sure that the Zambwanan scum are *here*, yes, General?" the king's tone was somber and menacing enough to make most men flinch, shiver, and wet themselves.

"Yes, my king" was the immediate response.

A three-star general butted into the conversation. "Yes, we know they are currently encamped right here, thanks to the reports of our operatives from behind enemy lines—from within the Zambwanan army. Tomorrow they will continue their advance right along here, on the path of this arrow *here*," he said, pointing at a hand-drawn mark on the map.

Up until this point in time, Mandebala had managed to keep his mouth tightly shut. Unable to contain his thoughts any further, however, he yelled, "Come on! How do you know that the Zambwanans will travel along the path you have drawn? Are they under your command? Are you omniscient?"

Pointing at the map, he asked, "Why might their army go this way or that way? And why haven't we attacked them yet? The enemy is fifty kilometers into Maleziland and we haven't fired a single bullet nor killed a single Zambwanan. This is madness!"

The king smirked but remained silent.

The three-star general cleared his throat and addressed the prince. "Mandebala, we have been modeling this attack for decades. We have simulated the most likely incursion routes that would be taken by our sworn enemy. We have intelligence on their precise location."

"But how can you know they will move in this direction?" demanded Mandebala for the second time.

"Ah, now I see. Apparently Your Highness has never set foot outside of the royal palace, other than in the comfort of his Range Rover," said the general, a slightly mocking intonation in his voice. "Once the enemy is here—where they are encamped—they would have to backtrack for several hours to go around the steep walls of the valley in which they are encamped. No, they have no choice but to forge ahead, just as our arrows indicate."

Mandebala could no longer focus upon the discussion. How *dare* the general speak to him in such a manner? He noted the name on the general's resplendent dress uniform badge. *NKAMBA. Your name will be forgotten once I erase you and it from history.* Vaguely he heard them all speaking about ensuring that they, *not* the Zambwanans, chose the battleground and that reports were confirming that Zambwanan heavy vehicles and equipment were breaking down. Mandebala vaguely heard discussion that Zambwanan logistics support lines were fragile and stretched thin and that all concurred it was time to launch their first counteroffensive. Mandebala saw only rage.

"So,"boomed King Mabanda, "it is unanimously agreed that General Jibwa's Mpini Ekundu—literally the 'Red Daggers'—will be the first to engage the invaders." The thousand-soldier-strong Mpini Ekundu were indeed viewed as the fiercest and best-trained armed fighting force on the continent. *We'll see if these men live up to their reputation*, thought Mandebala, though he might have whispered it aloud, as his father turned toward him with his eyebrows raised.

Mabanda spoke. "So, it is agreed. Now that the enemy is deep into Malezi territory, our Red Daggers will systematically destroy their communication and resupply lines, stranding and outflanking the Zambwanan dogs."

"Yes, my king," said the three-star general, "we will cut off the entire Zambwanan army, such that it can fight only with its available resources and within its own internal command structure. And then, God-willing, we will crush the Zambwanans from all sides."

"Done!" said Mabanda in his most imperious, commanding tone. "Commence the operation!"

Mandebala, Mabanda, and the generals in the Situation Room sat silently watching the screen. The big screen shifted into five different helmet camera perspectives, each camera identified by a small tagline in the bottom-right corner of the screens. Jibwa's aide's camera still focused solely on the general, and Mandebala found himself staring at the man. General Jibwa was an enormous behemoth of a man, with charcoal-black skin and an appropriate amount of silver in his hair. "GO!" said General Jibwa.

Through a headset, and equally audible to the generals around the glass table, Jibwa and the Situation Room were being fed live audio. The unmistakable sound of machine gun fire tore through the room, and Mandebala and the rest watched live as Zambwanan men fell lifeless to the ground in hails of molten lead. "Kill-kill-kill!" was shouted by multiple Malezi assailants as they bore witness to the same. And less than a minute after it started, the camera feeds all turned off—but for the feed focused on General Jibwa—and once again the televisions on the wall created a single giant image of the general.

"Good King Mabanda," the general began, then continued without waiting for a reply, "cutting off the Zambwanan dogs has proven to be a rather simple task. Most of the troops left as guards along the supply lines or were otherwise designated to perform resupply tasks with fuel, food, and water, and they were not prepared for the stealth or the lethality of my Red Dagger attack. In fact, most died without knowing a bullet was about to vaporize their brains, entering between their eyes and turning their cognitive thought processes into gelatinous, misfiring neurons."

Interesting, thought Mandebala, *this General Jibwa is both impressive and ambitious, for he thinks of the Mpini Ekundu as "his" own.*

The general continued, "Clearly the Zambwanans had not anticipated that their logistical support lines would be so extended without a battle being fought. My plan—I mean, your magnificent plan, my king—worked to perfection. Now, within minutes, we will commence our attack on the primary Zambwanan incursion force."

Mandebala knew from prior discussions that General Jibwa's remaining Red Daggers had taken up positions on high veldts opposite one another, overlooking an ancient but moderately steep riverbank. The Malezi generals knew that with proper training and discipline, the Zambwanan tanks would have continued their horizontally linear and well-spaced approach, eventually with each of them being forced to trek up an embankment and lead the following men, still spread in their ranks, up the hill. But precisely as General Jibwa and his peers projected, the outer tanks in the Zambwanan force began crowding into the flat terrain of the valley, obviously the path of least resistance, with the concomitant result that the troops were also being squeezed into the valley and were much more concentrated than proper strategy would dictate.

The camera feed split again and this time included two new camera views from troops stationed high on each side of the banks overlooking the advancing Zambwanans. One of the generals safely ensconced in the Situation Room said, "Jibwa! You must attack now!"

"Tut-tut," said General Jibwa dismissively. He let the Zambwanan troops get deeper into the valley, and the command group could see that Zambwanan men and equipment were becoming increasingly concentrated. "Rest easy, my friends," said Jibwa into his headset. "I need to launch my counteroffensive with perfect timing." As it turned out, his timing was perfect, for as the Zambwanan commanders, tired after three days of marching, began to sense the danger inherent in their positioning and called their men and equipment to a halt, the first mortar shells began to fire.

The generals and their king and prince watched as Jibwa beamed with macabre pleasure. It was going to be a great day for him, his king, and his country.

⸻ ◆ ⸻

Shigeku and the rest of the Zambwanan army had marched toward the Malezi capital for well over three days, but it felt like much longer. No amount of training could have prepared Shigeku or any of his fellow fighting soldiers, some thirty thousand strong, for the physical, emotional, and mental drain of their task—fully seventy-two hours of life on the edge of attack. They did make camp for four hours each night, but all rested in mortal fear of imminent attack, and few slept at all. In the afternoon of their fourth day, in the full heat of summer, as they marched along a narrowing river valley, the attack came. Having grown up in the slums, Shigeku thought he knew hell, but he was mistaken. Hades was, it turns out, the sudden whistle-scream of the mortar shells, followed by explosions all around and fire searing the hair off his body as shell after shell exploded in his vicinity. Shrapnel in the form of molten, fiery slags of metal and partially cremated body parts flew all around him, with minor bits searing into his clothing and skin. If this wasn't hell, he would prefer the Land of the Eternally Damned to what he faced there on earth.

It seemed like an eternity before the Zambwanan generals organized their men, but it was actually less than thirty seconds. Strategically, Shigeku wondered if the command given to storm up a hillside was the most advisable tactic, but Shigeku assumed that they had little choice. They had to negate the killing power of the distant mortars by getting themselves into the close range of the Malezi forces, which indubitably had to be positioned on the ridges that were now apparent to all. Their only chance to survive their precarious strategic position was to rely, presumably, on superiority of numbers to overwhelm the defending army.

As the Zambwanan forces began to storm up one side of the river valley, it appeared to Shigeku that the Malezi had made a mistake. A significant contingent of Malezi forces appeared to have been poised on both sides of the valley. By maintaining control and storming up one side, rather than both, of the valley, the Zambwanan forces had negated half of the Malezi ambush. It appeared that General Jibwa had underestimated the ability of the Zambwanans to maintain control over their men.

Shigeku's platoon leader was taking orders, and the necessary discipline was quickly reestablished and maintained by General Zumba. Without discipline and following orders, all would surely perish.

Shigeku and the rest of his unit found themselves at the rear of the advancing Zambwanan forces. Ahead, Shigeku could see the carnage due to the elevation upon which the primary battle was taking place. It seemed that wave after wave of their ranks were being methodically mowed down, despite frenetic offensive hot lead being spewed forth from the Zambwanans' front line of fire. Yet the strength of the defensive firestorm being mounted by the Malezilanders did not diminish, and the order to Shigeku and his men did not change. *None of us will live*, Shigeku thought, but he knew they must press on. To further compound their attacking and ascending efforts, the mounting pile of corpses impeded their progress. Shigeku recognized many of his fellow soldiers, as he and his mates stepped over their bullet-riddled, lifeless corpses. *Fuck, it's impossible to move forward! And we're like sitting ducks in a shooting gallery!*

So many bodies! Shigeku was sure that they had lost at least one-third of their force, yet they pressed forward unrelentingly. More and more bodies piled up. *Will this stop before the men behind me are climbing over my dead body?* As the thought passed through his consciousness, Shigeku thought that the strength of the resisting fire seemed to wane, if ever so slightly. *YES!* The Zambwanan men were quickly spurred into higher gear by Zumba, sensing that a breakthrough might be forthcoming. And then the firing stopped completely.

The Zambwanan army had survived a strategic impossibility and was still intact! Shigeku joined twenty thousand other voices in a spontaneous screaming roar of victory. Its sound was primitive, raw, and wild, and a shiver went up Shigeku's spine. Men jubilantly fired their weapons into the air, though this feting was quickly stopped by the commanders, who were clearly cognizant of limited ammunition supplies.

As the men charged forward to loot the bodies of their victims, Shigeku noted that there were comparatively few enemy casualties. Nevertheless, his spirit ran high, for the army had faced sure defeat at the hands of Africa's most feared and respected fighting force, and they had forced them to retreat!

Shigeku rejoined the other men in their spontaneous, bloodthirsty war whoop.

The group gathered in the Situation Room were arguing fiercely among themselves. "Attack! We must attack from the other side of the hill, as the Zambwanans have all headed one way!" screamed one.

"No," yelled another. "Then these men risk losing their covered positions!"

The men all watched and heard as the Zambwanan advance up the hillside began to gain momentum.

Mandebala joined in the intense debate, screaming, "I agree! the Mpini Ekundu on the far veldt need to advance and engage!"

King Mabanda's deep voice rang out. "No!" he said, drowning out all other voices. "General Jibwa has not engaged these men for a reason." He pressed on the communication link button. "General Jibwa, why have you not ordered your remaining Red Daggers to attack the Zambwanan rear?"

"My king," said General Jibwa, whose calm face suddenly appeared on the screens before them, "your Red Daggers are an amazing fighting force, but to order them down into the valley would subject them to the same tactical disadvantage that the Zambwanans also faced—the high ground is always favored. No amount of training, especially against a numerically superior force, could negate that disadvantage. With your permission, I am ordering my Red Daggers to retreat. It is clear that the Zambwanans will manage to crest the veldt. The fools will think they have won a battle. Yet fewer than fifty of your Red Daggers sacrificed their lives for you, my king. By our estimates, the Zambwanans have lost approximately ten thousand men—fully one-third of their forces. No, we must retreat."

Mandebala's father roared, "Sound the retreat this instant!" The men in the Situation Room watched, open-mouthed.

General Jibwa barked a command into his walkie-talkie. "Retreat! All retreat to fallback position two! I repeat, all retreat to fallback position two!"

The king turned to the generals. "Dead soldiers have no value."

Mandebala didn't dare argue his point, nor did the generals. The men silently turned off the AV equipment and filed out of the Situation Room. Mandebala marveled enviously at his father's power.

Once the celebration had subsided and the men had finished pilfering everything of value they could get their hands on, Shigeku paused to reflect quietly upon what had happened. He was quite impressed with the ability of General Zumba to hold his men together and organize them into a disciplined, coordinated counterattack. Clearly, without the quick reaction and well-orchestrated response, their entire force could have been lost. Shigeku was pleased that Zumba had confidence that his fellow soldiers were well trained enough to attack into an unfavorable position, knowing that eventually superiority of numbers would carry the day.

Shigeku took a further moment's pause from his camp setup duties and looked around. The devastation wrought upon the Zambwanan forces was significant. He noticed that the sound of twenty thousand men was appreciably lower than that of thirty thousand. Fewer tents were being set up. The wounded were being triaged, though only those with the most superficial of wounds were worth treating, as they were capable of rejoining the fighting force. Those who were wounded so badly that they couldn't immediately serve a useful purpose in armed combat would have to survive on their own and would be left behind when camp broke. Without a proper medical team to treat them, and facing abandonment in the heart of enemy territory, many took their own lives rather than allow themselves to be captured, tortured, and humiliated.

Shigeku and his crew bedded down as quickly as they could. He was grateful for his troop's positioning during the clash, for he and his mates had survived unscathed. He wanted to call out to Moto, Mobuto, Zansha, and Chala, but before he could formulate something witty to say, he fell fast asleep. Virtually every Zambwanan soldier slept soundly for the first time in three days.

Shigeku was roused from his deep sleep by the standard clanging of the bell. It was dark yet, and the fog in his brain told him that he had managed nowhere near sufficient sleep. They were being ordered to move out less than two hours after they had fallen asleep. Shigeku was still dead tired, hungry, and, after the initial euphoria and adrenaline had worn off, quite lethargic. He sighed.

On the move again.

The sole remaining Malezi spy was also taken aback by the sudden order to break camp and start marching eastward. He knew that it was incumbent upon him to try to report this movement to the king and his generals. Unfortunately, despite the fact that it was still absolutely dark, the local vegetation had thinned. They were no longer traversing through the jungle but were actually about to move through a high grassland plain, with rather sparse vegetation and thin, drying grass. He had no opportunity whatsoever to make a quick sat call, and he knew that if any of his other fellow transplants had survived, they, too, would lack a similar chance. The spoor of the Red Daggers was still fresh, and General Zumba was obviously going to attempt to catch their foe unaware. The spy hoped that sentries had been posted, and that if they had, their warning would be sufficient to permit King Mabanda's men to be readied for the attack.

To Shigeku's surprise, the troops made quick time across the plains, despite their significant number, and they moved quite stealthily. This was due in part to the fact that most of their noisier machinery had long since broken down, been shelled, or run out of fuel due to lack of resupply.

The sounds of the African night were quite familiar to Shigeku; nocturnal birds hooted and chirped, and the buzz of crickets and other hard-winged insects had an almost electric sound. Yet when the sound of a bellowing lion pierced the monotony of the more constant din, Shigeku froze. Deafeningly loud, the roar was close, very close. A nearby lion pride was on the hunt, or at least on the move, having been disturbed by the massive body of humans moving through their territory.

Other lions roared in response, causing Shigeku to come perilously close to breaking ranks and fleeing for his life. Indeed, the scent of lion musk drifted through their midst, and the men closest to Shigeku scanned the plains beside them more than they looked at the ground ahead. Shigeku hoped that the pride had been well fed that day, as their roars got ever closer and closer. He didn't want to be anywhere near a pride of hungry lions in the dark of the night. Shigeku's hair stood on end with each successive roar, and he was completely unable to suppress his visibly full-body shivers. His fear of becoming lion fodder dwarfed his fear of being shot.

From but a few meters away from Shigeku on the northwestern flank of the advancing group, one of the men gave a bloodcurdling scream. The lions would feast on human flesh tonight.

Shigeku heard unnatural sounds—man-made. He strained to listen. The forward scouts returned, confirming that the Malezi enemy encampment was less than a kilometer away. Their commanders halted their progress, and soon the sounds of an army were audible, being carried toward them by a surprisingly firm westerly wind. God had favored their silent approach with His favorable breath.

Shigeku was preparing for their attack by checking and rechecking the firing mechanisms and ensuring access to loaded cartridge refill clips when a disconcerting sound emanated from the enemy encampment ahead. It was the sound of silence. Not just a quieter volume of noise, nor the blending of many noises into one, but a sudden, absolute silence.

General Zumba responded by immediately sounding the attack. Shigeku's heart pounded with adrenaline and excitement as he and twenty thousand men launched an all-out assault on their yet-unseen enemy's encampment. Immediately, fire was hailed down upon them, but it wasn't nearly as strong nor as lethal as Shigeku was expecting. *Something's wrong.* He saw the men just ahead of him fall; however, within a few short minutes, the sound of shooting completely stopped. All was dead silent once again—even the sounds of the jungle.

Shigeku helped count the enemy dead—only one hundred bodies. A minor company of troops had mounted the entire resistance to their surprise attack. *Not much food here for the pride of lions.*

CHAPTER 7

The king seemed elated with the day's events. He relaxed in his library in his favorite chair with his favorite libation and smoked a massive Cuban cigar. Mandebala sat beside him, his spirits equally lifted by the day's events and his father's ebullient mood. Only the fact that the king's Cohiba was largely burning on its own without the king drawing on it regularly would have indicated to the astute observer that he was preoccupied. Mandebala was matching his father drink for drink, and the haze from his own cigar mixed with the king's to fill the room.

The voice of an unknown attendant behind them beckoned.

"My king, General Jibwa would like to speak with you."

"Put him through," boomed Mabanda.

Not even his top generals had his cell phone number.

"Well, you've had quite the amazingly successful day, General Jibwa!" said the king, beaming broadly as he leaned into his phone so that the speakerphone would pick his voice up clearly.

"Thank you, my king," said Jibwa. "We lost over eleven hundred men today, which is a tragedy."

"Come now, General, men can be replaced easily! But how many of my Mpini Ekundu were lost among that number? And how many Zambwanan dogs were sent to hell today?"

"You lost less than fifty Red Daggers, my king. The cur Kureba's army is more than ten thousand fewer in size, my king. Some, of course, were Malezis who had crossed the border," stated Jibwa.

Prince Mandebala knew that on a less glorious day, this would have enraged the king.

"We owe much to our operative behind enemy lines," asserted Jibwa to his king. "I do believe he has earned his promised promotion, should he survive the rest of this campaign, which, somehow, I think he has the wits to accomplish."

A spy? The prince wondered who it could be.

"Agreed," stated the king. "From this moment forth, he carries the rank of general. Whether or not he ever knows of or exercises the rights and privileges of his new rank is in God's own hands."

As the Zambwanans strolled into the abandoned Malezi camp, Shigeku and the men were quite thrilled to find luxury accommodations: new tents with bug screens without holes and fresh food—meat, dairy, and vegetables—waiting for their arrival. Some of the food was abandoned mid-preparation, obviously having been left behind as the departure was ordered with haste. In fact, most had not yet even been overcooked or otherwise wasted. It was as if a great feast had been prepared for them, and Shigeku dug into his first full meal in forty-eight hours like a hyena on a zebra. Within thirty minutes, he and the others were fast asleep, always knowing that sleep was necessary wherever and whenever possible.

Shigeku found that he was very much growing to like Moto, and it seemed that Moto felt the same. Perhaps the battlefield had a way of drawing people together. Theirs was a forum of combat where every man was fighting as an individual and relying, to an extent, on his own fire-power to eliminate the enemy threats to his life. Nevertheless, Shigeku felt certain that Moto, on more than one occasion, was watching his back. Shigeku's innate survival instinct had told him several times to turn about to face a previously undetected threat, only to see that same threat falling, dead, with Moto's weapon having eliminated him.

Shigeku's crew were sitting around a small, makeshift firepit, cleaning their weapons and allowing their overfilled stomachs to process what they had voraciously consumed.

"Hey, pup," said Moto, "you know that you owe me for dropping that Malezi dog who had his sights on you yesterday, right? I think that taking the honor of your first daughter should be sufficient . . . that is, if you ever find a woman desperate enough to fuck you and bear your child." The giant man grinned.

"Says the man who wouldn't know the difference between a virgin's flower and a goat's ass!" said Shigeku, dodging the cuff to his head that Moto amiably threw his way.

Their close circle of friends nestled around the small fire was diminished by one, however. "Do you really think that Mobuto will be okay?" Moto asked of the group.

"Almost certainly," replied Chala. "The wound to his stomach was superficial and clearly missed any major organs, or he would have died on the battlefield. He's actually Malezi, like me. We grew up not far from where we left him. There's a missionary hospital nearby, so he should be fine."

Zansha stared blankly ahead at the fire, obviously troubled. Chala began to dance rhythmically around the fire—the youngster in the group clearly had energy to burn, and his adrenaline-stoked body was still on a high.

"I cannot wait to kill more Mpini Ekundu pussies!" he sang.

Mobuto barked, "Chala, sit the fuck down before I shoot you myself. You're making *me* tired!"

Shigeku laughed with his friends. *It has been a good day.*

Shigeku awoke to the bright sunshine of midmorning, feeling refreshed and energized by the sleep and nourishment of the previous night. He knew the enemy was on the run, and Shigeku felt optimistic about their campaign.

He remained puzzled, however, by something he had seen during the lion attack the previous evening. After seeking out Moto in their tent, Shigeku asked, "What were you doing during the lion attack? You dropped to your knees and grabbed something out of your pack." Shigeku saw a momentary flash of shock register on Moto's otherwise blank face, but it was so fleeting that Shigeku couldn't discern it with certainty.

"Come here, my friend, and I shall show you," said Moto, bending over into his now resting backpack. Shigeku peered closer and watched his countryman dig deep into the pack, whereupon Moto whipped out a wild-looking—but clearly lethal—half-meter-long blade. With a quick and precise upswing as Moto stood up, the tip of the assegai knife expertly nicked Shigeku's nose. Shigeku jumped back in surprise. A tiny droplet of blood fell to the ground at his feet, creating a little ring in the loose dust where it lay.

Moto grinned down at the smaller man, who grinned back. "For thousands of years, our people have faced lions. I wanted to ensure that I had my assegai in hand if they decided to make a meal out of you and me, my friend, and to fight them off like a man with a traditional weapon. Our rifles are, of course, quite useless at close range against *samba* in the dark."

The prick to his nose didn't hurt, and he was quite in awe at the skill with which his friend had wielded the killing dagger. *Not bad for such a beast of a man.*

⁂

Crown Prince Mandebala was roused from his peaceful sleep in the dead of night, as none would dare awaken the king at this hour. The comm link alert had flashed in the Situation Room, and an attendant told the prince that General Jibwa was calling in on the sat phone/cam. The duty attendant had used his cell phone to roust the on-call general, who was asleep in adjacent quarters.

Mandebala threw on a luxurious robe of the finest silk and headed through the heavy mahogany double doors of the Situation Room. A three-star general named Kingame soon appeared through a small, inobtrusive door at the far end of the Sit Room, rubbing his eyes and donning his gold-braided general's hat, which completed his full dress uniform.

The wall of televisions lit up with the now-enormous face of General Jibwa, and a loud humming noise filled the room as the sat phone's audio transmission began. "General Kingame," said General Jibwa with a nod, "I have decided that it is our turn to utilize the element of surprise. Our own scouts have watched the progression of the Zambwanan army. They have confirmed that the dogs are, indeed, encamped for the night. These same scouts returned to our own camp at a pace equal to their uppermost physical capability, as they knew that their intelligence should be acted upon immediately."

General Kingame scowled. "So, you are *sure* that the Zambwanans are encamped for the night?" Mandebala knew the general's emphasis on the word *sure* would raise the severity of his and General Kingame's punishment should they reach the wrong conclusion. General Jibwa, and the camera on the sat phone, swung toward a still-panting scout behind him.

"Absolutely, General Kingame, sir," the scout blustered. "To make sure, we followed their scouts back toward their camp for three kilometers before returning to you to file our report, sir."

"And your conclusion is?" demanded General Kingame.

General Jibwa spoke with firm conviction. "Sir, it is my humble conclusion that the Zambwanan scum believe our forces to be out of range for an attack. Their scouts traveled far without finding our camp. It will be their report that our men are at least six hours away."

⁕

Shigeku felt the best that he had in over a month as he lay back on his sleeping pad. Optimism was high in the camp, and the Zambwanan commanders had let the men relax. The enemy forces were far away; Shigeku had heard that their scouts had come back after a six-hour sortie without encountering the Malezis. The nick on Shigeku's nose, which barely bothered him, had stopped bleeding. Shigeku also took comfort knowing that multiple sentries had been placed strategically around the perimeter of the camp. These sentries reported in regularly, every fifteen minutes, an interval that Shigeku knew provided for a high level of security.

Shigeku got up to take a leak, annoyed with his own bladder for interrupting his rest. As he strolled past the security tent, the various sentries began reporting in, one by one, at their appointed time. When the outer perimeter sentry to the west failed to report in perfectly on time, the watch commander paid no attention, though Shigeku felt uneasy about it. He called out to the watch commander, "Hey, comrade, aren't you concerned that the west post didn't report in? Aren't you going to call him?"

The watch commander replied with a chuckle, "The west post is Toto. He naps half his shift. Don't worry—there's a backup sentry on the inner west perimeter. I will reprimand Toto for dozing off after breakfast."

Shigeku was not pleased with these responses. He walked quickly back to his tent, grabbed his AK-47, and headed toward the western perimeter silently in the full darkness of a cloudy night.

———— ◆ ————

As Shigeku made his way toward the inner west perimeter post, he was quite relieved to see the red glowing ember of a cigarette hovering in the distant darkness of night. *Good, perhaps my concerns were unnecessary.* He watched the glowing ember jettisoned to the ground, obviously having sated its smoker's craving.

Shigeku kept advancing toward the sentry, his own sense of alertness lowered after confirming the sentry's well-being. "Hey!" he called out quietly in Zambwanan dialect, a form of their common tongue simple for him to master and understand. He hoped he wouldn't alarm the sentry and wind up with a bullet between his eyes.

What's that? It wasn't so much that he saw movement up ahead. It was almost as if he sensed it. He wasn't seeing objects move . . . but . . . he was pretty sure he could see trees and shrubs being momentarily and intermittently blocked from his view. *Fuck!* He was sure he had seen it again. And again. He strained his eyes to focus and dropped to the plains floor. *Fuck!* An attack force was moving toward his camp.

Shigeku knew that if he raised the alarm, he was dead. As he crawled toward a shrub for cover, he almost knelt upon the still-glowing ember of the sentry's cigarette and was forced to climb over his corpse en route to cover. *Fucking idiot—sentries should never smoke! Talk about making yourself an easy target!* Clearly the outer sentry was now "napping" eternally thanks to a silenced bullet. Shigeku could now see nigh invisible shapes, perhaps a dozen strong, moving to within attack range of the camp. *All our sentries are dead.* He knew that the Malezis' main force would surely follow. He had to warn his comrades, but to do so would ensure his instant death. As he struggled with his predicament, the security/communications array and tent blew up right before his eyes, close enough to singe the hair on his face. *The fucking Malezis knew exactly where the comms tent was located!* It had obviously been obliterated with an RPG.

"FUCK!" yelled Shigeku as the sounds of hundreds, if not thousands, of men filled the air, impossibly close to him to the east. Artillery shells began streaking through the sky westward, with every single one hitting on target. After sixty seconds of mortar fire, the sounds of voices began advancing toward him and his shrubbery cover, and soon floating military flares lit up the sky over the Zambwanan encampment. Hundreds of men strode into camp, some of whom were carrying heavy machine guns, tripods, and ammo cases. Shigeku watched in horror as first the tripods were opened, the machine guns affixed, and then bands of ammunition fed into the weapons' breaches. Shigeku hoped that Moto, Zansha, and Chala were scrambling to arm themselves.

As soon as each of the Malezi gunners' setups was ready, they fired wave after wave of molten lead, semi-vaporizing tents and people in their fields of fire.

Shigeku could hear sporadic gunfire coming from the far side of the Zambwanan camp, and he was certain that the resistance was going to be too little—and far too late. As he watched in fearful terror, he could see that the ammunition was almost ready to be loaded into the nearest Malezi machine gun—a weapon that would soon be trained upon his friends.

Shigeku readied his AK-47 and burst from his sanctuary bush, gun blazing. There were now three machine gun setups within his visual range, all of whom were faced, of course, toward the Zambwanan encampment, their backs toward Shigeku. With three rapid bursts of automatic fire, Shigeku mowed down three teams of four in less than five seconds. He sprinted to his tent, feeling very exposed. "Moto! Chala! Zansha! We've got to leave NOW!" he exclaimed as he burst into the tent.

"Thank God it's you!" said Chala. "What's the situation?"

"Not good!" said Shigeku. "We've got to bust out now or we're as good as dead, if it's not already too late. Then we have to try to organize our men to fight back!"

The four of them formed a tactical formation and moved out, with Moto and Shigeku in the lead.

Moto looked over at him and smiled. "Are you scared yet, pup?"

Barely able to yell over his heavy breathing, Shigeku yelled, "Come on! We've got to organize our men. So far they've hit us with mortars and machine guns, but I haven't seen any regular troops yet. Maybe they aren't sending them in and we can take out the machine gunners and be done with them!" As the last words left his mouth, bullets began whistling past them, followed by the unmistakable sound of AK-47 fire. Moto hit the dirt immediately and beckoned Shigeku to follow. Zansha and Chala sprinted in the opposite direction.

"No! What are you doing, Moto?" shouted Shigeku. "We have to kill these attacking dogs!"

Shigeku saw calm on Moto's face. *What is wrong with him?*

"No, my little friend," Moto said. "This battle—indeed, this war—is already lost. I know the ways of these men."

Shigeku hit the dirt, praying to be spared. As he faced away from the oncoming fire, he watched as first Zansha, then Chala, were mowed down by automatic weapon fire. Shigeku winced, closed his eyes tightly, and didn't move a muscle.

On the side of the camp farthest from the action, Shigeku heard a helicopter come screaming in, hot, engines whining to keep the rotor speed high. He opened his eyes wide enough to watch a late-model black Bell JetRanger civilian helicopter come in at top speed. Without the metal bird ever alighting on the ground or even slowing its rotors, General Zumba, who had not had the courage to even show his face to rally his troops, clambered aboard. Shigeku knew that it must be President Kureba's personal helicopter, as the Zambwanan military could not afford such refined transportation. Although she took many hits, the big metal bird carried away its precious cargo.

Coward. Shigeku briefly considered standing and unleashing a volley of lead into the side of the aircraft.

Shigeku knew they would all be slaughtered. It mattered not whether they surrendered peaceably. Shigeku had no idea how Moto intended their deception to save them, as surely the two of them would be slaughtered where they lay the moment their ruse was discovered. The entire battle was over in less than five minutes from the first shot. It was a complete bloodbath.

The only sound of gunfire came as Malezi troops finished off the wounded Zambwanan men. The scouring party was proceeding through the camp, poking and prodding the fallen and wounded, pistols in hand, finishing off all who breathed or otherwise flinched when kicked, poked, or otherwise prodded. As the pistol shots came so close as to cause Shigeku's ears to ring, and as Shigeku squeezed his eyes shut as tightly as he could and began his final silent prayers to God, Moto jumped up and shouted, "HOLD YOUR FIRE!"

Shigeku kept his eyes closed, knowing Moto was dead where he stood and knowing he was next. *Some plan . . . Now I cannot even die a proper warrior's death.*

Someone shouted, "Lieutenant Moto! Thank the gods that you're safe!"

What? Shigeku opened one eye to peer over at the soldier speaking to his friend. *"Lieutenant" Moto?*

"This little dog on the ground lives," Moto spat out, pointing at Shigeku.

Me?

"Bring him with me," the lieutenant said, scowling at Shigeku. "Full custody. He is my charge, and if he can give me good cause, I may spare his life. Actually, I doubt that very much, but I will see how well the little pup can beg."

Shigeku was half dragged along behind an unknown but large number of Malezi troops, somewhat in a daze. Not ten minutes earlier, his entire combat unit of twenty thousand men had been annihilated, and now he was evidently the only one left alive. His friend Moto was apparently a high-ranking spy for the Malezi armed forces. Shigeku's head spun, and the memory of the flash of shock that Moto had registered when Shigeku had questioned him about the lion attack suddenly made sense. Moto had used the diversion of the lion attack to alert his comrades in the Malezi military that an attack was imminent—*that* was how the Malezi army had escaped the surprise assault on their camp, even if just barely. Shigeku was angry, but as he marched along, that anger turned to fear.

Soldiers died on the battlefield all the time, but when death came in that fashion, you didn't have time to think about it, and as such you didn't have time to develop fear. Now, handcuffed and held captive, he began to truly fear death. No, death wouldn't come quickly and honorably; he would be lucky to not be tortured before dying. And what did Moto mean when he said that he might spare Shigeku's life? As they bumped along in a command jeep, Shigeku saw the look of satisfaction on Moto's face when he was informed that he'd been promoted to general, and as such with that rank, he merited travel by escorted jeep. Shigeku began wondering how he might save his own life.

CHAPTER 8

Shigeku watched disbelievingly as Moto entered the front double doors of a large, impressive building that he knew to be the headquarters of Maleziland's military.

The edifice looked incredibly out of place in East Central Africa, with ornate pillars and a grandiose, wide staircase leading to an artificially elevated building. It was rumored to house an extensive military prison, though in a land where incarceration was more expensive than bullets, no one had yet lived to tell whether or not the rumors were true.

Immediately after General Moto departed his escort, the jeeps whisked around the building to a back entrance. In a few short minutes, Shigeku had been led down cool, damp stairs into a dungeon-like cell. Though shackles hung from the stone walls, eagerly anticipating their next ward, none were placed on Shigeku's wrists. Odd. But then, what wasn't odd about any of this?

Time dragged by—exactly how much time, Shigeku didn't know, as there were no windows and no natural lighting whatsoever permitting him to discern day from night—but it certainly went by exceedingly slowly, irrespective of the actual ticking of a clock he could not see. His senses were heightened by depravation, and he swore that on several occasions he could smell food being cooked, but none was brought down. He could hear a tap dripping in the distance. Actually, perhaps it was more likely condensation collecting and falling. By his estimation it dripped regularly, every forty-eight seconds or so, and as time went on, it seemed to pick up its pace a bit, as if the moisture from his own body had raised the humidity level in the chamber. After counting it down several dozen times, he was quite sure that it was now dripping every forty-six seconds or so.

He heard a set of footsteps coming down the stairs. Moto's legs came into view. Then the rest of him appeared, carrying a rather impressive-looking meal by Malezi standards—chicken, rice, and some sort of leafy green vegetable. Instantly, Shigeku's mouth began to water precipitously.

Moto's general uniform was absolutely resplendent, with gold-braided epaulettes, shiny gold buttons, and multiple medals, including several medals that could only be bestowed upon someone who had seen active duty. Shigeku wondered if any had been given out for "rescuing fellow Malezilanders while under enemy fire." He decided not to ask.

Several minutes of silence passed. Despite his hunger and anticipation, Shigeku wouldn't beg for the food. Moto spoke first. "Here, my friend. Eat." And with that, Moto opened the door to his captive's cell and set the food on the floor in front of him. Shigeku was neither shackled nor handcuffed, yet Moto had walked unarmed into the cell. Shigeku was certain there were multiple armed guards at the top of the stairs; nevertheless, Moto's confidence unnerved him. As he ate, ravenously stuffing food into his mouth with his bare hands—of course, he wasn't provided with weapon-like utensils—Shigeku never failed to keep at least one eye trained upon his captor and former friend.

As he downed the last morsel, Shigeku finally spoke. "Why play with my life as if it were a toy? And why deny me the right and decency to die an honorable death?" He tried to sound braver than he felt.

"Little pup, do you not understand? If I wanted you dead, I would have given you that honor and put a bullet through your head myself. Although you do not seem to believe it, I do indeed consider you to be a friend. Maybe that's odd, but the truth of it is undeniable. Though I am a powerful man, there are limits to what I can do, for you are a known traitor to your king and your country. No, help me to help you, Shigeku. Give me a reason that will allow me to spare your life. Save yourself, Shigeku. Help me to save you."

As Moto watched intently, Shigeku felt the fear and trepidation that must have permeated every pore of his existence begin to transform into a confident posture and radiant smile. He straightened his back, his head reached the apex of his height, and his shoulders unslumped.

Shigeku knew how he was going to save his life.

"Ask the king if there was a fire in the missionary hospital the day his son was born," he said with a smile.

King Mabanda relaxed in a sumptuous leather chair in his library, smiling at the thought of the breasts of the young peasant girl his motorcade had encountered earlier at the market. His pulse raced when he remembered the fear on her face as she'd jumped out of the Range Rover's path.

His fantasy was interrupted by an idiot aide. "King Mabanda, sir," the lanky boy said.

Mabanda scowled. "This had better be important to so rudely interrupt my most important thoughts regarding future sources of funding for our country's infrastructure," he said.

"Yes, sir, yes, sir, it is," blurted the aide, wringing his dark hands. "Your new general, Moto, insists on seeing you. I told him that you were not to be interrupted, even by a general, and that he could pass his message on to me and I would relay it to Your Highness. He insisted, and I do believe that he would have pushed right through me had I not acceded to his request and agreed to inquire whether or not you would see him."

The slight young man began to tremble. The king smiled at the poor boy's physical manifestation of intimidation. *Excellent indeed.*

"Did not this man give you *any* indication as to the nature of his business with his regent?" asked Mabanda.

"No, s-s-s-sir, he said that he could not, that his message was of the gravest importance, and that he could only deliver it to you personally."

King Mabanda decided the boy was sufficiently terrified. "Fine, send the general in." He would have gladly taken the meeting with General Moto, "urgent matter" or not. He wanted to personally thank the man for his heroic service to his king and country and pepper him with questions about what he had learned behind enemy lines.

The aide creaked the door open slightly, presumably with General Moto in tow.

"Bring him in, you fool!" the king bellowed.

The aide looked as if he would wet his pants as he led the general into the room.

The king widened his eyes and glared at the young man. "Well?"

The waiflike boy went pale and exited the room with haste as King Mabanda turned to the large general with a hearty laugh.

"Good King Mabanda, I apologize for this rude and unscheduled interruption," began Moto with a grin.

"Not at all, General Moto. With what you accomplished while among the Zambwanan scum, you have earned the right to speak to your king! Come, join me! I have some beautiful Cuban Special Edition Cohibas and some Courvoisier XO that are a match made in heaven. Come! Sit with me!"

"Sir, I thank you for your kind offer. That said, I interrupted you for but one specific reason. May I speak?"

Mabanda frowned. It was bad form to turn down the generosity of the king. Having found somebody to indulge with, and by putting it at the forefront of his consciousness, Mabanda was already beginning to look forward to the numbing pleasure of the smoke and drink. "Speak," he said soberly.

"King Mabanda, I wish to ask a simple question of you, but I must first preface the question by giving you some background. As you know, I spent six weeks with the Zambwanan army, training with them as if I were truly loyal to the Zambwanan dog Kureba. As agreed, I swore a false oath of loyalty to him, as did all your other agents, none of whom apparently survived.

"While training among them, I became friends with a Malezilander who had also sworn allegiance to Kureba and was fighting for their forces. I'm not proud of this fact, but I suppose it was quite natural under the circumstances. We were together twenty-four seven. I watched his back; he watched mine. I killed to protect him; he killed to protect me. It is fair to say that without this little pup, I would have been killed and my mission would have failed. Indubitably, our superior military would have prevailed, but that victory most certainly would have come at a much higher cost in terms of money and men. As such, I decided to give this young pup the opportunity to plead for his life, and we took him prisoner under my orders."

"YOU DID WHAT?" roared Mabanda, leaping off his seat. Though Moto was a full thirty centimeters taller than Mabanda and had several kilos of muscle for every kilo of royal fat, the king was pleased when Moto took a step back. "That is UNHEARD OF!" Mabanda shouted. "What were you thinking?"

Moto cleared his throat and straightened his shoulders. After a deep breath, he said, "Sire, I understand your anger, as it was indeed an unconventional step to take. I fully anticipated that I would take the traitor's life myself; in fact, I expect that he will be dead by nightfall, by my own hand if you insist. However, after he saved my life in battle, and indeed helped me achieve my mission, contributing to your glorious victory over the Zambwanan dogs, I wanted to give him the opportunity to plead for his life. And he did just that."

"General, my patience is being *severely* tested here. What on God's earth does this have to do with me?"

"Sire, he said but one thing to me. He said, 'Ask the king if there was a fire in the missionary hospital the day his son was born.'"

The king's jaw dropped. He fell back into his chair.

"I must say, sir, that from the confidence in the way he spoke, and his behavior and mannerisms subsequent to speaking the words, he is very sure that the message will have meaning to you. What exactly the point of the fact of a fire may be, he would not tell me."

"Bring him to me *now*." The king's cigar ash fell guillotine-like to the floor.

⁂

Shigeku had fallen asleep on the cold concrete floor. He found the room intolerably damp and humid. He was completely unaware of whether it was day or night, and though he was tired, his sleep was far from sound. He was haunted by dreams of his maman, dreams he hadn't dreamt for years and years—the look in her eyes when she asked him to pledge to look after his soon-to-be-born sibling; the frantic rush to the hospital; the realization that she was dead on arrival; the spill of her guts and womb as the doctors cut her open to save a babe that, unbeknownst to anybody but him, had become the crown prince of Maleziland.

Shigeku tossed and turned on the hard floor. Half-consciously, he hoped that Maman would forgive what he was about to do. Half-consciously, he defended his imminent course of action against her accusing but imaginary stare. Half-consciously, he was happy to finally end the charade and to end the privileged life he had given his brother Mandebala.

Shigeku was awakened by the sound of Moto's voice. "Shigeku! King Mabanda wishes to see you immediately."

Moto stood at the door to the cell. "If you embarrass me in front of the king, I will cut off more than the tip of your nose this time, friend or not," he said.

"You have nothing to fear, *friend*," said Shigeku, smiling. He was *really* looking forward to this.

◆

Moto hauled Shigeku into the king's office. Shigeku's hands were cuffed behind him, and he staggered awkwardly before the king when Moto thrust him forward.

"Speak your tale, you treacherous little gutter rat, and see whether you can save your life," said Mabanda.

Shigeku slowly looked up at the king. Although he wore no crown, Shigeku could not imagine anybody possibly looking more kingly. King Mabanda wore rings and necklaces adorned with massive, sparkling gems, each of which was unknown to Shigeku, and his robe itself looked to have been woven from the same golden metal.

"Before I do, I need your word that if my story proves true, I will be freed." Shigeku knew that King Mabanda could, and would, go back on his royal word without a second thought, but nevertheless, he felt the need to secure this bargain.

King Mabanda silently got up from his seat, walked around his massive ebony desk, and brought his being to within millimeters of Shigeku. Although they were the same height, Mabanda's girth and presence made Shigeku feel puny; however, Shigeku neither flinched nor slumped.

Without a word, Mabanda took one step back and kicked Shigeku in the testes as hard as he could. Shigeku doubled over as the king cupped the crown of Shigeku's head and crashed his knee into his chin, *muay Thai*–style, and everything went black.

Faint light and echoes of words slowly came back into his consciousness, and Shigeku saw a dark and menacing shadow looming over his body.

"You are in no position to bargain with your king," Mabanda growled from above.

Someone began splashing water on Shigeku's face and slapped him about. When he had regained enough of his faculties to speak but not stand, Moto and another of his men held him upright. He faced the king, who was now perched on his throne. He had been moved to the throne room of the royal palace. Few Malezilanders had ever seen the ornate gilded throne in person, though all would recognize it from the televised state speeches Mabanda would often give. The royal perch appeared to have been crafted from solid gold. King Mabanda himself did not come close to the height of its silk-woven chair back, and jewels of every color and shape adorned its gold frame.

Wide-eyed, Shigeku peered around the room as best he could without moving his head even slightly. He could see all forms of art in the form of expensive-looking paintings and sculptures; interestingly, he noted, none looked tribal or indigenous in any way.

Shigeku forced himself to smile even as his head thudded with every heartbeat and pain flowed through his body. The king blanched, though on so dark a skin tone, it was nearly imperceptible. Shigeku started his tale, without properly addressing the king with titles of deference.

"My brother was born on the same day as your son, at the missionary hospital. He was born to my mother, who had already died before I delivered her to the doorstep of the hospital; the doctors cut my brother out of her dead body.

"Maman made me promise to look after the child about to be born. As you know, the soul of a mother who dies in childbirth is transferred to that of the child who caused her death. It was my death pledge to my maman, and one that I have honored right up to this very day."

King Mabanda had inched forward to the edge of his ornate perch.

Perfect. "I was a young boy then," Shigeku continued, "and I was burdened by my mother's request. How could I say no? Then I saw my opportunity. I could make good on my pledge and honor my mother. With quick action, I was able to relieve myself of that awful burden for all time.

"I heard you bellowing—"

The king frowned, and Shigeku cleared his throat.

"Um . . . speaking—in the room next door and saw a doctor with a newborn in his arms. I realized I was staring at Queen Carolanda's baby, the new crown prince of Maleziland. The entire country knew that she would soon give birth; everyone was hoping for a boy. When I saw the royal babe, I knew what I had to do.

"I set a fire in a wastebasket. The doctors were too busy to notice and were headed back to you. I screamed, 'FIRE!' and in the chaos that followed, I switched the queen's baby with that of my dead maman's. Your son, Crown Prince Mandebala, is my brother, a street-rat, lowborn bastard like me."

The silence that followed was so complete that Shigeku could hear the blood coursing through veins in his head. It was the last sensation he remembered before the butt of Moto's sidearm crashed into the side of his skull, the third time in less than a month that he was rendered unconscious by a blow.

Shigeku awoke in his familiar cell, his head throbbing like the beat of a timpani orchestral drum. When he reached up to rub his head, he touched a sticky mass at the base of his neck and winced at the sharp, electric pain compounding the constant, drubbing malady. A patch of his skin and hair had been cut off—to what end, Shigeku couldn't imagine.

Days passed, and Shigeku counted one day for every three visits by the guard bringing his meals. He grew quite restless, yet thankfully, his meals were a diet that Shigeku's wiry frame found decadent compared to his slum-dwelling days. His feelings of ill ease were primarily a function of wondering what would become of him in light of the story he had revealed. The horrible throbbing in his head had finally subsided, though a dull ache remained. Shigeku still had some difficulty forming thoughts.

It was many days—twelve, in actuality—before someone other than the guard came to see him again. Shigeku's spirits soared as he heard an unrecognizable gait descending the stairs into the holding area outside his cell. A visitor! He hoped it was his "friend" Moto, who he presumed had been responsible for the crushing blow to his head.

Moto approached and Shigeku smiled. The general opened the door to his cage and began to speak.

"I am sorry, my friend, for the blow to the back of your head. You must understand that you had just spoken the most preposterous story imaginable, and it seemed like the right thing to do at the time. I would have shot you myself for your affront to the king, but King Mabanda himself intervened. He demanded that I hack a piece of skin and hair from your head to send for testing. Something about your story made him believe it to be true. We sent it off to South Africa for DNA analysis; we do not yet have such diagnostic equipment in Maleziland, though the king now seems very much interested in acquiring it."

"And?" asked Shigeku.

"Your story has been confirmed. Mandebala is your brother. You are a free man," said Moto.

CHAPTER 9

Mandebala's life as a young man couldn't have been much better for anybody anywhere on the globe. It was filled with good food, fine alcoholic beverages, and schooling administered by private tutors, always female and always attractive and available. Yet what he liked best was being with his father.

Late one night, after an evening of drinking French Bordeaux and fine single malts, Mandebala was roughly roused from his bed at 4:00 a.m. by a dozen men in military fatigues. As his sleep-and-chemical-fogged brain tried to process what was happening, the soldiers dragged him from his bed.

"What in the name of God, Jesus, Lucifer, and Beelzebub do you vermin shit think you are doing?" howled Mandebala. "Unhand me this instant, and I will plead on your behalf to have your testes spared the knife!"

A leather-gloved backhand crushed his nose, sending shooting splinters of white light through his cerebellum as nerves fired and misfired in a way he had never experienced before. When his faculties recovered enough to process what had just happened, he took advantage of the momentary lessening of his captors' grips to lunge for his bedside table. He managed to break their hold, quickly seized his hunting knife from the drawer, and brandished it malevolently in front of his face, his back to the bed, waving the knife at his aggressors.

"I know how to use this knife, you soon-to-be-lifeless pieces of shit," screeched Mandebala, his voice rising an octave. "NOW GET THE FUCK OUT OF MY ROOM THIS INSTANT!"

Mandebala's mind processed a quick flash of light, then he watched in horror as his hunting knife and the first segments of his index, middle, and ring fingers dropped to the floor. The sword had been raised and flashed with such speed that he hadn't fully registered its presence or threat. Though he didn't feel any pain—that would come later and with a vengeance—the physical fight in him was completely gone.

"You fucking idiots!" he screamed. "I am the crown prince of Maleziland, the future king! How dare you! Quick, get ice and collect my fingers, you fools! They must be sewed back on!"

His captors wrapped a towel around his maimed hand, more to protect the flooring than out of concern for Mandebala. He had no idea why these men refused to obey his commands. Surely, they must be enemy operatives. It was the only plausible explanation. *How in the name of God-fucking-on-high did they breach the palace?* Mandebala adopted a slightly less hostile approach. "Look," he said, "it's clear you're not going to kill me or you would have done so already. I'll pay you double—triple, quadruple, whatever you wish—to set me free unharmed."

His captors ignored him. Mandebala hoped their silence meant they were considering his offer. "At least get me medical help! My fingers need to be reattached STAT!" His captors allowed him to tear strips from his nightshirt, from which he fashioned a tourniquet of sorts around his arm, just above his elbow. Only later that day would he begin to wonder why he bothered to save his own life.

The military men threw him roughly into the cargo space of a military jeep. From his prone position, Mandebala was able to see the solitary outline of his father, gazing blank-faced from the window of his high palace floor suite as his son was being dragged away like a criminal. "Father!" screamed Mandebala as loudly as he could, though he knew the king could never hear him through the thick bulletproof glass at this distance. His confusion could not have been greater. *Surely Father will send guards for me now!* Yet he knew something was grievously wrong, and he wept convulsively for the first time in his life.

After a treacherously bumpy, seemingly endless ride, he was dumped at the steps of the missionary hospital, bleeding and alone.

The dryness of the night air made the blood start to cake almost as fast as it seeped out of the space where his digits used to be. Flies fed hungrily at this most welcome source of nourishment, and though sickened by the sight, Mandebala made but a feeble attempt to scatter them away.

Oh, how Mandebala could now feel the pain! Elevated adrenaline levels had subsided, and sheer agony coursed through his body in waves of pain that almost made him lose consciousness. He began writhing on the hard steps, his hands between his knees, flopping back and forth in the dirt and dust. A male voice shouted through Mandebala's dark unconsciousness. Mandebala felt hands grabbing him as he remained tightly curled into a fetal-like ball. He was put in a wheelchair and pushed through some doors.

Inside, he was lifted to a gurney, unwilling still to unwind from his protective, defensive ball. He felt a sharp stab into his relatively ample buttocks. Mandebala began to feel a lightness envelop him as the pain disappeared. His tightly coiled position began to relax, and he regained the ability to speak again.

"You filthy pigs, can you not see who I am? Get me into a private suite *now*, I command you!" yelled Mandebala.

The ER staff snickered. "A private suite," one said with a chortle, "for a street dog with no fingers? You reek of booze."

Mandebala began to curse but felt another sharp pain in his rear.

"A well-fed little feisty one, eh?"

The drugs then won their battle with Mandebala's consciousness.

When Mandebala awoke several hours later, every set of dark eyes in the emergency room were trained on him. He even saw one patient, a young girl of about eleven, start to shake when he caught her eyes.

"Yes," Mandebala muttered, "this is more like it!" Clearly, they had finally figured out who he was, and he would start getting some action around here. "Doctor!"

Three men wearing stethoscopes exchanged looks before one of the three, the eldest in appearance and presumably the senior among them, sighed and walked over to the hospital bed.

Mandebala grinned. *The crown prince should never have to speak with a subordinate, even in a missionary hospital.*

"Inform me of the status of my fingers immediately! And get me out of this ward with these pigs and street vermin! Their smell is making me nauseous."

"It is the antibiotic that is making you feel unwell," the doctor said and then smiled. "Indeed, it might be your own smell turning your stomach, truth be told. As for your hand, you have lost the initial segment off your first three fingers of your right hand. Clean cut— must have been a sharp weapon brandished by a powerful man. You should have no further complications with the hand, as it was well sewn closed. I did it personally."

"What do you *mean* I have lost parts of three fingers?" Mandebala roared. "Why did you not sew them back on, you fucking idiot?"

"To have saved your digits, we would have had to have been provided with the severed pieces," the doctor said without expression. "When we found you in a heap on the front step, we found no extra pieces along for the ride. So, you no longer have three fingertips on your right hand. Further, you no longer have any status here, as we simply do not tolerate abusive patients. You are welcome to stay until your fever and infection clear; however, one further outburst toward me or my staff and you will exit in the same fashion that you arrived."

"How *dare* you threaten me like that!" Mandebala shrieked. "You are not worthy to wipe my shitty asshole, yet you dare to threaten me with expulsion from this piss pot you call a hospital? Why, I'll have you—"

The doctor nodded at two large orderlies, who lunged at Mandebala and hoisted him up with a firm grip under each arm. Instantly, Mandebala was en route toward the front doors of the hospital, legs flailing and kicking helplessly at his captors. As his gown opened, he felt a breeze across his buttocks, exposed for all in the waiting area to see. Many patients smirked and others laughed openly. *How are they not terrified to see the crown prince being handled in such a fashion?*

For the second time in half a day, Mandebala landed crumpled up in a ball on the front steps of the missionary hospital.

⸺ ◆ ⸺

The light of daybreak was getting stronger as Mandebala picked himself up from the hospital steps and began trudging down the hill. He wandered quite aimlessly down the road leading from the missionary hospital. His mind raced, and his eyes shifted left and right anxiously, surveying for danger. *Nothing makes sense!*

Of course, Mandebala suddenly thought. *This is all but a test for me. Father is staging this elaborate ruse as some sort of rite of passage, for me to prove myself as a man. As someone worthy of the royal lineage. Of course!*

Mandebala felt certain that the moment he made his way back to the royal palace, he would have survived and passed the challenge and that his father would welcome him back, arms wide, prouder of his son than he had ever been before. Yes, indeed, this was the reason for what had happened in the last twelve or so hours—there could be no other explanation. Knowing, finally, what was happening picked up Mandebala's spirits and helped put a bit of spring back in his steps as he trundled down the hill toward Kashatown. The fact that he was walking along a public road for the first time in his life did not bother him. It was all part of his father's test. *But the guard who severed my fingers will pay dearly with* his *life—once I am done torturing him for weeks on end!*

The walk back to the royal palace was going to be a long one—some twenty kilometers—but Mandebala was undaunted. He could probably cover the distance in four hours or less. He was not, however, looking forward to the walk through Kashatown, among the poorest of slums in all Maleziland. On the rare occasion that Mandebala had been in Kashatown—exactly why, he couldn't remember—the prince had been completely overcome by the lurid stench permeating the air. His sensory memory was dramatically more violent than the reality of the occasion, and he dreaded revisiting the smell. The crown prince didn't think about his safety. Why would he? No one would dare harm the crown prince of Maleziland.

He didn't hold the fact that he had forever lost the tips of his fingers against his father, and he again relished the thought of the guard who had struck the cutting blow paying for it with his life. *Indeed, his progeny too must be eradicated from existence.* Satisfaction swept over his entire being at the thought. No, the fingertips were a small price to pay for the respect of his father. It would be his own personal badge of honor.

As Mandebala reached the ditch at the foot of the hillside, where once ran a beautifully fresh stream of water, he began entering the outer borders of Kashatown. As he did so, he encountered children playing in the ditch who looked at him blankly, without recognition. Once he got farther into the slums, virtually all adults who looked up to see him acknowledged him instantly, with fear and questions registering in their eyes. Mandebala interpreted their curiosity as natural, for indeed it was an unlikely sight to have their crown prince strolling among them, especially in such a disheveled state.

A small crowd began to form and follow his steps as he walked. Mandebala was able to discern that the group was formed mostly of younger men, many of whom bore the scars of two decades' worth of scrapping and fighting for survival. Mandebala avoided eye contact with them. These men were not worthy of that ocular honor.

The men began to close the distance. Mandebala did not know what they could possibly be thinking or doing, daring to get so close to their future regent. When three or four of them passed him on the road on either side as he walked, warning alarms started to ring in his head. These men were suddenly blocking the path in front of him, and Mandebala found himself surrounded. The dust kicked up by the mob drifted forward through their midst as the group stopped, causing Mandebala to cough and choke. When he had cleared his throat, he looked up at his confiners, all of whom were smiling.

"You pieces of cow dung, get the fuck out of my way!" Mandebala roared.

His interlopers said nothing, but they held their ground. Several sneered malevolently at Mandebala.

How dare they?

"Surely to God you recognize your prince and future ruler, you filthy pigs!" Mandebala said, his voice starting to squeak, a bit higher and less imperious than it was a few seconds earlier. "NOW GET THE FUCK OUT OF MY WAY OR PAY WITH YOUR LIFE UPON MY RETURN!"

The tallest and most menacing-looking young man in the posse spoke. "We see no 'prince' in front of us—just a stray street dog, and a well-fed one at that, that seems to have lost his way."

"What is wrong with your eyes?" Mandebala screeched, his voice once again losing its composure. "Or is it your *brains* that are somehow being affected by the heat of the day?"

The young man took a step forward. His bare, barrel chest was now only a few centimeters from Mandebala's nose, and his head towered above him. Mandebala didn't flinch. The man spoke, quietly and deeply. "You're nothing here, outside of that fancy palace and without your bodyguards to protect you."

Without speaking, and before Mandebala could possibly react, the young man grabbed the prince's head and yanked it downward into his right knee, which crashed into the middle of Mandebala's face. Pain again shot through Mandebala's head for the second time in his newly defined life, and he crumpled into the dust. As he lay there in the street amid the filth, each member of the group took turns spitting and pissing on him, in addition to kicking him with all their might. After what seemed like hours, the crowd tired of their sport.

Mandebala lay in the dirt, moaning loudly. He realized he had several broken ribs. Mandebala knew well the sound and feel, having cracked many ribs of his playmates in the past. Further, he was likely concussed and was beginning to suffer from dehydration and loss of blood. He opened his eyes weakly and was startled to see a solitary man standing above him, silently watching.

"Don't just stand there like an idiot," Mandebala said, but this time in a whisper. "Help your prince!"

The lone man, who looked to be in his mid-twenties, said nothing and showed no emotion. He reached under Mandebala's armpits and hoisted him upward. Roughly, and somewhat incredibly given the man's slight build, he slung Mandebala over his shoulders. Mandebala's broken ribs screamed out in pain, and his voice did the same. He cursed his benefactor for being so rough; still the man said nothing.

After carrying Mandebala this way for several hundred meters, the man ducked behind a piece of corrugated aluminum siding into what appeared to be a shelter of sorts. There, from under a rough bench, his new friend pulled out a military-issue emergency medical kit. The man cleaned and bandaged Mandebala's wounds and sides using alcohol wipes and bound his gashes with seemingly expert ability and speed.

The man stood Mandebala up and walked him to the opening that was the door. Then, placing his foot on Mandebala's derriere, he shoved him roughly outside, almost knocking him back down to the ground from which he had picked him up earlier. In the light, and feeling somewhat refreshed, Mandebala looked upon his new friend for the first time. "You seem familiar to me," he said. "I know that it's near impossible, but have we met before?"

A fleeting smirk registered on the man's face, but he said nothing.

Mandebala said, "Your assistance will not go unrewarded. When I get back to the palace, I will send a group of men to find you, and you will be handsomely paid."

The man remained silent but smiled slightly.

CHAPTER 10

Mandebala began slogging along the road that led toward the royal palace. No longer was he supremely confident in his safety or security. That said, he seemed to pose little threat and was of little interest to the various slum dwellers as he staggered past. A few children took the opportunity to throw small stones at him, but they soon tired of their game when it generated no response from their target. On top of the bruises already covering 99 percent of his body, the stones had little impact, as the throbbing pain couldn't have been much worse.

Nevertheless, Mandebala remained at a heightened sense of wariness and continuously looked over his shoulders to see what dangers lurked behind him. Mandebala sensed that he was being watched or followed. He did not appreciate the sensation of unease that filled him and his newly fragile psyche.

Mandebala had barely made it halfway to the palace when he saw a security escort tearing up the street in his direction. Of course, he was used to being carried *within* the luxurious black Range Rover, flanked by jeeps. "Yes!" he shouted, his spirits soaring. "Finally, Father has sent someone to fetch me!" He stopped his forward progression and waited in the middle of the street for the escort to arrive.

The Range Rover seemed to be making great time on the rudimentary dirt road— Mandebala knew it rarely dropped below 70 mph, other than for the most cavernous and lethal of potholes. Mandebala usually enjoyed traveling at this high speed, maiming and killing scores of citizens. In the past, Mandebala had convinced himself that the people the drivers hit and killed had meant themselves to die—a way of committing suicide and terminating their miserable existences. In ways, the detail was doing these poor fools a favor, helping them do what they did not have the courage to do themselves.

Yet as Mandebala stood and watched the progression of the escort bearing down on him, he could not command himself to get out of the way, even as he willed his legs to move. The shock of what was happening, and the speed at which the threat approached, caused his legs to cease functioning. Mandebala froze in the middle of the dusty road, closed his eyes, and winced at the prospect of his certain death, preparing for the unequal impact of metal on flesh.

The expected collision came and knocked him sideways. Mandebala was vaguely aware that the impact had been less severe than he'd expected and that, oddly, he'd been thrown sideways into the ditch rather than a hundred meters back in the direction from which he'd been coming. He also was hazily aware of three vehicles roaring past him.

He opened his eyes, not believing that he would be able to accomplish this small task but succeeding. The stranger who had helped bandage his wounds earlier in the day was standing over him in the ditch, brushing himself off. The man left, without saying a word.

Mandebala didn't attempt to speak with him this time.

⎯⎯ ◆ ⎯⎯

Darkness fell before Mandebala could make it home to the palace. The prince was terrified. He had long left the squalid density of Kashatown, but he still had some ten or so kilometers to cover. Mandebala decided to stop walking along the road, feeling very exposed to the familiar but now malevolent sounds of the African night. Animal noises that sounded so normal from the safety of one of his father's hunting lodges took on a new, sinister, and terrifying trill.

Mandebala's imagination ran wild with the fear that the reincarnated souls of the many big game animals that he and his father had shot would come to exact their revenge. Mandebala knew he could never survive in the wild. He had no hope of finding nourishment, water, shelter, or fire. He was, however, lucky enough to find a large boulder. By trying to sleep with his back against the rock, he found that the rock retained some of the blazing heat from the sun of the day, and he was at least safe in one direction.

He awoke with a start and looked around in a panic. He saw no immediate threat, but every bone, every joint, every muscle ached—and that was before he attempted to move. When he did begin to stir, every neuron fired in an extreme electrical protest to his brain. The African sun had begun to rise, and with the early dawn, despite all of Mandebala's trials of the previous day, hope and optimism also rose within his soul. Soon, with any luck, he would be back in the palace where he belonged, having survived his test and won the respect and admiration of his father. After all, what more could possibly go wrong now?

Mandebala began to walk. As he got closer to the palace, the vegetation began to thicken, and with that he was able to benefit from the shade thrown by the trees in the still low sun. His gait was extraordinarily slow at first, as the residual stiffness and soreness worked its way through his body. As time went on, however, his stride began to regain purpose. A steady flow of traffic, mostly in the form of supply lorries, began to pass him on the road as they headed toward the palace. Mandebala didn't try to flag them down—he knew that he was now thoroughly unrecognizable to all but the most observant of passersby.

Mandebala was particularly pleased to avoid any interaction, based on what happened to him without the benefit of a security detail over his thirty-six-hour string of difficulty. He did, however, begin to worry whether he would be able to speak at all, as his throat was ridiculously dry after an entire day without so much as a drop of water. Just to make sure, Mandebala said out loud to himself, "Father!"—hopefully the first and last word he would need to utter before being given a beautiful, clear, cold drink of water, followed by a healthy dram of single malt to take the edge off his pain. If his body had any superfluous retained moisture at all, he would have been salivating at the thought.

Finally, the palace emerged into view through the morning mists. Carved out of the dense riparian jungle, the massive twin corrugated steel doors rolled open and closed with surprisingly rapid swiftness. These doors closed before another set of similar interior doors would open, preventing a proper glimpse of the incredible edifice inside. Yet the upper floors and rotunda were clearly visible above the gates and walls. It seemed to be built in heaven upon the clouds each morning, and indeed, its promise for Mandebala seemed greater than eternal paradise at this moment. As he strolled the final stretch, Mandebala felt triumphant. He had succeeded! He had suffered incredibly, yet he, Mandebala, had survived.

The fingertips, the broken nose, the broken ribs, the bruises—none of it had been able to break him. He felt invincible, as the crown prince should feel, given that he had been chosen by God to one day lead His people. He began waving at the passing lorries. He had no intention of trying to flag them down but felt the need to acknowledge their presence, much as if he were Julius Caesar returning to Rome, waving at the crowds in his triumphal procession.

As he marched up toward the entry gate, he was a bit surprised, though not utterly, that the massive metal gates didn't begin to roll open. He knew that, from a distance, the remote security cameras wouldn't likely project an image that the guards would be able to recognize. The lenses would simply be trained upon a curious-looking and bedraggled pedestrian who couldn't possibly have any real business at the palace. Any time now, of course, upon recognition, the gates would begin their slow roll sideways.

They did not.

Mandebala grimaced and squared his shoulders as he marched up toward the CCTV camera trained upon the intercom box, something used only by supplicants and others whose vehicles didn't carry the palace-issued RFID chip to communicate with the unseen security force within the gates and walls. This was *his* palace—why was he not being admitted? They should be sending transport out to meet him immediately, lest he must walk the final few hundred meters to the palace itself.

He pressed the intercom. "Open these fucking gates *immediately* and I won't have you flogged for your inattentiveness." *That should do it.*

No response came back from the black squawk box.

He cleared his throat and pressed the button again. "Is it at all possible that you blind idiots do not recognize me? Can it also be possible that your ears have gone deaf? Do you not recognize the voice of your prince? It is I, Mandebala! Now open this gate immediately and send me some transport!"

The box failed to squawk.

Mandebala began to shake; his fists were clenched so tightly that he saw fresh blood beginning to stain the tips of his finger stumps on his right hand. So much adrenaline was pumping that for the first time in thirty-six hours, he felt no pain. Still, there was no communication from the box, and the gates did not budge.

Fortuitously, one of the regular delivery trucks began rumbling into range of the RFID receiver for its ID transponders, and the gate began to roll open. Mandebala darted through the gates behind the gourmet butcher's truck.

Ahhh. Mandebala's stomach began to growl. He could almost taste the beautiful tenderloin that would soon grace their plates and sate their palates that night. He grinned, lost in fantasy thought, as three military jeeps flew into sight at top speed and screeched to a halt in front of him just as he darted through the second gate.

As the dust cleared, Mandebala looked up to see no fewer than nine AK-47s trained upon him.

He froze, waiting for the guards' moment of recognition.

"If you move, Mandebala, you die," said the captain of the guard, obviously a former mercenary from Uganda or Niger, as his skin was as black as the beret that he wore.

My name.

Mandebala's world began to crash and swim in circles around him, downward into a pure and lightless black hole.

"You . . . know . . . who . . . I . . . am."

Two men who weren't sporting AK-47s jumped from a jeep and pinned both of Mandebala's arms behind his back and shoved him into the dirt. One guard put his knee sharply into the back of Mandebala's neck, and the other jammed his knee into the small of Mandebala's back. The captain of the guard came closer and pressed his foul face close to Mandebala's ear.

"If you are *ever* spotted within a kilometer of this building, you will be shot on sight. Is this clear?"

"But my father . . ." Mandebala glanced up toward his father's bedroom suite high on the third floor and once again saw the outline of King Mabanda in the window, staring calmly down at the scene. This time, during the light of day, he could see his father's massive arms folded across his barrel chest. Mandebala knew, at that moment, that his life had forever changed.

CHAPTER 11

Mandebala sat alongside a narrow ditch and stared at the long dirt road stretching out before him. His mind was not racing. His heart rate was down significantly, and his breathing was deep and regular. He felt nothing; he was numb. The sun had begun to fall, yet he perched on the side of the road, blankly watching everything and nothing, all at once. He didn't linger out of hope. Without his processing even a single subsequent thought, the sight of his father watching him from the window had driven the full and true message home.

Mandebala knew he would never, ever set foot in the royal palace again.

He began to wander down the road. Mandebala had no destination in mind and no plan. He did not register landmarks, distance, vehicles—nothing. The advent of complete darkness found him back at the rock where he'd spent the previous night, offering him a small measure of warmth and nocturnal security. He fell asleep quickly and slept like the dead for nearly fourteen hours, his mind vacant of thought or danger, though his physical reality carried extreme peril. Many passersby presumed that he was dead, no longer of this world, and none paid him any heed.

When Mandebala awoke, his mind cleared, and his senses returned.

First and foremost, he felt pain—the pain of multiple wounds, of rejection and loss and extreme hunger and thirst. Mandebala knew that without liquid and caloric sustenance, he would soon die. One hope remained in his bleak and desperate world: He needed to find his guardian angel. The man who had shown him kindness was most certainly his only slim hope. Mandebala was finally aware that he was ill-equipped to survive outside of the palace walls.

Not only was this a foreign world to him, but it was also actively and maliciously hostile toward him. Ghosts of the outside world reared their menacing heads: children whose bones he had broken and whose ears he had bitten off; women deflowered and tortured and maimed; servants he had treated like disposable objects, to be tossed aside carelessly once their purpose had been served. All these memories flooded back to haunt him now, and Mandebala began to experience an emotion he had heretofore never encountered in his young life: regret. No, he didn't regret *doing* any of these things. He feared their return to haunt him and, worse, to get even.

As he reached the outskirts of Kashatown, Mandebala heightened his personal alert level from green to yellow. No one paid him too much heed, though he was quite sure that various groups of people, all of whom seemed to be clustered tightly together, talking animatedly, recognized him. Often, all heads in the group would turn simultaneously and continue to watch him as he passed. None followed; worse, none offered to help.

Mandebala considered asking for water, but after his reception the previous day in Kashatown, he thought better of it. He had no accurate location toward which he was traveling, but he thought he knew the general vicinity where he had been beaten and subsequently treated by the silent Samaritan stranger. Mandebala was quite certain that he needed to get to the center of town. When he reached an alarmingly large splotch of dried, caked brown blood in the dirt, Mandebala's intuition was confirmed.

At that point, Mandebala sat on the edge of the roadside and watched. He had no better plan than to hope that his rescuer would, at some point, walk past. Mandebala felt certain that he would indeed recognize the man, as he had been struck with an eerie sense of familiarity about his benefactor.

The day was in full swing now, and from his observation point alongside the road, Mandebala noticed things about his former subjects that he had never noticed before. Several things struck him so hard that he had difficulty processing or understanding them.

Amid the squalor of the slums, children and adults laughed and teased and played and joked with one another. Mandebala was left wondering what they could possibly be so happy about. He had always presumed that people living outside the sanctity of the palace were content, albeit just barely. Yet he had never considered the wild possibility that they were happy.

He also noticed that everyone he saw, whether the youngest of children or the adults, wore impeccably clean clothing, though this was but a temporary state for the youngest children as the day went on. His imagination could not grasp the concept amid the filth of the street, yet the evidence was all around him. Not only was the clothing clean, but it even looked to be pressed! Most of the women were wearing *chitenje* wraps around their waists in bright print colors in red, green, and black.

Last, and he realized that his other two major insights were all a function of his last, he was dumbstruck by how *proud* the people looked as they milled busily about him. Mandebala would have fully expected the people of Kashatown to have the posture and bearing of the oppressed and downtrodden, but nothing could have been further from the reality that he saw all about him. Despite their horrific economic circumstances—Mandebala knew that Maleziland was among the poorest countries on the entire planet—all that he saw evinced people that were both happy and full of pride.

Furthermore, he was certain that he sensed an even higher energy about these people. They were excited about something—even *optimistic*. Mandebala could see it in their faces, in their animated chatter, and in their eyes and souls.

After hours had passed without the Samaritan showing his face, Mandebala knew he had to shift his strategy or perish. He would have to begin asking around for the man, and he would also have to ask for water. He had quite long ago gotten past the sensation of hunger, but his thirst would not and could not abate. He dreaded the consequences of asking for help from the very people who had beaten him senseless and left him for dead not twenty-four hours ago. Mandebala knew that he had no choice—it was either death or risk humility.

Mandebala decided that he would ask only women for help. As far as he could recall, only men and adolescents had participated in the beating, though he did remember the sight of many women onlookers, most smirking as he fell. His logic, though, was sound. He was unlikely to be beaten by women whose aid he solicited.

A particularly large, kind-looking woman—how a woman living in the slums could be corpulent was again, like many things in Kashatown, beyond Mandebala's comprehension—was lumbering toward him, and Mandebala left his roadside position to step into her path.

"Woman," he began imperiously, but quickly changed his tone and softened his approach when she frowned at him. "I mean, kind lady, please help one who is desperately in need. You must recognize me as your crown prince Mandebala. The most unfortunate of events has befallen me, and somehow, in ways unknown to me, I have fallen out of favor with my father. I find myself cast out of the palace with nary a drop of water, a bite of food, nor a place of shelter over my head. I ask not the impossible of you—only that you give me some water so that I do not die of thirst." The woman politely listened to his impassioned plea, shook her head no ever so slightly, and lumbered around him on her path. At least she hadn't beaten him, which was entirely possible given his current physical state.

Mandebala attempted this approach with several more women, some of whom didn't even bother to slacken their pace when he began to speak. Even though he was ultra-cautious not to offend them with a demanding or regal tone, his pleas went unanswered. In fact, no one even bothered to speak as much as a single word to him.

Finally, on somewhere around his fifteenth attempt, Mandebala met with success. An elderly woman trudged slowly up the road. When Mandebala approached her, though his eyes must have been deceiving him, he was almost certain he recognized a faint smile on her lips. Before he could speak, the woman said, "Well, I suppose someone should welcome you home, Mandebala."

Briefly at a loss for words, and utterly confused by what the old wretch had said, Mandebala stammered badly as he began his prayer for help. "K-kind lady, p-please help. I-I-I need water—"

"I'm sure you do, young man. After what you've done to your own people for so many years, I may regret helping you, but you've had only a brutal and ruthless tutor. Out of respect for my friend, your mother, I will help you, Mandebala."

"But how could you know Carolanda?" Mandebala asked, astonished that an old slum dweller such as this woman could have ever met his beautiful mother.

At this, the woman burst out laughing. "Things are different than they appear, Mandebala. Much different." The woman ceased talking and beckoned him to follow.

She led Mandebala down a path of sorts—it couldn't have been called a road, as it was barely wide enough for two people to pass side by side. Its purpose seemed only as an access path for the shanties that pressed right to its very edge as it snaked among them. The slum dwellings had no street numbers, the "streets" had no names, and quickly Mandebala was lost in a maze that he knew he could never leave unassisted. The woman darted into an opening of a shack and, without word, returned to offer him a drink of water from a battered, thermos-like container.

Mandebala gulped it, despite the warning alarms being triggered through his nasal cavity, sounding the alarm that this was not Evian or anything remotely similar. He resisted his stomach's urge to immediately expel that which hit its lining, but only barely, as wave after wave of convulsions erupted from within. Despite himself, Mandebala couldn't help but react. "Good God, woman, what foul piss have you given me to drink? I should think it would be better to die of thirst than continue to drink this vile pseudo-liquid!"

Again, the woman broke out into raucous laughter, as if this were the funniest thing she had ever heard in her long life. "You'd better get used to it, Mandebala, as it's the best Kashatown has to offer." Mandebala could scarcely believe his ears and did his best to resist the urge to drink more, but he finally gave in to his body's urgent need for liquid. As he plugged his nose with his fingers while he drank, the old biddy broke into laughter once again.

Despite the nauseous feeling in his stomach, Mandebala felt somewhat refreshed. When the woman had stopped laughing and recovered her composure, she started up the path, beckoning him to follow.

"Where are we going, old woman, and how is it possible that you know Carolanda?" he asked, almost shouting to cover the distance that had already formed between them.

"To your home, of course!" said the woman almost happily.

"To my HOME?" Mandebala roared. "Woman, how could you possibly be taking me to my home? I have no home—the only home I have ever known is the royal palace!"

Again, the woman began to laugh, but this time it wasn't quite as raucous, and as it finished its course through her lips, a look of pity seemed to replace it.

"As impossible as it might seem, both you and I have just spoken the truth, yet to you, one excludes the other. You have no idea, do you, of what has befallen you?"

Mandebala was beginning to tire of the twisted, riddled, and knowing way in which she spoke, and having been rejuvenated somewhat by the water, he said, "Of course I have no idea of how any of this has happened, or of how what you speak could be true. Quit trifling with me, woman; I've had a very bad day, and I do not need your games to make it any worse. Explain the meaning of your innuendo to me."

She pointed beyond Mandebala and said, "Ask him. He's your brother."

Mandebala turned to see, standing in the doorway of a familiar-looking shack, his Samaritan.

◆

Mandebala stared at the smiling figure in the shanty's opening.

"Are you mute or are you going to speak to me this time?" he demanded.

"I can speak," the figure stated, nodding. "Most often I choose not to."

Mandebala had a thousand questions for this verbally challenged person, and he knew that it was going to be a painful and painfully slow process. Not knowing what else to do, he reckoned that he might as well get started.

"Why did you help me yesterday?" Mandebala asked.

A silent shrug was the slight man's reply.

"Have we met before?" Mandebala asked.

"Not really," the man said.

Progress. "Do you live in this shack?"

"When I am in Kashatown, yes. As do all my brothers and sisters, when they are here."

"Where are they now?" Mandebala felt that he was starting to make some headway and the stranger was beginning to open up a bit. He didn't care where the man's siblings were; he simply wanted to keep him talking.

"Some have moved out. Some are out working. Some have died."

Mandebala was indeed on a roll with his interrogation and pressed on.

"What is your name?"

"My name is Shigeku."

"Ahh, okay, Shigeku, when others struck me, kicked me, and beat me nearly to death, only you came to my aid. People of this town seemed content to leave me dying in the street. Why did you not do the same?" Mandebala asked, desperate for an answer.

"As much as I despise you, you are my brother. I could not let you die in the middle of the street like some animal that has been hit by a car."

"Don't be daft!" Mandebala said. "That is impossible! I have many brothers and sisters, but all live in the royal palace or in one of the other royal residences with my father. Where did you come up with such an absurd idea?"

"Poor little Mandebala. I guess no one has taken the time to explain things to you, have they?" said Shigeku.

From the cat-eating-canary grin on his face, Mandebala knew he was relishing this conversation. "Indeed," Mandebala said, "no one has, nor likely can, explain why my father has done this to me."

"Tsk-tsk," said Shigeku, shaking his head. "Well, I suppose I am the cause of all this, so perhaps I should explain it to you. You think that it's impossible that we're brothers? It is not. Forty-eight hours ago, you were living in the royal palace as crown prince of all Maleziland. Now, you are in a hut in Kashatown with no guards, no money, and no king to cover your royal ass.

"So, Mandebala, sit the fuck down and shut up for the first time in your life, and listen carefully to what I am going to tell you. I will not repeat it. Every word I tell you will be the truth. If you don't believe me, leave, and never show your face to me again," Shigeku said.

And with that, Mandebala sat.

"You have no father, at least none that is known, for I guess we all have a father somewhere. You were born fourteen years and seven months ago in the missionary hospital at the top of the hill, though you probably didn't know even that. Our mother, Shileza, died while giving birth to you. In fact, she was dead when I dropped her body on the front step of the hospital. They cut you out of her lifeless corpse and saved you. Maman made me promise to look after you, given that her soul would pass to you when she died, and you were born. I gave her my word, though I have long since decided that the belief that her soul somehow took up residence within you is utter crap."

"This is not possib—" Mandebala began.

"Be quiet. For once," Shigeku said. "Our mother was a sweet, gentle, and caring woman. You, however, are a cruel, uncaring, selfish, and unworthy scrap of garbage and perhaps should have been thrown out with the trash after I let you die in the street. I was a young boy at that time, only eleven years old. I was worried about how I was going to be able to fulfill my promise to our maman."

"*Our* maman? Queen Carolanda is *NOT* your maman!" shouted Mandebala.

Shigeku laughed. "Nor is she *yours*. When I realized that King Mabanda and Queen Carolanda were, for some strange reason, also at the hospital to deliver their baby, I thought I saw an opportunity. Very foolishly, I thought that to honor my pledge to our maman in a simple way, I could switch babies. I lit a fire in a wastebasket and, in the confusion, made the switch. I switched you from your bassinet into the royal babe's bassinet and moved the royal babe into mine."

"Wh-what are you saying?" Mandebala's heart sank.

"You, my brother by birth, were taken by King Mabanda to the royal palace. Of course, Carolanda's son, a boy we called Mateyo, was given to my care. Sadly, for my pledge to Maman to be fulfilled, I had to carry on with the ruse, and that required that I look after Queen Carolanda's son as if he were indeed my own brother. Otherwise, it would have been both unnatural and unthinkable here in the slums of Kashatown, where all must look out for one another. I was sure the little bugger was going to die anyway, with no mother's milk to feed him. But the mothers in Kashatown saved him. In fact, he thrived—on bits and drips of milk from scores of nursing women. Soon he was eating scraps like the rest of us, and just as we got by, so did Mateyo, the true crown prince of Maleziland."

Mandebala sat on the dirt floor of the shanty, stone-faced and grimacing silently, feeling as if he were being crushed by the weight of a thousand universes.

"Of course, my secret was not known by anyone else; I was the only one alive who knew. However, I was taken prisoner a few weeks ago while in the service of the Zambwanan army, and to bargain for my life, I told the story to one of your generals. They took a couple of weeks to verify my story—with DNA testing, I know now—and when my story turned out to be true, they agreed to set me free.

"That was three days ago. Yesterday, they—we—plucked my brother, I mean, Queen Carolanda's true son, Mateyo, off the street and took him off to the royal palace. I was set free. I presume that at the same time, they tossed you out on the street. I must admit, I didn't see that coming. I didn't think that Mabanda could be so cruel as to throw you into the gutter. That said, it amuses me greatly." Shigeku smiled. "After years and years of living off the backs of the people, you now will know what it feels like to go hungry. You will know pain; you will know suffering. You will know what it is like to be an ordinary Malezi, for that is *exactly* what you are."

It would be hours before Mandebala spoke or moved. His mind began to plot his revenge. He knew it would have to be an intricate, tumultuous, and lethal plan, but he *would* have his place back in the royal palace—or die trying.

*　　　　◆　　　　*

Try as he might, Shigeku could not shake Mandebala. *The fat fuck formerly from the palace won't leave me alone! I can't even take a piss without him watching and asking me questions!* He began to regret his decision to save his brother's life. Shigeku could not stand his brother. As the days moved on, he was absolutely certain that Mandebala could see it in his eyes and from the way he scowled at him—yet the former prince still followed Shigeku through the streets of the village and yammered on about life in the palace and the king and shit that was never, ever going to be relevant again!

Yet somehow Shigeku was unable to throw him to the mercy of Kashatown. Oh, the thought crossed his mind. Mandebala's odds under such a scenario would have been better had he been thrown with two broken legs to a pack of starving hyenas, which unfortunately was roughly equal to the temperament and ferocity of much of Kashatown toward him.

Yet Shigeku noticed that Mandebala's coal-black eyes showed no joy. Shigeku turned toward his brother, who sighed and sat on the edge of the dirt road. Shigeku saw the intent look in the eyes of his young brother and the aggressiveness in his posture. The hatred was clear on Mandebala's young face.

Interesting, thought Shigeku. *The young pup has a strong back, for his will is not yet broken. Perhaps that hatred will be useful someday.*

"Can you fucking believe it?" Shigeku muttered.

"What?" Mandebala asked.

"My brother from this village . . . ," Shigeku said, his arms spread wide at the dusty nothingness around them, "is now the prince."

"No, it is unnatural," Mandebala said with a growl. "Someone born to and raised in the gutters has no right to be in that position! Royal authority is God-given. God would never have let His chosen son live as a dog for fourteen years!"

Shigeku frowned. *I thought I would feel better once Mandebala was stripped of his title.* It had been amusing to see him thrown out of the royal palace and abandoned to his true lot in life. Yet today, all of Shigeku's hardship in raising Mateyo as his brother was being rubbed in his face! Now that his brother was the exalted one, one day to be king, and all of the people who had helped raise him still lived like vermin, drinking piss water and eating grubs and scraps. Mateyo was now leading a life of grandeur. The bile rose in Shigeku's stomach.

This was all *Mateyo's fault.*

CHAPTER 12

King Mabanda had agonized over his decision for a week before he'd discarded his son—a virtual eternity for a man who was used to making instantaneous decisions and having his decisions acted upon equally quickly. He had truly loved the boy, Mandebala, at least in a way that he thought was love. It sickened him to think of his former son, now a village street rat, living in the slums, eating maize and scraps, and sleeping on a straw mattress.

Anyone who had seen the two of them together—even his least competent and observant staff—knew that Mabanda's love for his son was real. *Fucking gutter dog, not the God-given heir to my throne!* he reminded himself.

Mabanda reflected on his fourteen happy years with Mandebala. Never had he been so proud as on the day he was born. Never had he been so enamored as on the first occasion that Mandebala barked at a servant. Never had he been so happy as the hunt on which Mandebala shot his first elephant, though it was far likelier that the guide's second, simultaneous shot between the charging bull's coal-black eyes struck the killing blow. No, Mabanda loved the boy. But he was in actuality a lowborn street dog, unworthy of the royal throne.

The king spat on the pristine floor. He couldn't ignore that which he knew was true.

His operatives had produced photos of the boy who had proved, by modern and irrefutable science, to be his son. There was no denying the genealogy of the lithe, tall, and fair beauty the boy had inherited from his mother. Even at the young age of fourteen, he was already a good thirty centimeters taller than King Mabanda, and based upon his broad shoulders, he would grow into a physically impressive specimen of a man.

But didn't Mandebala resemble his father as well? For fourteen years, King Mabanda had believed that Mandebala was his own spitting image, the obvious fruit of his loins. The realization that he was not had knocked the breath from his lungs, if not the blood from his heart.

For four days subsequent to the return of the DNA test results, King Mabanda had remained in agony. Over and over in his head, he went over his life with Mandebala. So much perverse joy they'd shared.

And then a sudden realization had dawned upon him. Why did he have to do it? Why did he have to do anything? Who could force him to cast out his son?

The king smiled warmly for the first time in days. *No one. I answer to no man—only to God . . . if there is one higher than me.*

King Mabanda smiled, but it soon faded. *My divine omnipotence cannot pass to someone other than my son.* The crown prince inherited not simply the office of ruler but also the divine right to rule.

No, my status can only pass through my bloodline. No subterfuge, no deception could change the fact that God had bestowed heaven's mandate upon Mabanda and his issue. The right to rule simply could not pass to Mandebala because the king wanted it so. The decision was not, in fact, his to make. God was the only one to whom King Mabanda had to answer, and God could only rule through the king's blood.

Over the next few days, King Mabanda began to work up the courage to do that which he knew must be done. With the decision having been made for him, he began to recall dozens, if not hundreds, of occasions where Mandebala's lack of genetic perfection and divine-right authority resulted in what now, with clearer thought, had been distinct evidence of his low birth. Mandebala had been slow to begin to speak, and then, when he did begin to talk, it had been mostly gibberish.

The boy had also been clumsy and never excelled at anything, physical, mental, or sportive. Indeed, with the benefit of hindsight, Mandebala had proved to be what everybody else had known or suspected all along but had not dared to say: *average.*

King Mabanda finally knew in his heart that his decision was appropriate. By the time a week had passed, he no longer cared for the only son he had ever known and loved. His heart had hardened, and its openness to love and care was slammed firmly shut. As he later watched the dog as he was dragged from the royal palace and thrown roughly into an awaiting jeep, the king felt nothing. His heart was empty again, and the feeling comforted him.

After passing out in the dining hall with King Mabanda, young Mateyo had finally recovered his wits. He remained stationary, with his eyes shut tightly, as though if he refused to move, the nightmare would go away. Four large men, presumably "orderlies," arrived with a stretcher in less than sixty seconds. Mateyo was quickly hoisted onto the stretcher with the most minimal exertion.

At the age of fourteen, despite being tall, Mateyo was incredibly thin, and the ten-kilo or so burden that each man hoisted was nothing. They wheeled him down a long hallway to a room labeled "Infirmary." Mateyo wondered at the multiple huge machines and other computerized equipment, the likes of which he had never seen before. Beeping noises seemed to be ringing out all around him, despite the fact that he was indubitably the only patient there. There, a man whom Mateyo presumed to be a doctor, thanks to his white coat and "in-charge" demeanor, wrapped a thick band around his arm and told him to relax. This same man shone the brightest of flashlights into one, then the other, of Mateyo's eyes. He examined the boy's head carefully, smiled, and then patted Mateyo's shoulder.

"He's just fine," the doctor said.

Mateyo desperately wanted to dispute this fact but did not.

He sat upright and waited on a recovery bed, dreading what he knew to be an imminent encounter with the king. Scanning around him, he saw that he was in the cleanest, whitest, most sterile-looking and smelling room he'd ever seen. Above him were huge, adjustable overhead lights and equipment that looked like something from a mad scientist's woodworking shop. Flashing lights, monitors, and computer screens also surrounded him. Mateyo was almost as afraid of the room as he was of the king. He quickly took to trying to figure out the devices around him, and yet his head was still spinning. What was the king thinking? Surely the man had gone mad, for all of Maleziland knew that Crown Prince Mandebala was the rightful heir to the throne. What on God's good earth had the king been talking about? Mateyo decided this was all some form of a sick ruse and that the king was toying with his prey before slaughtering it.

Heavy, lumbering footsteps trod toward the infirmary, and Mateyo stiffened his back and braced himself for impact, physical or mental.

King Mabanda threw the double doors wide open, as if he needed to make more of an entrance than his sheer physical presence would do without the dramatic gesture. Sweat beaded down the king's forehead, despite the very cool temperature in the room.

Mateyo began to quiver. *Please just get this over with!* Though being seated with the king at the other end of a long dining table was intimidating, having the king not more than two meters away induced sheer terror. Mateyo's rapidly racing heart felt again as though it would cause his body to again collapse, but somehow he managed to maintain consciousness. The monitors the doctor had hooked up to him beeped and blipped frenetically.

"They call you Mateyo, right, boy?" the king thundered.

Mateyo's eyes widened, and he nodded. He then forced himself to shut his eyes, realizing that he had been staring so intently that he had forgotten to blink, and his eyeballs felt as if sandpaper was being dragged over them.

"Can you not *speak*, boy?" the king roared.

Mateyo mouthed the word *yes*, but no sound came out.

King Mabanda roared with laughter. "So, the boy thinks he can speak, and he can form words with his tongue and lips but cannot actually make a sound! That is the funniest thing I've seen in years!" The king's hearty chuckle and big smile eased Mateyo's tension, but only slightly.

"Come now, lad, let's walk, you and me, and start getting to know each other. I will show you around the palace. I hope you'll find the accommodations suitable!" And with that, King Mabanda laughed again, as if he had just spoken the world's funniest joke. Mateyo failed to see the humor.

The king beckoned Mateyo with a simple, sweeping gesture, and Mateyo found himself hopping off the bed and following along, almost against his will, as though he'd been hypnotized by the king's deep and beautifully resonant voice. The king walked out of the infirmary and out into a long hall with a gleaming, high-polished floor, and like a lemming to a sea cliff, Mateyo followed.

As the unlikely pair walked down the hallway, with Mateyo's taller outline being dwarfed by the king's despite being a full head above that of His Royal Highness, the king was in full tour guide mode. "Look at all of these beautiful *objets d'art!*" he said, grinning. "Although all are priceless, not one cost me a single Malezi! You see, foreign leaders—kings, presidents, dictators—all want to court my favor. These are gifts—every one of them!"

Though Mateyo tried to focus as best he could, he felt both lost and overwhelmed. "Look here, Mateyo," the king said. "This is a painting by the Dutch master Rembrandt. It is the only 'masterpiece' ever painted by Rembrandt anywhere in the world that is not on public display in a museum. The only one! And it was a gift from the queen of the Netherlands on the twenty-fifth anniversary of my ascension!"

Mateyo stared at it blankly.

"This is a sculpture by Michelangelo—you might recognize it!" The king guffawed, as he obviously realized that Mateyo had absolutely no idea whatsoever as to the master artisan's name or work. "It is, in fact, a 'study'—a smaller working model—of his most famous sculpture ever, *David*. Few in the world know of its existence. From the prime minister of Italy, of course." The tour through the hall—which the king referred to as the Hall of Tribute—went on and on.

King Mabanda stopped to point out dozens of similar artistic paintings, sculptures, and portraits. He explained to Mateyo the historic, cultural, or diplomatic importance behind each of them. Few of his words registered with the boy.

Mateyo knew nothing of the affairs of state, or even countries and worlds outside his own. The names and dates and countries bounced quickly off his consciousness. Mateyo's state of mind was actually trancelike, as it was simply too much information for him to process.

They got to the end of the long hallway and stopped before a towering set of mahogany doors. The king looked back over his shoulders and smirked. He pushed them open and declared, "This is the royal den."

Mateyo's mouth fell open at the sight of the enormous room lined with several thousand books on six-meter-high solid mahogany bookcases, all accessed by a huge ladder on a track. Wheels at the base of the ladder were locked into the track, and a similar set of wheels and tracks anchored the ladder to the ceiling.

Mateyo followed the king inside, noticing the supple leather of one of the six wingback chairs clustered in discrete areas about the room. Mateyo touched them as they passed, seduced by their lustrous beauty. Multiple rugs, desks, and animal furs abounded. There was a central, extremely fancy-looking bar stocked with expensive, heavy-looking glasses and large glass containers with already-decanted liquids. Three natural wood-burning fireplaces, all perfectly stoked and burning idyllic fires, completed the amazing scene. Mateyo was silent as he took in the room, but after a while, his unblinking eyes began to hurt, and he became aware that his mouth was still hanging open.

"*Good!*" King Mabanda said. "I can see that you *like* your den!" He clapped his hands together. "Mine is much bigger and more opulent, of course." He chuckled proudly.

Mateyo, once again, said nothing. *What in the name of God is happening to me here?*

⸺ ◆ ⸺

It was beginning to drive Mandebala crazy. Throughout the country, the news of his ouster from the royal palace, how he had been thrown into the streets like a common criminal, and the elevation of *Mateyo* to become the crown prince spread like a wildfire on a wind-whipped savannah. The speed of the dissemination of the story was viral but largely without electronic transmission. "The crown prince was an imposter," "Mandebala was a phony," "We *knew* he was different," and the like were being repeated hundreds, even thousands of times, on every street corner, around every firepit, and in every shanty.

Mandebala saw people staring at him as he roamed the streets of the village, beaten like a dog caught stealing table scraps. Officially, the royal palace had said nothing about his predicament. And the irony was not lost on Mandebala that most of the Malezi people loved their king—they couldn't help but love him and believe in him, for several thousand years of African history had taught them to do just that. Their love for his "son," Mandebala, however, was not as tolerant. King Mabanda was bad; Mandebala had bordered on psychopathic. Many Malezilanders feared the day that Mandebala took the reins of power from Mabanda. Until just recently, that fear was a source of great joy and pleasure for Mandebala. Now it was manifestly apparent to Mandebala that Malezilanders joyously believed that day would never come.

Mandebala seethed as Malezilanders everywhere took to the streets in a spontaneous and unplanned outpouring of excitement. Everybody seemed to want to talk about it. All wanted to speculate; no one lacked for an opinion.

"Will the king tolerate his true son?"

"Will the crown prince, truly a boy from the streets, soften his father?"

"Will the royal family see fit to share some of its obvious wealth with the ordinary people, now that one is among them?"

"How could our impoverished state be ignored now that a boy raised in the slums is marked to rule the country someday?"

"Will Mateyo be able to help the ordinary people he lived with his entire life, who suckled him as an infant and helped his family unit scratch out an existence in the shanties of the slums? Will he want to, once he tastes the lifestyle of the royal family?"

Mandebala could feel the energy transference that surged through the crowd. Indeed, all could feel it. It was easy to see optimism and hope on the faces of the people. Everywhere, people spoke of Mateyo—the People's Prince.

Mandebala absorbed as much as he could. How could he use what was happening to his own benefit? He now knew that Malezilanders were, despite their abject poverty, on the whole a very happy people.

They were largely, in fact, content with their status quo. But as he watched from the sidelines a strange sense of anticipation began to take root in their conversations. If asked about it prior to the strange events of the past days, he knew that the people would have somewhat routinely professed their love, admiration, and respect for the king. Yet with this unfathomable turn of events—one of their own elevated to the second-most-powerful position in the country—a seed of hope began to germinate.

Hope. The people of Africa's poorest country began to hope. Maybe, just maybe, they seemed to be thinking, the People's Prince could change things. Maybe, just maybe, he would use his influence to help find the resources to put a bit more food on their plates.

<hr>

The king strode into Mateyo's den late in the evening of the true prince's first day at the royal palace and sat himself down in one of the leather wingback chairs clustered near one of the fireplaces. Why there was a fire burning in a palace with cold, man-made air pouring into it was beyond Mateyo's comprehension, but he didn't question it.

King Mabanda beckoned him to come and sit beside him.

A servant appeared with a box of cigars, a glass of deep red liquor of some sort, and a cutter and torch for the cigars. The king spent an inordinate amount of time looking at and contemplating which cigar he might smoke, much as a child offered candy for the first time spends a great deal of time choosing between red, blue, or green.

With the king's choice made, the servant snipped off the tip of a tremendously long double-tapered stick that Mateyo thought to be solid wood rather than a smoke. The moment the stogy touched Mabanda's lips, a torch appeared from the servant's hand, already lit and sporting an almost invisible blue flame. As Mabanda drew his first deep and aggressive pull and exhaled a virtual cloud of blue and gray smoke, he sighed and sank deeper into his seat.

The manservant immediately turned his attention to Mateyo and propped open the mini humidor to enable Mateyo to choose a cigar as well.

"Go ahead, my boy!" boomed King Mabanda, smiling. Without thinking, other than to search out the smallest cigar in the ornate, filigreed box—still, it was at least twenty centimeters long and as round as his wrists—Mateyo pulled one out. Immediately, it was snatched from his hand by the servant, expertly clipped, and returned to his mouth, torch at the ready before he could widen his eyes.

Though Mateyo didn't, and couldn't afford to, smoke regularly, he was no stranger to the practice. No Malezi boy of fourteen years hadn't tried cigarettes, if only to look tough and cool. However, Mateyo had never smoked a cigar in his life. He drew on the now burning tobacco stick, expecting a similar taste, feel, and bite to the cigarettes he had bummed or found.

Mateyo's throat and lungs erupted in a fiery, involuntary exhalation that caused him to pitch forward in his seat and cough with such force that his head nearly hit his knees as he doubled over. For a good thirty seconds, he continued to cough and wretch, and he would likely have continued had he not become aware of another loud and guttural proximate noise. It eventually dawned on him that the sound was laughter—heaving, rollicking, thunderous laughter. He looked up and saw the king laughing so hard that his immenseness shook and jiggled, and tears rolled down his jowls.

Mateyo had no idea why, but he began to laugh too. At first, he chuckled quietly, almost inaudibly, but then his laughter gained momentum like a boulder starting down a steep hill, and soon it was similarly out of control. They both laughed this way for several minutes, and only sheer physical exhaustion caused them to stop, cheeks sore, eyes moist. Then, one of them would start with a little squeak, and again they would laugh uncontrollably like children sharing a hilarious moment in a secret fort, until once again they exhausted themselves.

Carefully, the king spoke but one word, and even that was tinged with potential explosiveness. "Port," he said and pointed to the ruby liquor, then to a similarly colored full glass of liquor that had materialized on a table at Mateyo's right. The king clearly was restricting the number of times and duration for which he opened his mouth, lest more laughter should erupt.

Mateyo had no idea what port was, yet he was keen to quench the remaining fire in his throat and ease the dryness associated with minutes upon minutes of laughter. He gulped some down eagerly, filling his mouth and throat before a burning sensation struck. Though most of it was too far down his gullet to be expelled, a high-speed ruby mist emerged from his mouth and nostrils, causing the king, and Mateyo, to again lose their precarious battle with laughter.

Uncounted minutes later, they both regained their composure. Suddenly, whether from having shared such a wonderful moment of hilarity together, or perhaps from the effects of the alcohol that had made its way into their bloodstreams, for a fleeting moment they felt as though they were two friends having drunk from the same cup of an intimate and wonderful moment together.

"I have to tell you how this has come about, my son," said King Mabanda.

For the first time, Mateyo didn't recoil at the thought of being the king's son, more for lack of focus than lack of caring.

"Fourteen years ago, almost to this date, your mother, Carolanda, was in the throes of birthing you. Our idiot royal physician, Kabanga, God rest and bless his soul, was out getting drunk and did not respond to our urgent pages. As such, rather than being born here, with every modern convenience, technology, and apparatus known to medical science at the time, we had no choice but to rush you to the missionary hospital outside of Kashatown to be born.

"At the same time, it would appear, a woman from the slums of Kashatown was dying during childbirth. In fact, as the story goes, she was dead upon arrival at the steps of the hospital. The doctors managed to cut her open and save her baby. That child was Mandebala."

Mateyo slumped forward, shocked at what was being relayed to him. He knew the story of his birth—Shigeku had told it to him often, and he knew indeed that his maman had died giving birth to him. Still, he listened attentively and said nothing.

"As it turns out, this gutter woman's eldest son, barely eleven years old, promised his terminal maman to forever look after the soon-to-be-delivered child. Apparently, many Malezi people believe that the soul of their mother passes to the body of a newborn child if the mother dies during birth—obviously a silly, lowborn superstition. In any event, with the mother dead, the young lad felt as if the weight of the world had come crashing down upon him, and he was afraid of how he was going to be able to discharge his responsibility and oath.

"At that time, *your* mother, Carolanda, had just given birth to *you* in that same hospital, and when the boy realized who we were, he started a small fire in a trash basket and, in the confusion, switched his wretched little brother with *you*, believing, in his child's mind, that in making the switch, he could fulfill in an instant his pledge to his dying maman."

Mateyo's head began to spin as the realization of what had happened began to sink in.

"Only seconds later, the boy realized that the deception, and its permanence, required him in any event to care for, nurture, and raise an infant—you—to carry on the ruse. The charade was maintained until two weeks ago when the boy, now a man, was caught serving among the Zambwanan military forces who so hopelessly invaded our country.

Pleading for his life to be spared, this man—I think his name was Shigeku—revealed his deception for the first time ever."

Mateyo was flabbergasted as everything fell into place, and for a moment, he forgot that he had intended to never speak.

"Sh-Shi-Shigeku, my b-br-brother?" was all the boy could stammer.

"No," stated the king, "he is *not* your brother. As I have just told you, you are the firstborn son of Maleziland, born of Queen Carolanda and me, infused by God's own will and seed to be the ruler of your people. Mandebala was the true brother of Shigeku and the son of the gutter sow who died giving birth to him. No, you bear no relation to Shigeku, nor his scum brother Mandebala. It is only because of the great service he did in righting the wrong that he perpetrated fourteen years ago that I have spared his life."

"S-so Shigeku lives?" whispered Mateyo.

"I suppose he does, unless his fellow dogs in the street have gnawed off his leg because they were hungry and he then bled to death," mused the king, a smile forming on his lips.

"But how could you ever prove the truth of such a story?" implored Mateyo, speaking with syntactical structure for the first time in twenty-four hours.

"I don't expect someone like you—" The king seemed to be choosing his next words carefully. "I don't expect you, with your minimal worldly experience and your lack of formal education, to know about or understand these things. It is possible to compare your molecular makeup, called DNA, with that of mine, your mother's, and Mandebala's. We had your DNA analyzed. We obtained a hair sample that contains DNA from your bedclothes in Kashatown and compared it to mine and Carolanda's. It is incontrovertible. You are my son. Mandebala is not."

Again, Mateyo's desire to speak vanished like a mist in a breeze, though his voice surely would have failed him had he the need.

As he lay in bed that evening, Mateyo had no hope of sleep. First, he found the bed uncomfortable. How could anybody be expected to be able to sleep on such a ridiculously squishy object? After tossing and turning for several hours, Mateyo finally climbed off the bed and lay prone on one of the furs he'd seen when first brought to his room earlier that day. He was pretty sure it was the skin of an eland—a common antelope—and he brought one of the poofy comforters to the floor with him but soon discarded it for another fur. Though he was now physically more comfortable, it didn't change the fact that his mind was in overdrive, trying to process the events of the day.

He knew the story of his birth—that of his maman dying en route to the hospital. Mateyo also had heard, on many an occasion, the villagers refer to his maman's "soul" being within him. Shileza had been her name, and whenever he did something kind or particularly gentle or generous, comparisons were invariably drawn, as that was how all who knew Shileza described her personality. He also knew that many Malezis did indeed believe that the soul of a dying parent passed to her newborn.

Mateyo knew that he didn't look anything like his other "brothers" and "sisters," a point few people ever noticed and fewer cared about, until, of course, this very moment. Now, Mateyo cared about it a lot!

And now he knew why Shigeku had always hated the royal family, especially Mandebala, with every fiber of his wiry frame.

CHAPTER 13

As Mateyo lay on the floor that served as his bed, he realized that he was ravenously hungry. He hadn't eaten a scrap of food since he'd been yanked from the slums by Shigeku and the men in the jeeps. *Well,* he mused, *if I truly am the prince, let's see if I can get something to eat besides snails.* The departing manservant had told him that if he needed anything, anytime, all Mateyo had to do was depress the pager button on his bedside table. *Let's see if this works,* he thought. He stood and reached for the button. When the servant had said that, he had winked mischievously, unsettling Mateyo. Nevertheless, Mateyo thought he'd give it a try and pushed the pager. There was no audible click, but he jumped back a bit when it glowed bright blue as he depressed it, fearful he would be subjected to an electric shock. Mateyo thought it quite amusing and began depressing it repeatedly until a female servant arrived, less than fifteen seconds from his first touch.

Mateyo was startled, first by how quickly she had arrived and secondly by how stunningly beautiful she was. He stammered, "I'm hungry," without taking the time to so much as learn the girl's name.

The girl, who looked to be around sixteen years old, asked, "What would the crown prince like to eat?"

Mateyo was again lost for words. He didn't know what his options were. Secretly he longed for a warm bowl of maize porridge, but he didn't know if his request was reasonable. He decided to ask her a few questions, hoping, because of their relative proximity in age, that she would level with him.

"Please, miss. What is your name?"

"Your Highness, sir, it doesn't matter what my name is. You needn't ever use it. In fact, neither the prince—I mean, Mandebala—nor the king has ever used the servants' names. It would afford us more respect than should be paid by royalty to people of my station," stated the girl, her head lowered.

Mateyo burst out laughing. "Of *your* station? Just twelve hours ago I was *nowhere near* 'your station.' As a matter of fact, I was considerably *below* your station, for I know that a girl as beautiful as you didn't grow up in the slums of Kashatown. You have to tell me your name."

"But, sir, it is not appropriate—"

"I ORDER you to tell me your name!" said Mateyo, trying out his princely authority voice for the first time.

"Kanzi," replied the pretty young girl, and both of them smiled. Mateyo felt his heart leap. She was pretty, no doubt, but when she smiled, she was beautiful beyond compare. Her skin seemed impossibly smooth. Her teeth were gleaming white. They were also perfectly straight, as was her hair. She was quite tall—almost his height—but perhaps that was in part due to her shiny, high-heeled black shoes, the likes of which Mateyo had never seen before. *How can she stand on those, let alone walk?* Her eyes were dark, and they sparkled with intelligence. Even her name, which Mateyo knew meant "treasure," brought warmth and feeling each time he said it in his mind, though repetition would be unnecessary for him to commit it to memory. She and it were indelibly etched on his heart from that moment on.

"Kanzi, you must help me," implored Mateyo, trying to convey the gravity and sincerity of his request through his eyes. Kanzi nodded almost imperceptibly before he continued. "I need your help to understand what's happening here, and to understand how things work, and how I can even survive. I know nothing of living in a palace. I know nothing of beds, of linens, of cigars—what the hell is *port*? I am a creature of Kashatown, not some high-born prince, and this world terrifies me! It seems that the king is convinced by some high-tech testing that I'm his son. I am sure this is wrong, but I'm equally sure that it matters not. I need help—I need *your* help. Will you?"

As Mateyo made his plea, Kanzi sat silently, her eyes softening more and more with every passing word.

"Of course I will help you, my prince. I will—"

"You must call me Mateyo. It is the only name I have ever known. I have to think hard and focus when someone calls me 'prince' before I can actually comprehend that they are talking to me," said Mateyo.

"I cannot do so in the presence of others," Kanzi said, "but if it is only the two of us, well, yes, of course I will call you Mateyo. Mateyo— see, I just did it!" She giggled and smiled the heart-capturing smile that Mateyo already longed for desperately.

Mateyo sighed. "You have made me so happy. I feel so alone right now—though there always seems to be an army of servants around, so I am clearly not alone." He laughed and brought Kanzi laughingly along with him.

"First, we must deal with your hungry belly, my prince—I mean, Mateyo. What would you like to eat?" Kanzi asked.

"You see, that's my problem!" blurted Mateyo. "I don't *know* what I want to eat! What are my options? Is it too much trouble to ask for a bowl of porridge? It's what I'm truly hungry for right now."

Kanzi laughed her beautiful, sweet laugh. "Silly prince boy, you can order anything under the sun. You could order lobster tails grilled over a barbeque and served with a white truffle and cognac sauce. You could order the finest Russian caviar and twenty-five-year-old white Canadian cheddar. You could order Coquille St. Jacques, French onion soup, a beautiful rack of herb-crusted lamb . . . anything! Even corn porridge!" Kanzi smiled.

"But again, that's my problem!" Mateyo almost shouted. "I don't know what a single thing on that list of food that you just spoke *is*! Not one. I need someone to teach me, to help me."

"I will do that for you, Mateyo. But first, let me wake the chef to cook your porridge."

"I have a better idea," said Mateyo. "Let's go make it ourselves!"

Kanzi's smile was all he needed to confirm her agreement. It was all he needed, period. They stole off together like two kids in the night to cook a royal meal.

Mateyo awoke happy, if a bit stiff, as the marble floor upon which his fur sat was considerably harder than the packed dirt floor and straw he was used to. Memories of Kanzi and her smile had permeated his thoughts all night long, and he couldn't wait to see her again. He had no clue when that would be. He had no idea as to what her duties were at the palace, when she worked, where she lived, what her parents did—nothing! He had been so caught up in the moment with her that nothing else seemed to matter, and he cursed himself silently and made a mental note to remember to ask her all these things.

The prince had barely opened his eyes when the bedroom door opened. How the hell did anyone know he was awake? His heart skipped a beat, hoping for Kanzi, soared, then crashed hard when a male servant entered the room with a luxuriantly thick-looking robe draped over his arm. The servant said nothing. This seemed to be some form of protocol: Say nothing unless spoken to. Mateyo wasn't sure that he liked this concept, for after he'd finally opened up with Kanzi last night, he found that he had a thousand questions. That said, he wanted to ask Kanzi alone each and every one of them.

Mateyo went to put his clothes on—clothes that felt odd and constricting. He saw the look of shock and horror register on the servant's face. It visibly elongated as the man's jaw dropped without his mouth hanging agape, and his eyes widened. This thin, waiflike man then returned his face to a neutral expression. He, too, wore a perfectly starched, formal, white-collared shirt, a black bow tie, and black trousers. Everything he wore was ironed perfectly smooth, and nary a spot of slight discoloration was visible anywhere.

Mateyo broke the silence.

"What? What am I doing wrong? Speak!" he ordered, realizing that unless he was direct, he might not get answered.

"It is customary for the prince to take a shower in the morning," the servant stated.

Mateyo could barely believe his ears. "But I showered only yesterday!" he objected. "Surely I can't take a shower two days in a row? That would be utterly ridiculous!" He certainly did not need to bathe more than once a week. The water available in the village for that purpose had been little better, if at all, than the smell and germs that it purported to remove.

The servant frowned. "The king would be highly offended if you did not shower each day. Each of us who works here must do so as well. 'Cleanliness is the rule when next to godliness,' the king says, and I know that he showers each day himself."

Mateyo shrugged and headed for the shower. Once again, he adjusted the water to be as cool as it could be flowing out of the rain-head device. He was certain that he would never get used to warm showers.

When he stepped out of the shower, the servant was right there to hand him a towel.

"What is your name, and what do you do here?" inquired Mateyo, remembering to learn a bit more about the hired help than he had last night.

"Chumba," came the quick reply, "and I am your personal steward."

Mateyo felt exasperated, as he seemed to take at least one step backward for every step forward he took. "Tell me what a 'steward' is, or does, please, Chumba," he said.

"A steward is your personal attendant. When I am on duty, I am your first point of contact for any request you might have, other than when you are in the presence of other servants who are responsible for the area in which you are seeking information or service.

"For example, if you wanted a glass of wine and knew what type of wine and which vintage, you would ask me, and I would either get it myself or procure it. However, if you had a question about different wines and the royal sommelier was in attendance—and he is at every meal except breakfast—I would direct your question to the royal sommelier and get your answers. Is that clear?"

Chumba looked at Mateyo imploringly, waiting for his next question. Mateyo rolled his eyes. If he had a pen handy, he would have jotted down a half-dozen words and terms that had been thrown out, rapid fire, by Chumba—the first being *sommelier.*

Mateyo had a great deal to learn. He longed, however, for his tutor to be someone else.

⁂

Breakfast for Mateyo was uneventful, as his father didn't join him. The meal was served in the breakfast nook, a bay-windowed area with impossibly tall, broad windows set deeply overlooking the royal gardens and directly blessed by the day's first sun. There were five large tables in the nook, each seating ten people, and Mateyo felt relatively small and insignificant, and very much alone.

He wasn't hungry, as his belly was still partially full from his midnight snack with Kanzi. Even then, he never would or could have eaten the plethora of food put before him. He'd never seen so much meat before! There was bacon, sausage, ham, and steak; there were eggs, cheese, and fruit of all sorts. No fewer than four bread products graced his plate as well. Mateyo placated himself, if not his staff, by gnawing absentmindedly on a piece of toast, which arrived piping hot but was as cold as marble by the time he completed eating it.

After he "finished" his breakfast, no fewer than four servants hovered over him expectantly. Just what they expected, Mateyo hadn't the foggiest inclination. He beckoned Chumba closer and whispered, "What's next?"

Chumba smiled faintly and responded in what seemed to be yet another riddle, "Whatever you want, Your Highness."

Mateyo sighed. Without Kanzi around, it was going to be hard to get straight answers, or at least hard to get answers that didn't in and of themselves create several more questions. He decided to command rather than ask.

"Chumba, show me the palace," said Mateyo.

"Which rooms would Your Highness like to see?" offered Chumba in his typical blasé fashion.

Mateyo nearly growled. "How the hell would I know? All of them!"

"But, sir," said Chumba meekly, "there are two hundred and ninety-seven rooms, not counting those currently under construction."

Mateyo's eyes widened for what would be neither the first nor last time that day. Though most Malezis knew that the royal palace was large and that the royal family lived in luxury, none save for the select few who lived or worked there truly appreciated its grandeur. Mateyo was certain that Chumba was exaggerating. Gathering his thoughts together, Mateyo directed, "Well, if there are indeed that many rooms, then we had best get started."

Despite having already seen several luxurious rooms, Mateyo was *not* prepared for the overwhelming spectacle he was about to explore. They traversed through room after room of opulent extravagance.

All were expensively accoutremented. The purposes for most of these rooms were a mystery. Mateyo had never before seen a bowling alley, let alone a four-lane one, and had no idea of what the purpose was or how one played the game. Chumba mentioned cheekily that the last time anybody had bowled there was three years ago. At the moment, several staffers were applying the biweekly waxing to the alleys.

Happily for Mateyo, his guide fell into a routine of explaining each room and its purpose rather than face the inevitable barrage of questions that issued from Mateyo's mostly agape mouth. Swimming parlor, media theater, games room, poker room (apparently built after the hold 'em craze quickly gripped, then fled the king's fancy), library, studies (*what the hell was the difference?*), dens, informal parlors, formal parlors, guest chambers, and servants' quarters.

They also saw dining halls, formal dining halls, and kitchens (a main one and several satellites). All but the king's suite were eventually toured by the two men. Mateyo had to continually remind himself to blink, usually after his eyeballs had become incredibly dry. He casually observed no fewer than eighteen bathrooms. He did not ask how many there were in total, wondering why the king needed so many bathrooms at the ready. *Perhaps His Immenseness has stomach issues.*

By the time Mateyo finished his tour several hours later, he was ravenously hungry. "Chumba," he said, "I think I could now eat the several cooked beasts that were laid out for my breakfast this morning. I'm so hungry. Can we get something to eat?"

"Something?" said Chumba, smiling. "I think for *you*, it can be arranged." Shortly thereafter, Mateyo was digging into the biggest, most tender steak he'd ever dreamt possible, its red juices flowing over his tongue like life-giving water for a man dying of thirst.

"This is *soooo* good! I could get used to this!" Mateyo said to himself.

And then Kanzi floated into the dining room, and "good" became a dream.

Mateyo's next few days were filled with joy. He didn't see his father—he learned later that Mabanda was out of the country on a "state visit." He most certainly didn't care, for every single waking moment of his days was spent either with or thinking about Kanzi.

One day, Mateyo summoned the courage to ask Kanzi about her parents. On previous occasions when the subject had come up tangentially, he could see the real and acrid pain in Kanzi's eyes. Yet Mateyo longed to know every detail possible about her life. As they sat in the palace garden on a particularly beautiful and serene morning, Mateyo took a deep breath, exhaled, and began to speak.

"Kanzi," he practically whispered, "can you please tell me about your parents?"

Immediately, Kanzi looked away, and Mateyo instantly regretted asking her the question. He had hurt her, or at least callously brought up a painful memory for her.

"Kanzi," he said quickly, "I'm sorry. I shouldn't ask. It is none of my business."

Kanzi turned back toward him and faced him with glassy, liquid eyes. "Mateyo, it's okay," she said. "I rarely speak of my parents, as it pains me very much to do so. I miss them both—so much—but I should be able to speak of them. In fact, I very much want you to know about my parents. They are a big part of who I am.

"My father was Kabanga—Dr. Kabanga, the royal physician. He and my mother, Zeela, lived in the royal palace. My father had been educated in Paris and London and was a highly skilled general practitioner and surgeon. He was on call twenty-four seven and was often awakened in the middle of the night if the king couldn't pass gas easily or had a splinter in one of his baby-soft fingers."

Kanzi carried on, her voice gaining strength as she spoke. "On the day you were born, in fact, my father learned that he had contracted AIDS. As you likely know, AIDS is a death sentence. At the time, no one really knew how it spread, but we now know it can be contracted in several ways, including through receiving a blood transfusion contaminated with the AIDS virus. Sadly, a few months earlier, my father had a ruptured appendix. During the emergency surgery, he received a blood transfusion that saved his life, only to end it a few years later. Maman died a couple of years later, having been infected by the same scourge through my father."

Mateyo said nothing. The two sat silently in the garden for over an hour. Mateyo held her hand, but no words were spoken. Mateyo knew now why he had been born in the missionary hospital rather than at the royal palace. Somehow, God Himself had connected his and Kanzi's fate. He was sad that he would never meet her parents.

❖

As the days went by and days turned to weeks, Mateyo soaked up both his experiences and information like a sun-wizened sponge. Also, his body soaked up nutrition in a similar fashion; where earlier there were only skin, bones, and sinewy muscle, there was now a thin, healthy layer of subcutaneous fat that smoothened out Mateyo's skin and made him appear healthier and more handsome. Mateyo didn't spend time contemplating his attractiveness, but he had seen many a servant girl swoon and twitter as he passed by. Mateyo had once noticed Kanzi try to catch her breath as she stared at him, thinking her gaze had been unnoticed. Most of the time she seemed to do her best to keep from staring. More than anything, however, it seemed as if Kanzi was powerfully drawn to his personality: his warmth, his undying curiosity, his love of life, and his ability to laugh and to make others around him laugh as well.

Mateyo had a natural, innate sense of caring and concern that Kanzi had never seen within the walls of the royal palace. Perhaps those who lived and worked there were somehow infected by the life of relative privilege it afforded them, or perhaps even they were infected by the imperious and uncaring attitude and disdain shown by the royalty toward all others. "Mateyo, you really seem to care about everybody you meet," said Kanzi one bright morning as they soaked up some sun in the royal garden. "You make the servants and staff laugh and talk—real talk, not just responding to orders or questions. And you're so darn curious about *everything*!"

Mateyo thought for a few moments before answering. "Kanzi, I grew up with nothing. Or at least so little that most would consider it nothing. Everything here is so new to me. I feel like a little child, except children experience new things gradually. New things in my new world come at me constantly! Without you, I do not think I could keep up. I really don't."

One day, while Kanzi and Mateyo were exploring the north garden, a teeny mouse scampered by them with a big chunk of dry bread, much too large for it to fit properly in its mouth, held precariously by protruding teeth.

"That's a large chunk of bread for so little a mouse," said Mateyo, first corralling and then cradling the little mouse in his hands. "See this, Kanzi? Feel under its belly. This little mouse is a mommy mousy. It has little babies that are still feeding—there, can you feel the little teats?"

Kanzi nodded vigorously, clearly pleased with their discovery. "Now run along, little mousy, and don't forget your bread. Your little ones will be depending on it." The mouse looked left, then right, and made a beeline for the closest foliage.

They watched the mouse scamper off until a large black, shiny leather boot crushed the creature into a lifeless, shapeless form.

Mateyo heard Kanzi gasp quietly.

"Clearly I must start your formal education NOW," boomed King

Mabanda as he lifted his boot and admired his bloody victim. "It is apparent that you care too much for all things, little and small. God looks after their souls, should we choose to terminate their existence. That said, as God's chosen representative on this earth, you must not let your judgment be clouded by concern for the little things. As king and ruler, you must do what is best for the betterment of all, not just the little things like individuals and mice. Indeed, some must suffer to keep those closest to God—their king and his family—in a fashion suitable for the human form of deity represented by the king."

Mateyo could scarcely believe his ears. Is this what the king thought of his people? Nothing, however, in the voice or the conviction with which the king spoke betrayed anything but absolute and wholehearted belief. Mateyo said nothing.

"Come, boy, it is time to tell the world about you. Girl! Go fetch my communications officer. We'll be in my den. And do not dare return to me without my Cubans. Go!"

Kanzi dashed off quickly but gracefully and cast a sweet smile and glance over her shoulder toward Mateyo as she disappeared into the palace.

King Mabanda caught the glance and smile. "Well, well, young lad, looks like you've been dipping your royal pen in that sweet little ink pot already! I'll never understand why Mandebala never fucked that little tease—God knows, she always wanted it badly enough—but something about her always seemed to intimidate his royal scepter. Ha! I hope she bled well for you and screamed in pain. Nothing like fucking a virgin, hey, boy?"

The king saw a look of sheer hatred that passed over his son's face. Perhaps he was angry that the former prince had even attempted to bed Mateyo's rightful virgin.

After four full days at the palace, Mateyo finally met his mother. Mateyo had discovered that Carolanda lived in a separate wing with all the other wives, thirteen in total. Housing all the non-heir offspring as well—all Mateyo's half brothers and sisters—the Wives' Wing was one of the few areas that Mateyo and Chumba had not toured. Although the king visited his wives' quarters frequently—the staff referred to it as "winging it"—few of his wives ever visited the principal portion of the palace of their own accord, save for Queen Carolanda.

Though she was the king's third wife, once she had sired the king a male heir, Carolanda was quickly made queen. Officially, the king divorced his first two wives to open the role and title for Carolanda, though the first two wives and their children still lived in the Wives' Wing.

There was a knock at the door to Mateyo's den, and the new prince glanced up with a frown from the game he was playing with Kanzi. None of the servants ever knocked, for to impose such a rule would make their jobs difficult and obtrusive. And Mabanda himself clearly had no need to knock anywhere, anytime.

Who in the world could this be?

"Come in," Mateyo shouted from across the room. When Queen Carolanda entered, Mateyo's heart skipped multiple beats. Carolanda's eyes widened, and in an instant, they both knew. Carolanda was the feminine version of Mateyo. She was definitively heavier than Mateyo—the years of soft living and childbirth having taken their toll—but without a grain of doubt, she was his mother. Their features were identical. His skin tone—more a smooth milk chocolate than a dark brown—replicated Carolanda's precisely.

Neither mother nor son spoke. Jaw agape, Queen Carolanda turned and left the den without saying a word. It would be a full hour of silently playing Bwana before Mateyo spoke to Kanzi once again.

"Kanzi, you know who that was, right?" said Mateyo, even though he knew she did.

"Mateyo, the entire country knows Queen Carolanda," she said. "She's very beautiful."

Mateyo nodded. "Not as beautiful as you are."

The following day, Carolanda joined Mateyo in the breakfast nook as he was eating his maize porridge and staring outside at the beautiful flowers of the garden. Carolanda glided into the room so smoothly and quietly that Mateyo didn't notice her until she loomed, respectfully, at the side of his table. Mateyo was struck by her regal, mature beauty. Though she was a bit heavier than she would have been fourteen years ago when she gave birth to him, and there were a few more lines etched into her face, she was undeniably attractive by any standard. She wore a flowing white gown of a fine silken material and a beautiful sun hat that added to her already impressive height.

"May I join you, Mateyo?" she asked. Mateyo noticed that she did not call him "Prince" or "sir" or "Your Highness"—just Mateyo. He liked that. Nodding vigorously, he gestured for her to sit down.

Carolanda leaned forward and began to speak, her voice barely above a whisper. "I very much had my doubts about the stories being told about you being my son. It just seemed too fanciful to be true, though I do vaguely remember some form of commotion in the room next door that night at the missionary hospital. I suspect, also, that you, too, had difficulty believing the story."

Mateyo nodded.

"I also know nothing of the 'science' that my husband says has proved your birthright. That said, all my doubts were vanquished the moment I laid eyes on you. I am your mother, Mateyo, and you are my son."

Mateyo stood. Carolanda did the same. They hugged each other fiercely, and years of separation were bridged in one powerful moment. For a few minutes, they held tight to each other, and Mateyo was just a little boy in his maman's embrace, not the crown prince of all Maleziland and nearly a man.

Queen Carolanda and Mateyo began meeting for breakfast every morning this way. Kanzi never showed up before noon, being on official "duty" late each night, though exactly what she did when she wasn't with Mateyo, the prince didn't know. Breakfasts soon stretched into entire mornings, with mother and son becoming more and more comfortable with each other. As was his way, Mateyo spoke little when he first met his maman, but once the relationship was established and the lines of communication opened, Mateyo chatted animatedly and excitedly with Carolanda as if they'd been together all along.

"Fourteen years ago," said Carolanda one morning, "I almost named the infant I thought to be my son 'Mateyo.' The king absolutely and outrightly rejected the name. He said it sounded too 'soft.' He was right, and that's exactly why I loved the name so much." Carolanda beamed. "And now here you are!"

"Wow," said Mateyo, exhaling. "I hope he doesn't ask me to change my name to Mandebala! I won't do it—he'll have to execute me first!"

Carolanda blanched. "You shouldn't joke that way, Mateyo. The king has killed many people, both via execution and by his own hand, though you are most certainly safe from that fate. As you are heir to the throne, he would never intentionally harm a single hair on your head. Not even Mandebala was ever in jeopardy of being intentionally harmed by the king, despite becoming an evil, foul, vile little miscreant. Of course, perhaps that is exactly why your father never harmed him." The queen sighed. "As Mandebala's mother, I could not love him, try as I might. But, Mateyo, promise me that you will never, ever push your father to the point of rage."

Carolanda continued, "You see, the king has a button, a 'switch,' if you will, that once flicked, throws him into a bloodthirsty frenzy. If this happens, your life will be in peril. I was once beaten senseless by the king—four broken ribs, a broken arm, and four broken fingers—crushed by his boot as I tried to keep him from kicking me." She held up her left hand to show Mateyo that none of the fingers straightened properly. "And yet I know that he loves me deeply. These are the perils, and contradictions, of the man who is your father."

Every morning, the two of them talked freely of palace life, about plants, animals, trees, and food. They talked about anything that might cross the minds of two thoughtful, caring people. Carolanda seemed pleased. "Mateyo," she said, "it has long troubled me deeply to have brought an animal like Mandebala into the world. I am relieved and grateful that I am, in fact, your mother and not his."

At around noon each day, when Kanzi would arrive, Carolanda would quickly and politely excuse herself and head back to the Wives' Wing, ostensibly each time to look after some semi-urgent matter. She would hug Mateyo warmly before she departed, and she and Kanzi locked eyes each time as she left, smiling, saying more words with the glance than could be spoken in a half-hour dialogue.

After Carolanda left each day and Kanzi glided to Mateyo's side, he scarcely remembered that the queen had spent the morning with him.

CHAPTER 14

The royal palace issued a statement confirming that the true crown prince of Maleziland had been discovered living in the slums of Kashatown and that the former crown prince, Mandebala, had been cast out of the palace. No further explanation was given. The king also declared the following Monday would be called "Prince's Day," a national holiday this day and every year forth. A grand parade through Kashatown and much of the remaining countryside would mark the occasion this and each subsequent year.

Mateyo dreaded the event. He did not feel that he deserved the attention soon to be directed his way, and he certainly did not yet feel that he had any right to the lineage to which he'd been told he was genetically entitled.

On the ensuing parade day, a beautifully bright, clear African summer morning, he stayed much longer in the shower than usual and didn't touch his breakfast. His stomach was so tightly wound that he couldn't have accepted nourishment even if he'd wanted it. Not even the warm, welcoming smile of Queen Carolanda, sweetly bidding him good morning as she joined him in the breakfast nook, could lift his spirits and ease his tension. "No, Maman," said Mateyo. "I am quite sure this will be one of the worst days of my life."

Mateyo was driven through every major city and town in the country in an escorted, heavily guarded Range Rover—black, of course. Two khaki-colored army jeeps led the way, and two identical jeeps followed. Three camouflage-uniformed military men in each vehicle scanned for threats in every direction, AK-47s pointing outward to the crowds, all at the ready. The procession was met by virtually every citizen of the country, cheering enthusiastically from the roadsides. They had dressed in their finest and most colorful clothes, and their hopes were high. Everywhere, Mateyo was met with cheers of "People's Prince! People's Prince! People's Prince!"

King Mabanda grinned as the cheers echoed through the car. "See? The people already love you. They are claiming you as their own."

In no way could Mateyo have imagined that he would enjoy the day, but to his utter shock and initial dismay, he found himself thoroughly enjoying it. He was caught up in the happiness of the people cheering him wildly in every town and on every street they passed. He was caught up in the moment with every other Malezilander and even forgot at times that everyone was cheering for *him*.

When Mateyo and the procession arrived back at the palace, fully eighteen hours after they had left, the king barked at Mateyo, "Wait for me in my den." Mateyo nodded and quickly went to the bathroom to first wash his face. By the time he arrived in the king's den, Mabanda had settled into one of the many comfortable chairs and sparked up a massive Cuban. The king had also gulped down several king-sized swallows from a large tumbler of port—his "evening water."

"You see, my boy," the king began, exhaling slowly, "the people of this country truly do love us. Why, I almost got the sense that they were cheering more wildly for *you* than for *me*. Preposterous idea, I know. But there is no doubt that they were enthralled with you. Did you hear what they were shouting? People's Prince! They already love you, much in the way they love me. Can it be denied that we are indeed divine-right rulers? After all, their love for us, including you, is pure and unquestioning, much as their belief and love for God is pure and unquestioning. That, my son, is how we know that our reign is blessed, nay, even supported by God Himself."

Mateyo sat quietly, listening but not believing what Mabanda was saying. He had never spoken back to the king. Indeed, he had rarely spoken at all in his father's presence since arriving at the palace. Mateyo was, however, feeling emboldened by the adrenaline surge from the crowds earlier, and without thinking, he met the king's eyes.

"You can't possibly believe this 'divine right' stuff, can you?" Mateyo said. "I can tell you from the perspective of ordinary people, like me, there is no such concept. They have never heard about the divine right, which you claim gives you authority to rule. They believe that it is important to have a strong ruler and that as such, you suffice, but the people of Maleziland in no way think that you are some form of earthbound godly representative." He chuckled until he saw the look on the king's face. Mateyo's heart began to race.

King Mabanda's eyes widened, and Mateyo could almost see the blood rushing up the king's neck and into his face and brain, fueling his rage. His veins began to course visibly, as though he were some freakish monster from a horror story. Mabanda was clearly struggling to contain his wrath, an internal battle he was unaccustomed to fighting.

"Leave," Mabanda said.

Mateyo nodded and, legs shaking, left the room. Having wakened the sleeping bear, he was more than happy to slip out of harm's way. When he arrived back at his room, Mateyo realized that he had been lucky to escape in one piece.

⊷ ◆ ⊶

The next morning Mateyo realized the king was undaunted by his transgression from the night before. In fact, Mabanda was apparently inspired, and he began tackling Mateyo's "education" with increasing daily fervor.

Mateyo had to endure countless and seemingly endless soliloquies. For the most part, he listened and did not speak on the various subjects, which included "divine right," "pack mentality," "the people's need for a strong ruler," and "Darwinian theory.'"

"My boy," said the king, "God blesses us and accepts us as His representatives on earth. When I was first elected, I did not rule with God's blessing. But the Lord God came to me in a dream and told me that He wanted me to rule over His people as long as I should be alive. When I asked the Catholic Church to bless my rule, they happily sent the Sword of Divinity to Maleziland for my swearing-in ceremony. Now, the Sword of Divinity is no ordinary sword—every pope since the fourteenth century has been sworn in with its graces. No pope would ever condone its use for any ruler without firmly believing those rulers to be God-anointed. And perhaps not without an eight-figure donation to the Vatican as well—hah!"

Good Lord, he really believes this! Mateyo nodded politely.

"My boy," the king said, "we need to chat about something called 'pack mentality.' People are animals, and in fact, we are pack animals. As with dogs in packs, leaders naturally evolve. Once the members of the pack, be they canine or human, learn their order in the pack, they are comfortable and happy. If a member of a pack doesn't know his social ordering, chaos can and will erupt. Similarly, if that order is somewhat assaulted or changed, animals get nervous and uncertain about their future. So, as you can see, all pack members—including all Malezis— benefit from establishing an order and maintaining it. We are the God-chosen leaders of our pack, my boy."

Mateyo could tell from the earnestness in the king's voice that he believed every word of this lesson. He pondered the king's words until he fell asleep that night.

King Mabanda found him early the next day, before Mateyo had completed his breakfast. "Son," he began, "for tens of thousands of years, the people of Maleziland, and even all of Africa, have been ruled by kings and chiefs. Democracy? This is a foolish notion. God chooses us, my boy, to rule over His people. And our people do not know of matters of state. They do not need, nor do they want, some form of elected representation. The people want to know that their king is strong and good and can defend them and their prosperity. The king looks after his subjects—this they know. So as a king today, I am like a great chief of years ago. This is all they need. This is all they want.

"In fact," the king continued, "it is important to our people that our neighboring countries, and even the rest of the world, see the strong leader that I am. Our defeat of the loathsome Zambwanan curs but a few short weeks ago proved to the people that we are strong! And it is that very type of threat that proves the need for a powerful and strong king. It had been over thirty years since we faced a military threat—and I daresay it may be that long before the next!"

Mateyo nodded, expressionless, and had only a fleeting moment before the king continued with his next royal lesson.

"Son," he said, "I know that this will be a new concept for you, but a further truism of science also supports our rule. Over thousands and millions of years, God's creatures have changed and adapted to their environment. The stronger, smarter, and better of those animals have better and more frequent breeding opportunities than the weaker, and the bloodline of all is thus improved. This is called 'Darwinian theory,' and it is widely known to be true. Clearly, our bloodline is more highly evolved. It is only natural for us to lead lesser humans.

"In fact, and I believe this to be true, my doctors have suggested that I am evolving into a godlike being." The king paused and smiled. "I am, of course, blessed and anointed by God—as you are, or will one day be. It is manifestly obvious that you and I are more intelligent, refined, and perfect than the average Malezi citizen. Only a man of royal blood could ever rule Maleziland."

It took all of Mateyo's concentration to keep his emotions in check. He almost burst out laughing as he looked at the short and stocky king. Instead, Mateyo nodded and said, "Yes, King Mabanda. I see."

The king broke into a broad, toothy smile and said, "Mateyo, you need not call me 'King Mabanda,' at least not when we're out of the public eye. You can call me 'Father.'"

The king grinned even more, clearly pleased that his young acolyte was coming around, learning, and believing.

On an early evening later in the week, the king strolled into Mateyo's den, clearly intent on teaching further lessons. Mateyo was this time settled quite comfortably, surrounded by the many cozy furs, fireplaces, and luxuriously large and soft leather furniture. As the king plodded unsteadily into the room, Mateyo could smell the stench from scotch and cigars on his breath. *He has started early today!*

King Mabanda plopped himself into a great leather chair, took a long drink from a huge tumbler filled with scotch, and began. "Son, you must know that as the crown prince, you can do anything, anywhere, anytime, with or to anyone as you please. This is your right, as heir to our divine kingdom. If you see a pretty girl, and your royal member is hungry, it is your right to feed it and fuck as many pretty young things as you wish."

Mateyo was listening absently, nevertheless trying to appear attentive, when Kanzi poked her pretty head into the den.

"GIRL!" the king boomed. "Come in here this instant."

Mateyo sat up straight in his chair. Nothing good could come from this. The king was volcanically volatile when sober, but when drinking, he was exponentially more so.

Kanzi's face registered pure fear, as she'd had no idea that the king would be with Mateyo in his den.

Kanzi drew back her shoulders, her chin up as she walked in, but Mateyo could see the trepidation in her eyes. She, too, knew the situation was beyond precarious. Nevertheless, Kanzi entered the den with quick and tiny steps, her head down, stopping at a safe and respectful distance from both the king and Mateyo.

"Take off your clothes, you little whore," the king said. "I've seen you prancing around my halls for years now. It is time somebody demonstrated the time-honored concept of royal prerogative to my son!"

Mateyo stood. "Father, I—"

"Son, this should be almost as much fun for you as for me! Don't think that I haven't noticed how you look at each other and spend so much time together. Why, I bet the little slut was coming to relieve the tension from your royal scepter this evening, weren't you, you little bitch?"

Mateyo's head began to spin.

"Well, worry not; you'll have your turn to fuck her—after I am done, of course. After all, I am the KING!"

"Father, no," Mateyo stammered, hardly believing his ears, which had grown hot from anxiety.

"Ha!" the king said, laughing. "Don't worry, son. They always fight and scream and cry a bit at first, but by the time we're done, she'll be moaning like a little whore and begging you to never stop! Now take your clothes off, girl!"

Kanzi, still looking at the floor, began sliding the straps of her white sundress off her shoulders.

Mateyo lurched forward and ran toward her. "Kanzi! No!"

She looked up and placed her hand on his chest. "No, Mateyo," she whispered. "It will be safer for both of us if you let the king have his way."

The king uttered a low, throaty growl. "Come here, you little bitch, so that I can suck those perfect tits and fuck you properly for the first time in your life."

Kanzi inched forward, hands shaking and legs wobbling. She knelt before the king, who grinned broadly and began to open his robe. "Now," the king said gutturally, "I will show you how *great* it is to be king!"

Mateyo snapped out of his stupor and lunged toward his father. "NO!"

The king's attention was very much focused elsewhere, and Mateyo caught his father with his shoulder in the middle of Mabanda's throat, knocking him hard and causing both the wingback chair and the king to topple over backward.

Although the king had probably not faced physical opposition of any kind in almost four decades, he was through and through a man of violence, and he responded with sheer blood rage. The king backhanded Mateyo across the side of the head with his massive, club-like hand. With one hundred and fifty kilograms of weight behind it, the crushing blow struck Mateyo with such force that his thin body left the ground as he reeled upward and backward from its impact. Mateyo's head felt like it had been cleaved in two. The king sauntered over, sneering, and kicked Mateyo in the groin—hard. Mateyo doubled over into a fetal position on the floor.

As Mateyo lay on his side, writhing, the king grabbed his son by the hair, wrenching his neck from its cocoon-like position, and laid one of his great paws on Mateyo's slender throat. King Mabanda then slapped his other hand on the prince's throat and squeezed mightily with both paws. The king then lifted Mateyo from the ground, paying no heed to his son's flailing and kicking legs. Mateyo's once bright world began to fade.

This is the end. Mateyo could see the murderous intent in his father's eyes. He could see the primeval, bloodthirsty rage flowing through the king's engorged, sweaty, pulsing face.

Mateyo knew he was drawing his last breaths. His legs stopped kicking wildly and went limp. As the room went dark, he managed to mouth "I love you" to Kanzi as she stood open-mouthed behind the king, watching in horror.

Mateyo crumpled to the floor as a huge weight fell beside him. Mateyo was suddenly able to suck in much-needed air.

Kanzi ran to Mateyo, grabbing him in her arms and sobbing.

"My prince, you're alive."

Mateyo's head, throat, and groin throbbed angrily in pain as he tried to understand what was happening. He turned to his right and saw his father—the king—lying prone on the marble floor, lifeless.

What happened?

Kanzi cradled Mateyo in silence as they both trembled beside the corpse of his father, the *former* king of Maleziland.

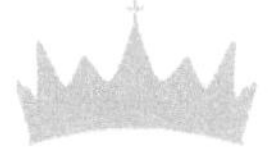

CHAPTER 15

Shigeku practically sprinted through Kashatown's decrepit streets, en route to Miss K's shanty, clutching a copy of the morning's newspaper. He already knew the gist of what it said, as news of the king's death had spread like wildfire, traveling mouth to mouth at lightning speed. But he wanted to know what the article said—every single word—and he knew that Miss K was one of few who could help.

He burst into her shanty. "Can you read this to me?" he blurted out.

Miss Kalibwa was obviously ready for that day's school session in her impossibly white, perfectly pressed blouse, and below-the-knee black skirt. She was seated at a little table drinking tea and looked up, startled, when Shigeku burst in.

"Good morning, Shigeku. How are you today? Indeed, yes, I *can* read it very well, thank you. Would you *like* me to read it?"

Shigeku recognized the lesson in politeness she was attempting to impart and hung his head. "Yes, please," he said.

"Well, it appears that the royal palace has issued a formal press release this morning, announcing Mabanda's death," she said. "It reads:

The Royal Family is grievously saddened to announce the death of King Mabanda from a heart attack at approximately 7:30 p.m. last night. King-Elect Mateyo has declared a week-long state of mourning, followed by a state funeral to be held at Our Lady of Grace Cathedral on Monday, June 7, at 10:00 a.m. King Mateyo will be officially sworn in by the Archbishop of Maleziland, His Worship Archbishop Sulamena, at the Cathedral at 2:00 p.m. on the same day."

What does this mean for us now that Mateyo is to be king? Shigeku's mind raced. He thanked Miss K and left to be alone with his thoughts.

Shigeku knew that the weeklong state of mourning implemented by Mateyo after his father's death would be extremely popular with the Malezi people. Although he couldn't fathom it, the people of Maleziland truly did mourn the loss of their king. Most didn't know or remember a time when Mabanda hadn't been king. Mabanda's cadaver was to be laid in state, open casket, for an entire week in the cathedral. For days he watched Malezilanders filing through Kashatown on foot, dressed in their finest. *Off to pay their respects to that piece of shit they call king,* Shigeku thought with disgust. They filed past by the thousands to pay their last respects.

Indeed, in part due to the small size of the country, and in part since everyone had a week off, most citizens were able to make the journey from the countryside to pay their respects to the king. Shigeku had come to the cathedral to see what was happening, though he had zero intention of setting foot inside. The queue to do so snaked for nearly five kilometers up the main street of Lalonga, up its massive flight of steps, through its hand-carved, massive twin wooden doors, and all the way through the central aisle of the massive colonial edifice. Built in the late 1800s with the blood, sweat, lives, and pennies of the local indigenous population, the church stood as a semi-eternal reminder to one of the principal underlying reasons for the original European settlement in Africa—the harvesting of souls. Its neo-Gothic architecture stood in stark contrast to the abject poverty of the rest of the city and country and reminded all that the promise of heaven and its eternal reward could only be accessed through its massive wooden doors.

The building appeared to be hewn from red stone but instead was made from locally fired bricks of varying sizes. It was easily the most impressive public building in all of Maleziland—second, of course, to the three royal palaces—but few of its populace had ever laid eyes on any of the palaces except from afar. Its spire was Gothic in design, and the cross atop was at least twice the height of the tallest tree Shigeku had ever seen. Stained glass windows with brilliant blue, green, and red hues depicted the scenes from the stations of the cross.

Shigeku remembered wondering as a child how such brilliant colors could be within the glass, and further how the colors simply did not fade—ever. A vibrant, circulating mini market of walking vendors hawked food, blankets, trinkets, and drink along the queue's route. Shigeku knew that as the day of the funeral and swearing-in ceremony approached, the crowds and queues would grow impossibly larger, with many from out of town hoping to both attend the funeral and the inaugural ceremony on the same visit.

Shigeku felt strangely compelled to study the crowd.

As the initial shock of the king's sudden death wore off on the populace, the realization that Mateyo was soon to be sworn in as king had caused a current of optimism and excitement to once again race through the land. It was palpable. When Mateyo had been feted only days earlier on Prince's Day, none of the Malezi people had foreseen how quickly his reign would come, despite King Mabanda's less-than-healthy, grotesquely indulgent lifestyle.

Shigeku decided he too must stay for the big memorial, despite that fact the ceremonies were not meant to take place for another three days.

He slept each night under a tree on the outskirts of town and watched the growing crowd of people intently.

The excitement in Lalonga reached a fevered pitch on the night before the funeral and the ceremony. Shigeku could see, in the immediate vicinity of the cathedral, hundreds of small fires that warmed those who were prepared to camp overnight to secure their seats at both events, basking the cathedral in a warm, flickering glow.

At dawn's first peek on the morning of the ceremonies, the long queue emerged from the night, snaking in a disorganized manner through the streets. Wisely, it allowed ample room for the inevitable motorcade of motorcycles, military vehicles, and cars that would most certainly herald and precede the arrival of the king's body, removed and refreshed the day before.

Shigeku peered down at the scene from a hilltop cemetery a few hundred meters away, thinking, *There's no way all these idiot people will fit inside that church!* Precisely fifteen minutes before the commencement of the funeral, a priest threw open the twin European oak doors. The crowds surged and pulsed through the arches, much as a living and breathing massive organism with but one sole purpose for existence. As the throngs entered, new bodies from the streets took their place in the queue, such that the church was jammed with people and the great doors were hopelessly unable to be closed. Shigeku strolled down the hill into the crowds, working his way to the doorway entrance with great difficulty.

Shigeku began to worry that he would not be able to gain entrance. So stationary and immovable were the crowds that it would have appeared to the casual observer that nary a soul had moved for hours. With five minutes until the appointed time for the ceremony, and once their potential for gaining entrance was thwarted, the crowds on the outside looking in then formed an enormous receiving line, staking places along both sides of the expected route of the motorcade and procession. The crowd stretched all the way from the top steps of the cathedral's primary entrance as far as the eye could see. All attendees along the outer perimeters of the line were nervous, as the potential for being inadvertently mowed down by the official escort or being forced by the pressure of the crowd into the path of the vehicles was real.

Shigeku looked at his watch. *Fucking royals always making the people wait.* Minutes past the appointed hour were ticking by, and the funeral procession had not yet appeared. By the time twenty such increments had elapsed, a general murmur began to rise from the crowd.

Shigeku heard the procession before he saw it. Or, in fact, what he heard was a collective hum that began to spread along the lines of the crowd as the motorcade slowly came into view. Two military jeeps, each with three machine-gun-armed men, led the shiny, long black Mercedes hearse, which was in turn followed by multiple black Range Rovers and two more jeeps filled with armed men. The vehicular procession stopped two hundred meters from the cathedral.

Shigeku strained to see what was happening, but the distance was too far, and multiple vehicles blocked his vantage point. Eventually, he could see the procession. A solitary shiny black coffin was being slowly and carefully transported up the street toward the church. Shigeku wondered who would be carrying the coffin, and it wasn't until the human procession was immediately next to him that he was able to recognize senior government officials, or "ministers," as Mabanda had called them, and generals from the armed forces.

Shigeku's eyes narrowed when he spotted Moto. He stood next to Mateyo himself, who was helping to carry the king's final resting box.

———— ❖ ————

Mateyo's staff had handled the plans for the funeral. The only changes that Mateyo had insisted upon were that he and the casket's pallbearers would arrive at the cathedral on foot and that the king's casket be as plain as an ordinary Malezilander's coffin. When an aide had asked why on earth he would do that, Mateyo shot the young man such a look that he immediately shut his mouth midsentence and did not raise any further objection. In Mateyo's mind, the underlying message and reasoning were clear—death humbles us all, and once dead, you are no better than the rest of the populace.

Mateyo and the most powerful men in the land trudged up the steps with their considerable load. The casket was heavy, despite being a simple pauper's box made of plywood, with the only luxury being that it was painted shiny black. As the procession disappeared from the view of the exterior of the church, Mateyo saw Shigeku burst from the crowd and start toward him. Within seconds, quicker than Mateyo could call out, the armed guards following the coffin aggressively tackled Shigeku to the ground, and no fewer than three AK-47s were pressed against his temple.

"NO!" shouted Mateyo. "That is my brother! Let him follow."

Mateyo turned forward and nodded slightly, and the coffin bearers began slowly marching their way toward the front of the great cathedral.

Mateyo did his best not to gawk and stare at the crowds as he and the other bearers of death marched toward the altar. The light coming through the stained glass and other ornate windows cast an eerie colored glow. Statues depicting religious scenes and saints were everywhere, and the wood carvings and other decorations on each of the massive wooden support pillars would have taken master carvers decades to complete. At the very front of the edifice, a wall of tall, thick pipes from an ancient pipe organ—one of the largest in the world—formed a panel against its back wall, with the pipes themselves first increasing and then, after the roof peak, decreasing in height in parallel to the lines of the roof.

Music was emanating from deep within the organ's pipes, with the deepest of notes resonating so low that the subsonic vibrations added to the crowd's general unease. The altar looked to Mateyo as though it had been cast of pure gold, yet surely it couldn't be so, could it? Although Mateyo, like virtually all the Malezi people, believed fervently in God and the Catholic Church, virtually all at the same time were overwhelmed by the opulence of the house of God. As the procession made its way up the central aisle, throngs of people closed in upon them, like the Red Sea closing in on the Egyptians. All stayed a respectful distance from the casket and the dignitaries, who stopped in unison at the foot of the altar and laid King Mabanda down with a bit of a thud. Once the casket was at the altar, nary a soul moved from his or her position within the cathedral. The atmosphere was stiflingly hot, and it felt as though there was limited oxygen in the air. The heat and humidity became unbearable—and intolerable for some. Those who fainted amid their friends and fellow citizens were passed over the heads of the standing crowd to the street.

Mateyo was quite relieved that he had no official role to play in the ceremony that marked, celebrated, and finalized his father's life and death. He watched intently as the most holy man in all of Maleziland, His Worship Archbishop Sulamena, ascended toward the altar, having suddenly and somewhat mystically appeared through a side entrance invisible to the congregation.

The archbishop wore a robe of the finest white silk. It was embroidered with gold banding, and his neck and chest were adorned with a cable-like chain and an enormous diamond-crusted cross. At the center of the cross was a deep blue, perfectly flawless, round-hewn tanzanite gemstone. Sulamena's archbishop headdress—peaked at the top— added at least two heads to his already impressive height. His skin was as pale as any native Malezi Mateyo had ever seen. *Clearly*, thought Mateyo, *this man has never seen a hard day's work under the sun in his life.*

The holy man stood before the altar and raised his hands toward God dramatically. He paused for at least sixty seconds, and the entire church seemed to squirm collectively.

"King Mabanda is dead," he stated, then paused lengthily once more. "Your king ruled not by the will of men but by the will of God Himself! Indeed, God favored your king and blessed his every act and deed as your regent and His representative on earth. All that your king accomplished in life—providing food and shelter and security for his peoples—he did with the grace of and glory for God. You—the Malezi people—exist for the king and for his Church. Why, you ask, is this so? The answer is and has been the same as it always was—for the glory of God!"

Mateyo noticed the skill with which the holy man spoke, frequently pausing for dramatic effect and raising the pitch, tone, and volume of his voice as his story continued.

"You, the people," said the archbishop, "have your place, your lot, and your role in life. Question these not, lest you question God Himself! And no, I need not beseech the Lord our God to have mercy on Mabanda's soul. He is already in heaven, chosen by God, at his Father's side. Go in peace to love and serve the Lord." And with a quick spin that flared his robe out magnificently, God's holy man disappeared through the same door from whence he had come.

Mateyo and the other pallbearers stood and re-hoisted their load upon hearing the archbishop's dismissal. The most powerful men of Maleziland marched out in somber silence, walking back down the long central aisle, out the front doors, and through the waiting crowds. They rendezvoused with the vehicles two hundred meters from the cathedral and were whisked away.

Mateyo had been told that the king would be buried on the grounds of the palace, behind its walls and out of sight of the masses, without ceremony and with only family in attendance, as was Malezi tradition. The crowd did not disperse, for in less than two and a half hours, a new king would be crowned in the same cathedral in which the country bid farewell to its old.

As he stood in Mabanda's favorite garden, Mateyo, with Kanzi by his side, felt confusion, sadness, trepidation, anger, angst, bitterness, and spitefulness as he watched his father's simple coffin being lowered into the ground. One emotion seemed to trump the rest, however, each time another fought for his conscious supremacy: relief.

Mateyo was relieved that his father was dead. Only the sweet, beautiful female companion at his side fully understood why. Only she knew of the sparkle and life behind his otherwise presently glazed-over eyes.

After the somber event of the morning funeral, everybody was in high spirits by the afternoon, eagerly anticipating the celebratory inauguration. Few could remember the last time there had been a coronation, and fewer yet were even alive when it had last occurred. The Malezi people, Mateyo knew, loved a celebration with its pomp, ceremony, flash, and bling. It was making Mateyo feel ill. The people couldn't wait to hear his speech.

What would he say? What would his voice sound like? Would he sound like King Mabanda or more like Carolanda?

Mateyo arrived at the church via motorcade. When he stepped out of the gleaming black Range Rover, the crowd cheered. Mateyo was resplendently dressed in a perfectly tailored and pressed white tuxedo, trimmed smartly in black. He turned back to the black-tinted truck to extend his hand to Kanzi, who gracefully stepped out of the car.

She emerged from the car in a sequined, form-fitting silver cocktail dress cut just above her knees. The crowd collectively gasped. Mateyo knew that all eyes were upon *her*, not him, for at least several long seconds.

Trying to hide his smile, he grabbed her hand, and they quickly glided up the staircase to the church doors. The crowds erupted into a perfectly coordinated chorus, shouting, "People's Prince! People's Prince! People's Prince!"

Kanzi had her most beautiful smile on display, especially when she looked at him. It appeared genuine, and Mateyo thought that she could not have been happier. By this time, Mateyo had definitively fallen for Kanzi. She shared his curiosity toward the world around him. She shared and loved his appreciation of the smaller things in life. She seemed to love his simplistic opinions on what was right and what was wrong. She seemed to love *him*.

Mateyo couldn't help himself, nor did he try. He hoped desperately that Kanzi shared the same emotion—Mateyo was quite sure that she did, but as they had never spoken about it and hadn't so much as even kissed, he didn't know. None of this mattered to him, though, for at this moment she was at his side, and he would rather have died than have missed this occasion and opportunity to be with her.

Mateyo had not discussed his reservations about the coronation ceremony with anybody. For the entire previous week, he had simply gone along with the suggestions, guidance, and advice of his advisors and staff in planning the details of the ceremony and the reception that would follow. They explained to him in great detail what had to be done, when it had to be done, and precisely how to do it.

No detail could be overlooked, from the tuxedo he was wearing to the style of cocktail napkins to be used at the royal gala planned for post-ceremony—to be held, of course, back at the palace for the elite citizenry of the country.

Mateyo and Kanzi proceeded down the center aisle of the great edifice. The similarity of the procession to a wedding was missed by no one. Mateyo met the eyes of Archbishop Sulamena, who awaited them at the foot of the altar. The holy man had changed from the funeral's white silk into a ruby-red robe of similar cut, once again adorned by golden brocades. Once they neared the great man of God, Kanzi gracefully stepped to the side and took up a position in the front-row pew, allowing Mateyo to continue toward the archbishop. *It is interesting that there are those who think Sulamena has his eye on the papacy*, thought Mateyo, recalling the lesson that Kanzi had given him on the Catholic Church in Maleziland. Indeed, many thought him to be well positioned to become the first Black, African-born bishop of Rome—the pope, head of the entire world's 1.5 billion Roman Catholics.

"I welcome all in the name of the Father, and of the Son, and of the Holy Ghost," said the archbishop loudly and solemnly, and in unison all present executed the sign of the cross, including both Mateyo and Kanzi. Mateyo knew that the coronation was no ordinary event, and as he expected, the celebrant had no "script" per se to follow. Unfortunately for all those gathered, it became quickly apparent to Mateyo that Sulamena had decided to use the ceremony as an opportunity to showcase his own superior education and oratorical skills. He went on for a full twenty-five minutes, beseeching this, beseeching that, encouraging the prayers and support of the people for their new king, and once again reminding the congregation that Mateyo derived his authority only through the Church. Mateyo got the very distinct impression that the archbishop was lecturing him, not the crowd, for he stared at Mateyo intently—almost malevolently—for most of the speech.

Finally, a priest brought over a jewel-bedecked gold sword and scabbard. The sword clearly weighed a significant amount, based upon the way the priest carried it with both hands. Mateyo had never seen so much gold and precious stones. A murmur issued from the crowd; they clearly wondered what a treasure and artifact like that was doing in the possession of the Church—and further, what need the Church had of such a weapon.

Sulamena spoke. "On your knees, Mateyo." The absence of formal reverence when addressing Mateyo was obvious to all, even to Mateyo. Nevertheless, he knelt at the feet of the big man of God.

"This sword is one of the Holy Catholic Church's most valuable treasures, and it is known to the world as the Sword of Divinity. It has been sent to us by Rome for our use today to confer God's will and authority upon Mateyo to rule, for without God's authority, Mateyo is no more than a man. This beautiful weapon was liberated from the Middle East by God's holy army in the thirteenth century and has been stored in the Vatican archive ever since. This very sword was used to ordain and swear in every king in the great country of France for over a thousand years, from Charlemagne to Louis XVI in 1774. Though its ability to impart authority to rule is only symbolic, as God alone has that ability, its symbolism is indeed powerful, and it serves to focus my ability to conduct God's will through its blade. Legend holds that if a regency candidate is not worthy of God's favor, the bearer of the blade will be compelled to strike off the head of the unworthy supplicant."

Mateyo, already on his knees, with his head bowed at the feet of the archbishop, trembled visibly. When the holy man whisked the gleaming weapon from its ornate scabbard, it created a disturbingly loud metallic ring. The sword's purpose may have been ceremonial; however, to all within close enough range, there was no mistaking the razored double edge of the lustrous blade. The shine reflecting off of its highly polished surface almost made it look like the blade was on fire.

Several dozen onlookers in the crowd screamed as the archbishop raised the Sword of Divinity above his head, two-fisted, as if he were about to swing an axe upon a particularly daunting-looking piece of hardwood. He held that pose for several long seconds, then began to speak once more. "Mateyo Mabanda, I anoint thee regent—"

Swiftly the archbishop began to swing the sword. Screams of horror surged from the onlookers as the weapon sliced quickly downward toward Mateyo's exposed neck.

Just as Mateyo expected to feel his head cleaved from his body, the archbishop froze the blade in midair, mere centimeters from Mateyo's neck. He continued, "In the name of the Father—" He touched the Sword of Divinity to the nape of Mateyo's neck. The archbishop flashed the sword in a great arc, causing further but fewer screams, and halted its blade to lightly touch Mateyo's feet. "And of the Son—"

He again swung the blade in a wide circle and tapped Mateyo lightly on the left shoulder. "And of the Holy Ghost." The archbishop brought the blade to rest on Mateyo's right shoulder.

The crowd exclaimed, "Amen!" and then erupted into raucous cheers. "People's King! People's King! PEOPLE'S KING!" they screamed.

Mateyo felt like he was going to black out, but he somehow managed to keep from crumbling to the hard, timeworn brick ground.

"SILENCE!" boomed Archbishop Sulamena, well above the boisterous cheers. Immediately, the crowd quieted.

The archbishop sheathed the great sword in a motion extraordinarily quick, professional, and efficient for a man of the cloth. He stated simply, "You are now king, Mateyo. Rule wisely and with God's counsel. You may address your people."

Mateyo shakily stood and faced his congregated citizens. He paused nearly a full thirty seconds before he spoke, and despite his long pause, when he finally spoke, his voice quivered.

"I do not accept the Church's authority to make me your king. There will be change."

And with that, Mateyo began a brisk walk down the central aisle of the great cathedral, quickly but demurely followed by Kanzi and his security detail. Before he strode down the central aisle and out of the church, he couldn't help but note Archbishop Sulamena's eyes burning with hatred hotter than the fires of Hades. Mateyo had made a mortal enemy with his first few words as king.

As he exited, Mateyo caught two sets of eyes staring at him intently. *Shigeku!* He was confused by the amused gleaming in Shigeku's eyes and then by the sight of Mandebala, hiding in the crowds quite far away from Shigeku. *Mandebala must have followed us into the church after the guards stopped Shigeku,* thought Mateyo. As much as Mateyo wanted to stop and speak with his brother, the new king carried on, breaking his purposeful gait only slightly.

CHAPTER 16

Shigeku had been shocked that Mandebala too had shown up at the cathedral for the king's coronation. "That is the last place I expected to see you," Shigeku said. "Why in fuck would you want to see 'your' crown handed to Mateyo?"

"Know thine enemy," Mandebala had said without the slightest hint of a smile or emotion.

Both Shigeku and Mandebala had voraciously observed how Mateyo's "speech" sent shockwaves through the cathedral. Shigeku had seen the look of hatred and fury on Archbishop Sulamena's face, and he knew it to be more than mere anger and embarrassment. Clearly, Sulamena considered the new king to be a threat to the Church's role and privileged position of power in Maleziland.

Shigeku and Mandebala had also seen the looks of consternation on the faces of the everyday folk in attendance. Shigeku knew what concerned them. Inasmuch as the Malezi people wanted a better life, to the people in this part of Africa, "change" was a foul four-letter word. Change made them uneasy. Sure, thought Shigeku, people hoped for a better lot in life under Mateyo than under Mabanda, but they certainly didn't expect change to include a rejection of the

Church's power to appoint kings, and by implication a rejection of the Church's role in the entire country. The brothers watched as the entire country's general spirit of elation and excitement over Mateyo's new reign turned into a sense of uneasy trepidation, bordering on outright fear, with Mateyo's utterance of those four short words: "There will be change."

Shigeku had watched in silence as it all unfolded, and drank in the sentiment and spirit of the moment thirstily. Neither brother had spoken until after all others had left the cathedral, with the statue of the Blessed Virgin Mary watching over them and blessing their ultimate egress. Simultaneously, each turned to the other and said, "Brother—"

Shigeku was shocked by the contemporaneous utterance of the word, coupled with the fact that neither had yet used the word *brother* to refer to each other. After three quick attempts to simultaneously resume conversation, and three seemingly pregnant pauses in between, Shigeku motioned for Mandebala to speak.

"Brother," said Mandebala slyly, "I am beginning to get the sense that you hate the interloper Mateyo as much as I do. Please tell me why this is so, as you raised him as your brother since he was a few minutes old."

"Brother," returned Shigeku, with full sincerity but in a sarcastic tone intended with his use of the word, "it isn't Mateyo so much as it is the privilege that he now gets to enjoy. I hated him as a child. My own youth was stolen the moment he became my responsibility. You slept in his imperial bed and led a life of luxury, while I barely scraped by, eating scraps and insects and maize. I had a tremendous burden imposed upon me by our maman. I resented you. Of course I did. And I did the only thing in my power that I could to unseat your fat, lazy ass. I joined the Zambwanan army.

"Your reasons to loathe Mateyo are quite understandable. He has what you used to have and what you obviously want back. The real question becomes, do you think that there is something we can do about it?"

The former prince smiled at Shigeku and said, "I'm beginning to think that you were spared execution in the slaughter of the Zambwanans by a higher power and for a higher reason. That reason is becoming much clearer to me by the day.

"If there's one thing that I learned as a royal, it is this: The weak are put on this planet for the exploitation of the strong. In times of change and crisis, people will latch on to anything or anyone that promises a better and stronger alternative. We simply need to figure out a way to use what Mateyo is doing to our advantage."

Smiling, Shigeku nodded. He was suddenly very glad that he had helped Mandebala and saved his life. He could use Mandebala to chip away at the foundations of Malezi rule and order.

"Well? Do you have a plan yet?" Shigeku demanded.

Mandebala raised a single eyebrow and said, "Oh yes, Shigeku, I most certainly do. It's going to take some time and effort, but its first steps involve two meetings. The first will be with Archbishop Sulamena, who today became the single greatest threat to Mateyo's reign. The second will be with Mateyo, your former brother. I presume that the first would not deny me a meeting, knowing who I am—or more properly, who I was—and that the second, Mateyo, would not deny you, his 'brother,' the same courtesy."

"Beyond that . . . ," Shigeku said, smiling wickedly, "we will make sure that Mateyo is cast from office and the two of us rule all of Maleziland."

Without speaking, Shigeku drew his assegai, and Mandebala simultaneously did the same. They cut lightly across their wrists—those who are suicidal cut down the wrist, not across—and each pressed their open wound into the other's at right angles, a dark Malezi oath forming the image of a cross: an oath that could not be broken without sacrificing one's immortal soul.

The preparation for the coronation party had begun the morning of Mabanda's death. Although Mateyo and Kanzi had technical oversight and approval of all planning, it was carried out by Mateyo's staff, completely in line and consistent with what Mabanda would have done on such an occasion. As such, even though Mateyo approved the importation of two kilos of white truffles from France; one thousand kilos of fresh lobster from the coast of Maine; two thousand kilos of beef tenderloin from Alberta, Canada; and the finest of beer, wines, and liquors from around the world, his head and heart had barely been present. In fact, Mateyo had rejected nothing, making for a party planner's fantasy and a night of gourmandism to remember for all fortunate enough to be on the invite list. And the list was impressive.

His staff went over the final version of the invite list. Mateyo saw that government officials made up fully 50 percent of the attendees at the reception. Other nongovernmental authorities—judges, senior police officers, doctors, and lawyers—made up nearly 40 percent of the attendees, with the balance being military generals and heads of state from friendly neighboring countries. Mateyo nodded his approval.

Although he didn't recall approving it, it appeared that no expense had been spared for decoration. Fresh-cut flowers, flown in directly from the daily flower market in Amsterdam, adorned the Great Hall where the reception took place. Mateyo couldn't believe the sight or smell of them all. Kanzi pointed out some that she knew—tulips, orchids, lilies, roses, and more—but most of them were unknown to the two of them. A palace senior procurement officer had flown to Amsterdam and purchased the flowers directly at the auction and then supervised their loading on the smaller royal jet, a Challenger series private jet. After a ten-hour flight, less than twenty-four hours had elapsed from the moment in time the flowers were snipped from their stems to the moment when their beauty, fragrance, and quantity were taking the breath away from the guests.

The larger royal jet, a 737-800 series, had also been busy. After off-loading its catering cargo from North America, it had headed south. A full 50 percent of the Johannesburg Symphony Orchestra had been whisked in for the event, with each individual—leads only, of course—earning more for his or her performance that evening than they did in a month. Typically, at private functions, the JSO was crammed into a hall that truly wasn't big enough for their instruments or their music, but as they set up in a corner of the Great Hall, it was clear their entire orchestra could have played without concern over space or acoustic quality.

Kanzi held Mateyo's hand as they watched the musicians setting up, and she squeezed it. "Are you excited about hearing them play, Mateyo?" she asked.

Mateyo simply nodded. He'd never seen any of the instruments, nor had he heard any of them in person. He couldn't grasp how they would sound all playing together, but was excited by the prospect.

It was the sub-Saharan party of the decade, if not the century, but King Mateyo's heart wasn't in it. Dutifully, he and Kanzi stood at the entrance to the Grand Hall and greeted each of the guests as they arrived. "Thank God that we have staff here to introduce these people to us!" he whispered into Kanzi's ear. "I have no clue who any of these people are! And why are there so many guests?"

"Mateyo, you approved them all. This is all your fault!" Kanzi said, playfully poking his side.

Mateyo was quite impressed with Kanzi's breadth of knowledge of people's roles in Malezi high society. On only one occasion did she fail to recognize a guest, and that was because the general, an impressive but younger-looking man named Moto, had only recently been promoted to the top ranks of the Malezi forces.

This same unknown military man leaned toward Mateyo and whispered into his ear, "I made you king."

What is this man talking about? Mateyo wondered.

He made a point to remember to investigate the facts, or fiction, to which this young general might be referring. A few minutes later, after the guests had all arrived, Mateyo sought out one of his palace advisors.

"What is the story behind General Moto?" Mateyo asked, avoiding mentioning what the general had whispered in his ear.

"Ah, General Moto," said the senior, gray-haired attendant. "He is now legendary within the armed forces. The story goes that he infiltrated the Zambwanan-dog army and single-handedly handed victory to our glorious country, both through subterfuge and conveyance of enemy information. In fact, the king handed him sole command of the Mpini Ekundu!"

Mateyo pondered this information. *Perhaps this is the man that delivered my brother from behind enemy lines. If so, indeed his actions have made me king today. I wonder what he wants.*

As Kanzi and Mateyo stood at the edge of the Great Hall, the JSO played some wonderful-sounding music that the king did not recognize, but it felt beautifully relaxing and engaging at the same time. Kanzi was smiling from ear to ear, as she had since the two of them had entered the hall.

She's far more comfortable with this than I am, Mateyo observed.

A servant stopped by with some hors d'oeuvres. Mateyo barely noticed until Kanzi prodded him. "Mateyo! Would you like a lobster tail skewer?"

Mateyo nodded and grabbed one of the dainty sticks. Kanzi handed him a cocktail napkin. "Hey!" he exclaimed after taking a somewhat oversized bite, "this is *good*! What did you say it was?"

"It's lobster," Kanzi said. "And you shouldn't take such large bites.

It's impolite." Mateyo raised an eyebrow but said nothing. Kanzi then asked, "Is everything okay? You seem distracted."

"Everything is fine," he replied.

Kanzi did not look convinced.

Mateyo pulled Kanzi aside. "You're right," he said, barely loud enough for her to hear. "I don't like this. It's too . . . fancy. Yes, the food is amazing, the music is amazing, and I love the fact that you are here by my side. But it seems wrong to be celebrating in this way. Most of this country—of *my* country—is always on the verge of starvation. How did I approve all of this? I don't remember it at all. How did you let me approve all of this?"

"Oh, my sweet, kindhearted boy king. You did indeed approve all of this, but it is quite understandable that faced with everything that has happened so quickly, most of your memory is a blur," said Kanzi with a warm smile.

At that moment, General Moto walked by, uncomfortably close to the couple. Mateyo watched his hungry eyes devour every centimeter of Kanzi's body, first down and then all the way back up again, lingering on her eyes for an uncomfortably long moment. Kanzi looked away, blushing. The fear and anger associated with his father's ill-fated attempt to rape Kanzi flooded Mateyo's consciousness, and he began to shake with anger.

Kanzi sensed his distress and quickly dragged him toward the bar for a strong drink. Mateyo, try as he might, could not shake a resulting thought; the image of her naked body was seared into his mind, and since that horrifying day, Mateyo had been reminded of it every time he saw her, every time he heard her voice, and every time he smelled the scent of her body nearby.

Mateyo snapped out of his mind's lustful prison as Kanzi tugged on his hand. "Mateyo, we can go now. The last of the important guests have left."

Mateyo nodded and followed her out of the Great Hall.

With the formal events out of the way, Mateyo relaxed, as much as he could, into his new role. From the moment he woke up and showered to the moment he said good night, Kanzi was by his side. Mateyo had officially "relieved" her of her formal duties as a servant to the king.

One particularly pleasant morning, before the sun's heat became oppressive, Mateyo and Kanzi headed outside to the royal garden after they finished their breakfast. Mateyo was both pleased and surprised to see his mother, Carolanda, enjoying the beautiful surroundings by herself. The queen smiled warmly as she saw them, and both Mateyo and Kanzi sprinted into her arms with affectionate hugs. Mateyo broke the embrace, stepped back, and looked at his mother somewhat crossly.

"Mother," he said, "why have you not been coming by anymore? You are meant to come every day, and I believe it has been almost a week since your last visit!"

"Oh, Mateyo, why would you want a meddling old woman like me around? Clearly you have your hands full with Kanzi," she said and winked. "And she indeed appears to have a lovely body to keep your hands full. You are a lucky man!"

Both Mateyo and Kanzi blushed and looked away.

A few days after their encounter with Carolanda, Mateyo asked Kanzi about what it had been like to go to one of the elite South African boarding schools.

"Well . . . ," said Kanzi, easing into her favorite position on one of the den wingbacks, her bare feet tucked underneath her, "apart from being away from my family, I loved school . . . at least at first. I was very fortunate that my father had set aside enough money for me to continue attending after he died—otherwise I could never have afforded it. And I've already completed enough of my O-level courses to gain preadmission to university in France when I turn eighteen."

"So, you liked school?" asked Mateyo. *Strange.* None of the children he knew ever stayed in school, if they attended at all, beyond grade four. Aside from the schooling given to him by his kindly neighbor Miss K, the schoolteacher, Mateyo had no formal education whatsoever, as he had been required to help the family unit survive from the earliest possible age. Children were often needed to contribute to the economic well-being of the family, especially when there was no mother or father to look after them. And *no one* he knew *liked* going to school—it was simply a necessary, repetitive, boring chore.

"Oh yes!" exclaimed Kanzi. "I loved reading about different countries, learning about different languages, and how to count, add, and multiply in my head. All these things fascinate me immensely! I also learned about different economic theories, different political systems, and the histories of many different countries."

Economic what? He shook his head. "But if you enjoyed it so much, why did you say you only enjoyed it 'at first'?" Mateyo asked.

"Um, well . . . it's kind of hard to explain, but . . ." Kanzi sighed, looking downward. "When I was younger and began attending the school, the fact that I was Black didn't seem to make any difference."

"The fact that you were *Black*—what does being Black have to do with anything?" Mateyo frowned.

"I was the *only* Black kid in my class. Actually, I was one of only a handful in the entire school for many of the years that I was there. In fact, I was the first Black 'Head Girl' in the history of the school."

"Are you kidding me?" Mateyo gasped. "How could that be possible? Why were there so few Black children? Are you going to tell me that there aren't any in the entire Republic of South Africa? I might be uneducated, but I'm not stupid."

"Mateyo, things are not the same in South Africa as they are in Maleziland. There, the Whites were in power for hundreds of years, and Blacks were essentially slaves, second-class citizens. For the longest time,

South Africa practiced apartheid—a formal policy that kept Whites and Blacks apart. Black people were denied basic rights—rights that only the White people of South Africa enjoyed. Even though Blacks are no longer second-class—they have the right to vote and every other democratic right that the Afrikaners have—they still have very little economic power."

"That's beyond ridiculous," said Mateyo. "In Maleziland, we barely even have any White people, and they certainly do not run our country!"

"The White minority still controls most of the economic wealth in South Africa. So, even though the boarding school cannot *prohibit* Blacks from attending, the fact of the matter is that few Black parents can afford to send their children there. As King Mabanda's royal physician, my father was one of few Black men this side of the equator who could actually afford to send his children to the school."

Mateyo frowned. "But that still doesn't answer *why* you liked it at first, but then it all changed."

"Kids can be cruel. Not so much when they are little. Then, the color of someone's skin doesn't matter. But as they grow older and are affected, or infected, by outside influences, they become less and less nice to kids whose skin is a different color."

"That's outrageous!" Mateyo said. "How could they treat you differently only because your skin is black?"

"Even though the discrimination of White against Black is no longer officially permitted, many people still hold the same views. Until we're economically equal, democratic rights mean essentially nothing. And people—including children—view Blacks as 'inferior.'"

Mateyo shook his head, as there were too many concepts and ideas competing for his neural pathways. He vowed to himself, though, that he would make a difference in *his* country so that kids like his beautiful Kanzi would never, ever have to feel that way. And once again, he found himself in awe of Kanzi's knowledge and understanding of the way the world worked. He couldn't believe how small his universe had been, growing up in the slums.

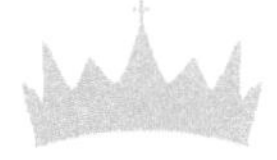

CHAPTER 17

Shigeku suggested to Mandebala that they simply call him "Bala," to help distance the people's memory of him as the hated, deposed crown prince of Maleziland. He watched his brother make his way from the latrine trench that flowed behind their shanty, pulling up his pants as he waddled up the bank.

"Just a few weeks ago you wiped your ass with silk cloths, unless, of course, you had one of your servant girls do that for you," said Shigeku with a sneer.

"Quit your whining about the past, brother, unless, of course, you want to wipe it for me yourself next time," said Bala, grinning from ear to ear.

In response, Shigeku cuffed his brother on the top of the head, just enough to hurt a little bit. Shigeku smiled slightly, mostly to himself. *He's come a long way from the imperious, self-entitled little pompous shit that showed up here with a bleeding hand.* Although at times Bala slipped into the unpleasant form of his former imperial self, Shigeku had noticed that, of late, Bala was quick to recognize it on his own and to make immediate amends. Now that Bala had been disentitled, Shigeku embraced him as an ordinary gutter rat like the rest of them—and indeed, he was a gutter rat of Shigeku's own blood.

Shigeku was pleased with how their planning was going. "Why would we meet with Sulamena?" he demanded of Bala one day, several weeks into their planning.

"Oh, Shigeku, sometimes I forget how small-minded you are," said Bala. "The Malezi people have begun to grow nervous, as little, if any, has been seen of or heard from the new king in his self-imposed palatial exile. This creates a power vacuum, and I know that the archbishop also has designs on power."

Shigeku was astonished at how easily Bala was able to get a private audience with the archbishop. Bala passed a private note to the shantytown's assigned pastor, and the archbishop's reply came less than twenty hours later. It was as if the archbishop could sense the malintent of their meeting before it had even occurred.

An aide, presumably a monk, junior priest, or acolyte of sorts, now ushered them in through an electronic gate upon their arrival at Sulamena's official residence. Shigeku noticed how plainly the archbishop was dressed; he wore a flowing black robe, although it was perfectly pressed and clean. Not a single visible piece of jewelry adorned him. As they walked through the courtyard, Shigeku took note of the high wall and razor-wire perimeter security. Armed guards patrolled the grounds. "Why do men of God need such measures?" he asked, with Bala nodding along as if the thought had been his own. His musing was soon answered.

Sulamena's private residence, or the rectory, as the people of the village referred to it, appeared relatively ordinary from the outside, although it was indeed quite large for a residential dwelling. It looked similar in size and architecture to one of the government ministry offices from many years prior—when the French ruled Maleziland—that had been repurposed into grander, more formal colonial residences now inhabited by some of Maleziland's elite. However, nothing from the outside prepared Shigeku and Bala for what they saw once they were ushered through its front doors.

Shigeku had never seen such opulence, and from the look on Bala's face, clearly he thought he would never see it again. Everywhere within the entrance foyer and beyond, their eyes were assaulted with gold showcases containing religious artifacts and jewelry and the finest of European art. All had a Christian theme, of course, though with much nudity.

"Ha!" said Bala quietly so that only Shigeku could hear. "I haven't seen tits like these in so long I think my royal shaft is going to get hard!" The paintings were obviously from a much earlier time, and Shigeku wondered when the Church had declared nudity to be displeasing to God. The works of the masters adorned virtually every nook, cranny, and wall space available.

After being led into a sitting room to wait for His Eminence, Shigeku and Bala took to exploring their environs. Original artwork from the Renaissance seemed to hold Bala's attention. With his formal education, Bala was able to identify for Shigeku many of the paintings—and he seemed to have an appreciation of their value on the world art market. As Shigeku and Bala were admiring a Rembrandt original, Sulamena swept into the room.

"It pleases God," said the archbishop, "to have such beauty created by the hands of His children to honor Him."

"It would have pleased my father," Bala said, "to have had this art adorning the walls of the royal palace!"

"It is indeed a shame that your *father*," said the archbishop, rolling his eyes, "has gone to be with God." The flatness in his tone further betrayed the insincerity of his statement.

"Your sentiments are appreciated, Sulamena," Bala said, "but, of course, he was not my father. Being surrounded by this level of finery made me forget, momentarily, that I no longer live in the palace."

"You may address me as Your Worship, Your Eminence, or Your Grace, young pup. Pray tell me, Mandebala, what brings Kashatown's newest gutter rat into my home?" Sulamena said sternly.

"Cut the bullshit," Bala said. "You know as well as I do that your privileged position here in Maleziland was dependent upon the support of the king. I was at the funeral. I was at the royal coronation. I saw the flash of fear on your face during Mateyo's speech. Your state-supported monopoly in its noble battle for souls, and the resulting Church tithes to fill your greedy, always-so-empty coffers, is at risk."

Bala continued, "You know goddamned well—and no, I'm not sorry I used that word—that Mateyo presents a huge threat to your personal wealth and life of privilege *and* to your chance of becoming pope. I might add, a mighty fine life of wealth and privilege it seems to be. Yes, I now live in a shanty, but that does not in any way take away my capacity to become a force once again in this country. So, *Your Eminence*, get off your fucking high horse and level with me if you want your best chance at preserving the sweet little gig you've got going here."

Shigeku had not been prepared for Sulamena's chastising of his brother. He was even less prepared for Bala's response. Had he known what was coming, he would have done his best to prevent his jaw from dropping open.

Though the archbishop had remained silent for Bala's entire rant, Shigeku watched as Sulamena reacted with exaggerated facial gestures and body language, acting as though he were shocked and even outraged by Bala's tirade. The holy man paused heavily and then drew in a deep breath.

"Well, you little piece of shit," said Sulamena, "it looks like your humbled position has not yet mellowed your tongue. So, tell me, 'Bala,' as I understand you now like to be called, how on God's great earth do you think that you, a cast-aside, battered boy trying to become a man, will be able to effect change that will somehow help me—and God's cause, of course—in this country? And all this from the slums of Kashatown? Please. You must think me, and the entire population of this great country, as stupid as your clearly mute brother beside you."

Shigeku did not engage with the archbishop, as he and Bala had agreed. But he watched Bala grin broadly and nod his head. Shigeku knew that his brother had the archbishop precisely where he wanted him. "That's where my brother here comes into play in this game, along with my knowledge and understanding of how to manipulate people in ways that only a former royal knows how."

On a beautiful morning, spent as always with Kanzi by his side, Mateyo spied a nameless servant girl eating what appeared to be a bowl of cold maize porridge. Mateyo called her over from her far-off corner, where she was tucked under a great acacia tree for shade. The young girl obeyed immediately and scampered quickly to her king. Mateyo saw the fear in her eyes, and it bothered him.

"Girl," he said, in a tone that caused Kanzi to frown. "What is your name, and what are you eating in the royal garden?"

The girl's voice quivered as she spoke. "I am Shala, and I'm eating my usual *nsima* for breakfast. I apologize, Your Highness. I . . . I . . . I just wanted to escape the heat of the servants' dining hall. I didn't mean to offend you. I will never eat in the royal garden again."

Mateyo was angry. Kanzi even took a step back. Mateyo looked up and down several times at the poor girl, who couldn't have been more than thirteen. She wore a perfectly pressed white servants' uniform, her hair was smoothed back, and her hands and face were clean. Mateyo now knew that years of service had taught the palace staff to be immaculately dressed and groomed, lest they incur the murderous wrath of King Mabanda.

Mateyo turned to Kanzi and demanded, "Why have you never taken me to the servants' quarters? Or to their dining hall?"

Kanzi's brow wrinkled, and she stammered out a response. "I . . . I mean . . . well, I didn't think it would interest you, Mateyo. I mean, *King* Mateyo. Shall I take you there immediately?"

"Yes," he said and followed Kanzi out of the garden without dismissing Shala.

Kanzi brought Mateyo to the servants' dining hall. Neither of them spoke as Mateyo entered the room. The "hall" was a tiny rectangular room whose entire length and width was filled by an unfinished wooden table and an odd assortment of mismatched chairs, twenty-four in total. Half a dozen servants were seated at the far end of the table, chatting animatedly. The murmur of voices ceased the second Mateyo walked through the doorway into the hall. All seated froze for a brief instant before scattering like a herd of gazelles startled by a bloodthirsty lioness.

What in the world?

Kanzi whispered, "Never did King Mabanda ever set foot in the servants' quarters. It would have offended him." Mateyo looked at Kanzi incredulously but said nothing.

Mateyo then followed Kanzi into the servants' quarters—a long unfinished corridor lined with roughhewn doors. Kanzi pushed the first one open—it had no latch nor lock. Crammed into the tiniest of rooms were four sets of triple-decker bunk beds, all perfectly made.

Mateyo finally spoke. "Why do our servants live like dogs?"

Kanzi looked away. After a few moments, she turned back to face Mateyo. "That's my bed—on top, in the corner."

She turned and fled the room quickly, leaving Mateyo standing alone, but not before he saw the tears in her eyes. Mateyo followed eventually, and his heart ached like never before.

Later that afternoon, Mateyo beckoned his butler Chumba closer. Kanzi had disappeared after their morning tour of the servants' quarters. As Mateyo had exited the servants' quarters, Chumba had reappeared and stayed by his side at the ready.

"Chumba," said Mateyo in his imperious voice, "I want to go to the slums of Kashatown. *Now!*" Chumba nodded almost imperceptibly and vanished.

He returned less than two minutes later and said, "King Mateyo, your car is ready."

Although Mateyo wanted Kanzi by his side, he could not wait for her. "Driver, take me to my former home in Kashatown."

Only minutes later, the shiny black Range Rover sped off toward the gate. Mateyo could see the main gate rolling slowly open in the distance and began to worry that it would not open in time. Just before they were about to exit the barely open gate, two black jeeps, each with a driver and three machine gunners, slipped in front of the king's car, and a third similarly manned jeep fell in behind. Each car in the procession of four followed so closely that Mateyo was uncomfortably nervous that a multiple-vehicle crash was a certainty.

All through the slum district, people who jammed the streets on foot parted almost magically at the last second before the motorcade streaked through. As the convoy flew through the village at ridiculously high speeds given the lopsidedly uneven path they called a road, Mateyo couldn't even recognize the blurred faces of his friends. The vehicles finally screeched to a skidding stop, slamming on their brakes in choreographed unison and kicking up clouds of red dust. King Mateyo flung open his door and tore into his former home for the first time in months, ignoring the protesting yells of his security detail, who scrambled to catch up with him.

As Mateyo burst through the doorway, he slumped visibly. Every detail of the shanty looked exactly as it had on the day he'd been dragged out of it, right down to the number and placement of bowls and cups on the board on the wall where they had always rested. The shanty was empty.

Of course, Mateyo thought, *everyone is working in the fields.* Mateyo looked around at the familiar barren walls; the stained, worn, thin sleeping mattresses; and the few other meager possessions of his household, including the highly valued but well-worn cooking pan. *Fuck. I should have brought some things with me from the palace!* Suddenly, as if a major pipeline had just ruptured, his nasal cavities were inundated with a horrific, acrid stench. It was enough to make his eyes water and his chest begin to heave.

Outside, Mateyo saw that a small crowd had now formed and were being malevolently held back by his security detail, with their guns lowered and the business ends pointed directly at the people. He recognized many familiar faces. "Guards, stand down!" he shouted.

None of them did. The captain of the detail looked back at Mateyo and said, "King Mateyo, are you sure?"

"*Yes, I'm sure!*" came the king's reply. "These people are my friends!"

The guards immediately lowered their weapons and opened ranks so that the people could pass through. Mateyo expected his friends to rush in to see him, but none did. Mateyo called out to several of them, but none approached. Mateyo finally spotted Metu, one of his closest childhood friends. Mateyo embraced his pal warmly, but Metu stood stiffly and did not return the embrace.

"It's so good to see you, Metu! How have you been?" Mateyo said with a warm grin.

Metu, who had never been much for words in any event, said, "Good."

Mateyo was a bit taken aback, by both Metu's lack of warmth and by his foul stench and dirt-caked hands and face. "Friends!" he exclaimed. "I've come home to see how you are doing!"

As he looked from face to face, all but Metu looked away. King Mateyo turned back to him and asked, "What is going on, Metu? Why are my friends acting so strangely? It's me! Mateyo! I grew up with each one of you! I am no different now!"

Metu stared at Mateyo for an impossibly long moment and then began to speak. "No, King Mateyo, you are different. You arrive in a motorcade; you live in a palace. You've grown fat off expensive food, you sleep on feathers, and you live in a mansion with untold riches and servants. You are not 'one of us,' Mateyo. You're little better than King Mabanda."

And with that, Metu and every other person who had gathered to see Mateyo walked away, leaving the king alone with his security guard in the middle of the usually bustling street.

CHAPTER 18

King Mateyo had been beyond elated when he'd heard from Shigeku. Shigeku had borrowed a cell phone, come close enough to the palace to be within Wi-Fi range, and called through on the royal palace's general number. As far as Mateyo was concerned, Shigeku was still his brother and, if nothing else, was the only real father figure he had ever known. Mateyo had thought of him often since he'd seen him at the coronation and had hoped to encounter him during his visit to the shanty.

What if his brother rejected him too? He was anxious to hear about how his other siblings were doing. He missed his family, his friends, and the camaraderie that was life in the Kashatown. And after his trip to his own home and the rejection by his friends, he had been absolutely crushed.

Although he didn't speak with Shigeku over the phone, as no outsider would ever be put through to the king, Mateyo instantly granted Shigeku's request for a meeting. He threw himself into his brother's arms when Shigeku was ushered into his palace office.

He was taken aback by the stiffness and rigidity in his brother's embrace and stepped back to exclaim, "Shigeku! God knows, it's so good to see you! How have you been? How is the rest of the family?"

Pulling stiffly away from the hug, Shigeku said, "All are fine, Mateyo—*King* Mateyo, I should say."

"Cut the king crap, Shigeku. It's you and me—brothers. Science cannot take that away from us. It cannot take away the fact that you were my nursemaid, provider, and protector and treated me always as your brother. I expect to be called Mateyo, as always, by you."

"As you command, sire," Shigeku said with a smirk and a slight bow, and both he and Mateyo burst out laughing.

"I apologize, my brother. I didn't mean that to sound like an order. It seems ridiculous to me, but everyone in this entire palace turns to me for orders. Nobody can think for themselves. Even my senior ministers and generals won't go for a coffee without me telling them to!"

"You must enjoy being such a powerful man," Shigeku said dryly, and again the two of them burst into laughter.

"Are you kidding me? This is terrible," Mateyo finally said. "I cannot take a shit without someone asking if I would like my ass wiped. It's insane!"

"But you are comfortable here, no?" Shigeku asked.

"Yes and no, brother, yes and no. I can't get used to sleeping on a mattress. It is disgustingly soft, and all the bedclothes wrap around your skin, making it hot and sticky. And the 'air conditioning,' as they call the fans that constantly blow cold air in here, makes it unbelievably cool. I've raised the temperature setting by six degrees in here since King Ma—since my father died, and still I find it quite intolerable. I eat well, but I'm beginning to get soft."

"You look good, Mateyo. You always needed a bit more meat on your bones, and it looks like you've grown taller . . . or is that just the 'crown' on your head?" Shigeku said, after which Mateyo launched himself at his brother, knocking him to the ground. As always, the wiry Shigeku won the wrestling match, though with a fair bit more effort required than during any previous jousts.

After the two of them stopped breathing hard, Mateyo asked, "So what brings you to see me?"

Shigeku put on a look of hurt that Mateyo had not foreseen. "Can a man not come see his long-lost brother, brother?"

The words jolted Mateyo, who then could barely believe that he had ever asked Shigeku the question. "Forgive me, of course you can. It is simply that I get so many supplicants coming to see me that it seems each and every Malezi soul wants something from me!"

"Ah," said Shigeku with a nod. "So that's what I am now?" He raised an eyebrow. "A beggar of sorts and not your brother? I see how things are."

"Please," Mateyo said, "I didn't mean it that way. You're twisting my words! It's just that—"

Shigeku punched Mateyo in the shoulder, then grinned.

Mateyo winced, knowing that it would bruise, but he was thrilled that Shigeku had been pulling his leg. Shigeku had always been smart about his customary brotherly swing, though, intentionally crippling Mateyo's punching arm with the first blow. The receiver was then entitled to mete out a return blow to the shoulder of the original puncher.

Shigeku closed his eyes, waiting, and gave a grunt when Mateyo paid back the shot.

Mateyo felt only mildly bad about seeing the wince of pain flash across his brother's face. He *felt* stronger.

"Stay with me for supper, Shigeku. I've got to tell you, the best thing about being the king is the food!" Mateyo beamed. "That, and I have someone I'd like you to meet."

"Well, well," said Shigeku, smiling, "has the king already been dipping his royal scepter in some honeypots? It's about time!"

"You sound exactly like my father! All you think about is sex!" Mateyo said. Images from his father's aggression and death flooded back into the forefront of his consciousness.

"One day soon enough you'll know, little brother, one day you'll know. And yes, I accept your invitation. *It would please me greatly to dine with thee,*" Shigeku said with a sneer.

Again, Mateyo slugged him in the shoulder, a huge smile on his face. It was great to have a sense of normalcy returning to his life. Mateyo almost skipped as he left his brother to head to the washroom.

⁘

Shigeku stayed at the royal palace for almost two weeks and thoroughly enjoyed it. He had status as King Mateyo's guest and was entitled to order the staff to attend to his every need. One morning, after a particularly late night of drinking port and smoking cigars, Shigeku's head felt like it was going to explode. Ordinarily, living in the slums, one would just grimace and bear it, but Shigeku had learned about the wonders of painkillers in the army and decided to ring for a servant. He wasn't impressed that the servant seemed to take *forever* to get there, and when he did arrive, Shigeku was feeling less gracious. "For fuck's sake, that took you a long time to get here. I need painkillers. Now!"

The attendant did not immediately depart and instead appeared to lower his head and slightly raise his right eyebrow. "Oh," said the manservant, "did we drink a bit much last night? Is your head hurting?"

Shigeku was in no mood for this. "Do you know who my brother is? How dare you?"

The servant raised his eyebrow fully now and quickly said, "Oh, I know who your brother is. I simply don't know who you think *you* are." He vanished out the door.

One morning soon after, Mateyo dragged Shigeku to a new area of the palace to which he had not yet been. Shigeku found himself ushered into a room filled with women and children of varying ages. Mateyo stopped in front of one and hugged her warmly.

"Shigeku," the king said, "this is Carolanda, my mother. I guess you've sort of met." Mateyo was pretty sure that Shigeku indeed recognized the queen.

Carolanda shook Shigeku's hand warmly and said very earnestly, "Well, Shigeku, I guess I could choose to be angry at you for what you did, but that is not in my nature. Instead, I thank you from the bottom of my heart for taking care of my dear son and raising him to be the fine young man that he is today."

Shigeku swallowed his anger and bowed to the queen. "Of course, Your Highness."

Later that day, Shigeku came to speak with Mateyo. "Brother, I must now leave," he said simply.

Mateyo said, "Why, Shigeku, there's no reason to leave! You can stay as long as you like! I am, after all, the king!"

Shigeku replied, "I have work to do."

King Mateyo said, "I promise to build you a new, proper home immediately, just on the palace side of the outskirts of Kashatown, so that you can escape the stench and despair of the village and be even closer to me to visit."

"Oh yes, brother, I promise to return," Shigeku whispered under his breath as he waltzed down the road from the palace and through its gates. "Sooner than you think."

⁂

Mateyo had not forgotten his momentous promise of change at his coronation ceremony; however, his vow had been a spur-of-the-moment reflection of what he'd felt and a reaction to the pompous Sulamena's lecture on divine right. He had been angry and frustrated. He had no idea of the epic challenge he would face to effect permanent, lasting change. Indeed, many a government had tried and failed. He was not confident, in fact, that he was going to succeed.

The visit to Kashatown and Shigeku's visit had inspired Mateyo to work in earnest on his plan to reform his country for the benefit of his people. Mateyo awaited Kanzi in the dining hall the morning after Shigeku left, and as she entered the room, he leapt out of his heavy, formal dining chair, almost knocking it over with his eager approach.

"Kanzi," he said, "how can we make our people better off? Can we just sell all this fancy royal property and things and give it to the people? Surely, they will all be rich then, no?"

Kanzi grinned and said, "Good morning to you too, King Mateyo."

Mateyo, feeling somewhat deflated, said, "Good morning, Kanzi. Sorry, I . . . I just—"

"It's okay. Your passion is one of the things that I most admire about you. And indeed, it is high time that we truly focused on developing your plan for Maleziland. To answer your question, well . . . it's complicated. There have been many transitions of power in Africa, some from colonial powers—like the British, French, and Germans—and some from kings and dictators like your father and his father before him . . . men who assumed power, whether by election or force. Some of these power shifts have been at least partly successful—for example, South Africa and Kenya. Others have resulted in a devastating economic reversal of fortune for the entire country, such that once strong, vibrant economies have been reduced to poor, crumbling societies, with dire consequences for the people of these countries."

"But how much money can we get for all of this?" Mateyo asked. "We absolutely do not need it! We can make everybody rich, can't we? There are jets and art and valuable buildings and cars and—"

"Mateyo, I know your heart is pure and that you would do this in a heartbeat. Sure, selling everything would help your people, but not nearly as much as you would think. There are twenty million people living in Maleziland. Yes, everybody would get a nice bit of money. But then what? How does that fix the underlying problems?"

Mateyo stared at Kanzi, suddenly devoid of his usual brightness. "Well, then what do we do? Because we can't do nothing. My people need me to help them, even if they do not even know it themselves."

Kanzi smiled her deep, beautiful smile. It gave Mateyo goose bumps. At that moment, Mateyo knew that he loved this girl. He would do anything to continue to make her smile.

Kanzi took a deep breath, exhaled, and started to speak. "This is going to be a long journey. Despite having taken economics and business courses at boarding school in South Africa, I don't think that my level of understanding is good enough for the task we must complete. That said, I think that I know somebody who can help."

Mateyo nodded quickly and said, "Who? We must speak with this person!"

Kanzi continued. "Well, my teacher, a woman named Jane Makiko, taught me these subjects for three years. She was amazing." Kanzi smiled. "She was born in the northern province—they say that people from the north are pretty smart, and she was! After I graduated from high school, she was invited to do a PhD at Harvard in the United States. Today, she does consulting work for various developing countries around the world."

"But, Kanzi, why would such a woman come to Maleziland to help us?"

"Oh, Mateyo, sometimes you forget that you're the king and one of the wealthiest men in the world! It's her job to work with people like us—of course, we would have to pay her, but her fees would be nothing as compared to the good that could be done. I've kept in touch with her, and I happen to know that she has just wrapped up a huge consulting project with the government of Rwanda. It is possible that she is available to us on short notice."

"Kanzi, reach out to this woman now. I want a royal jet in the air tomorrow morning to pick her up, wherever in the world she might be!"

Mateyo looked over at Chumba, who had been discreetly watching from a distance. The king nodded. Chumba scurried away to initiate the king's orders.

Kanzi smiled her beautiful smile, nodded politely, and did the same.

Mateyo grinned. *I like being king!*

It took thirty-six hours to get Ms. Makiko to Maleziland. She'd responded quickly to Kanzi's email and said she would be thrilled to come help, but the Tanzanian government had rejected the flight plan for a Malezi crown jet to fly through its airspace. Mateyo was initially quite annoyed, but his staff had quickly resolved the issue, and the shiny new red, black, and green Gulfstream soon took off and returned shortly thereafter.

Mateyo and Kanzi strolled onto the tarmac to meet the jet carrying the teacher, each of them holding a carry-on-sized bag. Mateyo had decided that working with Ms. Makiko at his second royal palace outside of Bandago would be more efficient, without the constant interruptions of normal palace life. Yet, as they approached the plane, Mateyo began to think his decision to take to the air foolish when staying safely on the ground would work just as well.

The aircraft door popped open from a bottom hinge, and as the top edge met the runway, Mateyo was surprised to see that there were stairs on the inside of the door, such that they had a perfect little staircase to ascend to the plane.

The captain of the plane greeted them as they alighted. "Good afternoon, my king. Welcome aboard Malezi 3. We like to think of her as the jewel of your fleet, even though she is the smallest."

"Th-thank you, sir," said Mateyo as he cautiously lifted up one foot to meet the first stair. He hesitated as the stairs settled in under his weight, and then proceeded up the steps slowly. "But please call me Mateyo."

Mateyo's eyes were wide as he took in the exquisite interior of the luxury jet. It was long and quite narrow, with six huge, beautiful tan leather-upholstered chairs on each side of a narrow aisle. Natural mahogany wood cabinetry and accents, polished to a mirrorlike luster, gleamed throughout the cabin. Mateyo reached out to touch the soft, supple leather and ran his fingers over the smooth-as-glass wood. He felt a tapping on his shoulder.

"Mateyo," whispered Kanzi, "can you please continue? I'd like to go say hello to Ms. Makiko."

Mateyo nodded his head and resumed his careful pace forward. As they neared the center of the jet, he saw the top of Ms. Makiko's lustrous jet-black hair, neatly pulled into a bun. He stepped in front of an empty seat and allowed Kanzi to pass.

Kanzi practically sprinted down the aisle to greet Ms. Makiko, who jumped out of her seat to embrace her. The two women hugged tightly and then stepped back half a pace each, without totally abandoning their embrace.

"Look at you!" said Ms. Makiko. "You're a grown woman now! And so beautiful!"

"Ms. Makiko! You look so . . . good! I've never seen you wear anything other than a schoolteacher's uniform! You look stunning!" said Kanzi.

Indeed, Ms. Makiko did look quite lovely. She had a beautiful silk blouse with an Asian-inspired red-and-metallic-gold dragon pattern sewn into its tight, shiny threads, and cream-colored slacks of some light material. She wore fashionable tan open-toed heels that perfectly matched her belt and purse, and there was a beautiful heart-shaped locket on a gold chain around her neck.

"Please, Kanzi, you're not my student anymore. You must call me Jane."

"I will try, Ms. . . . . I mean, Jane," said Kanzi with a shy grin. Kanzi then turned to Mateyo. "King Mateyo, I'd like you to meet Ms. Makiko."

Mateyo felt the blood rush to his face. "Please, Kanzi, just introduce me as Mateyo. Ms. Makiko, I'm thrilled to meet you. Kanzi has told me so much about you, and we have so much to do. Thank you for making the time for me and my country."

"I'm very happy to meet you, Mateyo. I've been hearing so much about what has been happening in Maleziland, and I'm extremely pleased to help advise you on your options moving forward," said the teacher.

How has she heard about Maleziland? wondered Mateyo as a voice over the intercom interrupted his thoughts.

"My deepest apologies, Your Highness, but if you wouldn't mind taking your seats, we're about to start our taxi to the runway. Our flight to Bandago will only take about twenty minutes, so we'll have you there shortly."

Mateyo's stomach knotted as the engines began to roar. Kanzi must have seen the look of terror flash over Mateyo's face, for she frowned and moved in closer to him. "What's wrong? You look almost White!"

Mateyo wasn't happy that Kanzi had spotted his unease. "Nothing is wrong," he said, a bit too sharply.

Kanzi looked at Mateyo with one hypercritical eye. "Really," she whispered, "what's wrong?"

Mateyo looked at the poshly carpeted floor of the expensive jet. "It's just that . . . well, I've never been in a plane before. I've never flown. The very thought of flying scares the life out of me. Birds fly. People don't!"

"Oh, Mateyo," said Kanzi, "flying is extremely safe, and it would take us eight hours to drive to Bandago. Come, let's take our seats. Once your seat belt is on, you'll feel better."

Mateyo took his seat, figured out how to buckle his seat belt by watching Ms. Makiko fasten hers, and sat back into his plush, comfortable chair. He decidedly did *not* feel better. He gripped the polished wood armrests of his chair so tightly that his fingers and knuckles were indeed white. "Why did we decide to fly to the other palace again? We could just as easily work from here."

Kanzi turned her head back to look at Mateyo. "My king, I know this flight is somewhat unnerving—"

"Unnerving?" Mateyo asked, his eyes wide. "*Unnerving?* There may be royal piss staining this beautiful carpet shortly if we don't stop this plane right now!"

Kanzi smiled her comforting smile. She caught the eye of the statuesque flight attendant and beckoned the comely woman over. "Double Macallan 25, one cube, STAT . . . *before* we take off."

No less than sixty seconds later, Mateyo was taking an oversized gulp of his now-favorite drink. The beautiful amber liquid poured out of a glass so delicate and clear that it seemed impossible it could hold its shape. As he swallowed the whiskey, Mateyo could feel his body relaxing.

"Thank you, Kanzi. You know me so well."

Kanzi looked across the narrow aisle toward Ms. Makiko. "I hope you don't mind the additional flight. Mateyo thought it might be easier to be productive with fewer interruptions at his second royal residence. Neither of us has ever been there, nor to the third royal residence in the north of the country. I have seen this palace from afar, though, as it sits high on the hillside overlooking Bandago, which is Maleziland's second city and its business capital."

Ms. Makiko said, "Oh, yes, I, too, have seen the palace perched on the mountain. It is amazing how much the city has grown up around it. Only fifteen years ago, it was surrounded only by trees. The proximate trees are all still there on the extensive grounds, but the city now meets its fences."

The whirring jet engines suddenly grew louder, and the sleek jet rolled forward. Mateyo gripped his armrests again. The plane made its way to the very end of the paved landing strip as the king stared fixedly ahead.

With the cockpit door open, Mateyo could see the runway stretched out before the plane once it did a 180 at the end of the runway.

Mateyo's mind raced. *Why does it take two people to fly the plane? Why is the airstrip so short? Does the pilot see those tall trees at the end of the runway?* The engines began to roar, louder than any sound Mateyo had heard in his life.

What is wrong with the engines? Why isn't the plane moving? The whole damn thing is shaking! Mateyo was just about to shout out to stop the engines when the pilot released the brakes and the small jet lurched forward. Mateyo was thrown back into his seat with such force that he could not have stood up to evacuate, as every neuron in his brain was telling him to do, even if he had wanted. Through the cockpit windows, Mateyo could see the giant acacia trees at the end of the runway, malevolently daring the little jet to try to get through their wall. The plane picked up speed at an incredible pace, and Mateyo knew they were doomed. He opened his mouth to scream at the pilot, but either nothing came out or the sound from the engines was so loud he could not be heard.

Mateyo closed his eyes, not wanting to see the trees come crashing through. Yet somehow, the plane suddenly lurched skyward, as though it had launched at a right angle toward the heavens. With the plane's wheels no longer on the ground, and the sound of the engines some-what diminished, a loud, somewhat manic laughter filled the cabin. Mateyo realized he was the one who was laughing uncontrollably. He didn't know why. Maybe it was the crazy sensation he felt in the pit of his stomach as the plane took off. Maybe it was the sheer relief and joy to be alive after thinking death was imminent. Mateyo also became aware that Kanzi, Ms. Makiko, and even the pilots were all laughing along with him.

"Oh, Mateyo," said Kanzi, "sometimes I forget that you haven't yet experienced so many things that the rest of us take for granted. I shall try not to forget this again."

Mateyo felt his cheeks grow hot. "It is easy to forget that I am really even king now, much less on a jet. Not so long ago, my entire world was only the village."

Kanzi placed her hand on his knee and smiled. "You have come far, my love."

"Well," said Ms. Makiko, clearing her throat. "Shall we get to work?"

Ms. Makiko reached under her seat and pulled out a beautiful tobacco-colored briefcase. Mateyo had wondered if it had been labeled with her name, but on closer inspection he realized that the polished gold plate under the leather handle read "Dupont." *Could she have taken this bag from someone named Dupont?* thought the king. She popped open the polished latch and pulled out some papers, handing a page each to Mateyo and Kanzi. Mateyo smiled as he looked down upon the thick, textured paper in his hands, thankful for his reading lessons back in the village with Miss K.

"I hope you don't mind," said the former teacher, "but I took the liberty of writing down the broad areas for reform that you can undertake to help Maleziland move forward and take her out of the bottom rungs of global poverty. You can adopt any such reforms as you see fit; after all, it is your country. That said, the more reforms you adopt, the better your results will be. We need only look at Rwanda to see how economic and political reforms can have a positive effect on a country and its people. It is argued that Rwanda was able to implement its reforms after its horrific genocide, in effect causing a 'reset' in how people think. I think that the death of your father, and the ascendance to the throne of the People's Prince, gives you a similar opportunity. We can, I believe, change the course of Maleziland's future with what we are about to do. I'm extremely thrilled to play a role in this!"

Mateyo nodded as he read the list, although he did not yet understand much of its content.

- Political reform:
  - Democracy versus constitutional monarchy
- Legal reform:
  - Independence of the judiciary
- Agricultural reform:
  - Granting title to farmland
- Financial/market reform:
  - US dollar currency lock and microfinance funding
  - Foreign aid

"What are all of these things?" asked Mateyo.

Kanzi jumped in. "There are lots of things you need to know about in order to understand the way things operate. Like the way markets work," she said.

Mateyo sat up straight. "Kanzi, I've been to a market. I *know* how they work." He wasn't a total fool, after all.

Kanzi smiled. "Okay. Now, imagine if all the markets in the world were combined—even imagine if all the markets in Maleziland were combined. You need to understand how events in Maleziland and even in the entire world affect what happens in the markets outside of Kashatown. You need to understand how the price for any item in any market affects how much of that item will be sold. For example, you would happily pay one Malezi for a papaya, right?"

"Oh yes!" said Mateyo. "Papayas usually are sold for four Malezi!"

"Right," said Kanzi. "But what if the market farmers decided to sell their papayas for fifteen Malezi each?"

"Well, then I wouldn't buy any at all!"

"Exactly," said Kanzi. "Or what if locusts came and stripped all of the leaves and flowers from almost all of the papaya trees when they were in bloom, and the harvest of papaya was reduced by ninety percent? Do you think the remaining papaya would be more valuable?"

"Well, of course they would! I love papaya!"

"Well, my king," said Kanzi with a big grin, "you have just learned the basic principles of supply and demand economics and price elasticity!"

Ms. Makiko cleared her throat. "I think this is where I step in. One of the biggest problems that Maleziland faces is inflation. So the concept is simple. When the prices of things go up, it's called *inflation*. Sometimes the prices go up due to scarcity—like Kanzi's papayas." Ms. Makiko smiled. "But often, especially when a country imports different goods — like gasoline—you need to pay for those things, right? Historically, the Malezi has been very unstable related to other currencies, and if traders of foreign currency think Maleziland is in trouble, the value of the Malezi falls—meaning it takes way more Malezi to pay for gasoline. If the value of the Malezi is pegged, or fixed, to another more stable currency like the US dollar, then the risk of the currency falling is greatly diminished. So if one Malezi always equaled one dollar, many problems are solved. This also promotes foreign investment in Maleziland, as dollars and Malezi are always exchangeable at a fixed rate. And of course, being such a poor country, Maleziland could use more foreign investment!"

"So simple," said Mateyo. "Why hasn't anybody done this before?"

Ms. Makiko smiled. "Many developing countries have," she said.

At that moment, the plane began a sharp descent. Mateyo's eyes widened, but then he relaxed. "I'll be okay this time," he said to Kanzi, smiling. "Ms. Makiko, let's pick this up this evening after dinner."

"Of course, Mateyo," said the teacher of kings.

The unlikely trio walked up to the great wooden double front doors of the palace. None were burdened by luggage, having been assured that it would be brought immediately. All gazed up at the impressive colonial edifice in front of them as they approached, with no fewer than three tree-height columns framing the entrance. Chumba stood at the front door of the terrace, smiling. "Welcome, King Mateyo," he said.

"Chumba? How did you get here?" asked Mateyo and then frowned. "Did you stow away in the belly of our plane?"

"No, my king," Chumba said with a grin. "Right after you had breakfast, a group of us boarded a transport and were driven here. It was a pleasant, albeit bumpy, journey. Of course, there are many staff who work here year-round, but twenty-five of us from the capital came as well to ensure your proper treatment."

Mateyo shook his head. Surely this had not been necessary, but he did not have the energy to discuss it at that moment. After leading the ladies to the front doors, Mateyo stepped aside and bid his guests to enter the main hall. He followed the women in, but all three stopped after entering.

"This is the Grand Reception Hall, my king," said Chumba. "As the original palace and first seat of government, Bandago was where both your father and his father held all state receptions."

The floors were made of black-and-white marble polished so smoothly that the reflection made it difficult to see the natural beauty of the stone. The coffered ceilings were three stories high, and in the center of the room was a chandelier bigger than four of the largest shanties in Mateyo's village. Thousands upon thousands of beautiful crystals hung from its shiny golden arms, each reflecting rainbow light beams all throughout the room as the sun hit each one.

"It was a gift from Russia," Chumba said. "It has over forty-nine thousand individual Swarovski crystals, and its arms are all eighteen-carat gold plated. It weighs seven and a half tons. The roof had to be torn apart and rebuilt in order to reinforce it for the chandelier's weight. Your father called it his Milky Way."

Mateyo saw Ms. Makiko and Kanzi nod at the name, but he remained silent, despite his total confusion over why this magnificent light had been dubbed the "Milky Way."

"May I show each of you to your quarters?" asked Chumba.

Mateyo answered for all of them. "Yes, please."

The three of them met in the king's study. Chumba had to lead each of them there. When Mateyo was shown into the dark wood-paneled office, Ms. Makiko and Kanzi already were waiting for him. They stood in the middle of the room, looking around in awe. Another spectacular, although smaller, chandelier hung in the center of the high wood-coffered ceiling. The carpet was plush yet very tightly woven. Mateyo felt his feet slide left and right a tiny bit as his weight bore down upon it. There was an enormous hand-carved mahogany desk at one end of the room, with a giant wingback leather chair on its far side. Both the desk and chair were in front of a five-meter-tall glass window, from which one could see up the mountainside into beautiful treed vegetation.

Miss Makiko and Kanzi sat down in much smaller upholstered chairs facing the desk, and Mateyo made his way to the throne-like chair on the other side of the desk. "Well, Ms. Makiko? What is first on our agenda?"

"Perhaps we should start with political and legal reform, King Mateyo," said Ms. Makiko.

Mateyo frowned slightly at her continued use of his title.

"First, a little history lesson. As no doubt you know, Africa was colonized by various European powers. For hundreds of years, the French, British, German, Dutch, Spanish, and Portuguese European powers divided up our continent and harvested her produce—including, of course, her people as slaves—in order to enrich themselves and their countries."

Mateyo did his best to not betray his total lack of historical knowledge and was grateful for the lesson. He cleared his throat. "And how was this considered acceptable?" he asked earnestly.

"The world was different then, though not all remnants of that era have been erased from people's minds and hearts, King Mateyo," said the former teacher, falling easily back into a familiar role.

"Eventually, each and every colony was given independence from her colonial power, with every new country forming a fledgling democracy. But in virtually every instance, democracy failed. The people of Africa didn't ask for democracy, and there were very few institutions in place to support democracy. Remember that for thousands of years, African traditional government was not democratic in nature, so few people wanted democracy. As a result, democracy typically reverted into a single-party, nondemocratic dictatorship—exactly as happened here in Maleziland."

"Yes," Mateyo said, "people seem to love their king, elected or not, even when they are poor and have little."

"Of course they do," Kanzi said. "It matters little to the people of our country whether there is a king or an elected president in power, as long as the king or president acts in the interest of his or her people. Democracy, however, is the rallying cry for Westerners hoping to 'fix' Africa, but after thousands of years of tribal law and rule, many have realized that democracy does not ensure that a government will act on behalf of, and in the best interests of, her people."

"Indeed," said Ms. Makiko, "democracy was forced upon our people. Today, many young democracies exist, but few have fair elections, and fewer still elect those who govern for the people. Many of these elected governments are plagued with corruption and hardly act in the best interests of their people. We want to avoid that, yes?"

"Of course," Mateyo said, and Kanzi nodded.

Ms. Makiko smiled at Mateyo. "The best form of government for Maleziland would be a transitional constitutional monarchy, a form of government where you would remain as king and head of state."

"No," interjected the king. "I have no desire to remain as king. I do not believe that God chose me for this role, and I reject the notion that it is my birthright!"

"I understand, Mateyo," said Ms. Makiko, "but please hear me out. Your role as king would be temporary. A new constitution would have to be adopted, one where the people had the right to vote in their own government. But every law that was passed would have to have your royal signature. Once the government was up and running and acting in the best interests of your people, the monarchy could be abolished—or it could be kept on forever but have little or no power over laws passed by the elected government."

"But I don't *want* to be king!" exclaimed Mateyo.

"I know, but I do believe that Maleziland's governing political system needs the check and balance of somebody who can be trusted to act in the people's best interest. Who better than the People's Prince . . . I mean, the People's King?" said Ms. Makiko. "We can always set a time limit in the constitution for how long your reign lasts."

"I'm not sure how comfortable I am with this," said the king. "But let's continue, please."

"It is also very important to establish the rule of law and of property rights. In nearly every country where White colonial powers have given rule to her native peoples, economies have failed, often spectacularly. For countries to survive and prosper, they need a legal system in place that protects people's property rights and freedoms. Who in this country would work hard to build up a business and wealth, if at any time the king could simply reach into such person's back pocket and take it all away?" asked the former teacher.

"But I would never do that!" said Mateyo. "Ask Kanzi."

"I know you would not," said Kanzi. "But your father certainly would have, and another king after you might do the same. Mandebala certainly would! So, whatever the political system of a country might be, every country that wants to encourage its people to better their own lives must prohibit the government, be it a king or president, from stealing the property of its citizens."

"Agreed," said Ms. Makiko. "And you must appoint independent judges to enforce the rule of law—people who cannot be bribed or threatened and who are not beholden to others such that they might rule in unfair ways. How else can a country preserve the rights and freedoms of its people?"

"I get it!" said Mateyo. "Why would anybody try to make their lives better and get richer if it could simply be taken away? This makes perfect sense!"

"And then, if we're talking about the people having rights to their own property, we must certainly address agricultural reform," continued Ms. Makiko.

"Agri-what?" Mateyo asked.

"Farming," Kanzi said with a smile.

Why didn't she just say that? Mateyo wondered.

"I believe that it is important for the people of your country—most of whom farm and live in the countryside—to be given ownership of the land they farm."

"How does that make sense?" Mateyo asked. "People can't own what is not theirs! People are *of* the land. We are one with it. It is not possible to own such a thing!" said Mateyo with a frown.

"I understand why you are saying that. But the idea of land ownership is something that is accepted in virtually every corner of the world. Land has value—significant value—and granting ownership of it to people who have cared for it and tended it for decades and even longer motivates people to improve their farming methods. It also gives them something of value upon which they can borrow and further improve their lot in life."

"But currently village chiefs already grant them land on which to farm. That is tribal law," said Mateyo.

"Yes," Ms. Makiko said, "but the village chief can also take it away at his whim."

"Okay, I think I get this," said Mateyo. "What else can we do?"

"Well, there are other financial reforms that can really make a difference to Maleziland's economic growth." Ms. Makiko went on to discuss how a fixed exchange rate for the Malezi could reduce inflationary cycles by linking its value to a major stable currency like the US dollar. She also explained to Mateyo and Kanzi how they could encourage the flow of foreign investment into Maleziland by eliminating or reducing taxes.

Mateyo's head was spinning. "But how can lowering taxes increase government revenues? This makes no sense!"

"I know it sounds illogical, but when you lower taxes, more investments are made in the country, and ultimately there are more businesses and people generating wealth and taxable revenues."

Mateyo nodded. Ms. Makiko must have noticed and quickly added, "I know that we're talking about a lot of new concepts here. Don't worry, we have many days to talk about these things. And we can stop at any time."

"No, please continue," said Mateyo.

"Ms. Makiko," said Kanzi, "can I talk about microlending now? I really liked learning about that in your class, and I think it has very real potential to help so many people here."

Ms. Makiko frowned and said, "Yes, I'm sure you are *able* to talk about microlending, and indeed you *may* begin."

"Sorry, Ms. Makiko," said Kanzi, lowering her eyes. "*May* I speak about microlending?"

Ms. Makiko nodded.

Mateyo was thoroughly confused by the exchange.

"So, Mateyo," Kanzi began, "there's a relatively recent way of doing business that has been experiencing some amazing success. It's called microlending."

"Microlending?" said Mateyo.

"Yes. Companies with lots of money have been giving small amounts of money to people all over Africa who want to start their own businesses. These people first submit plans for their business, and if approved, they receive money to start and run these businesses. The money given is called a loan because the business owners have to pay interest and repay them, but the success of these loans has been nothing short of amazing! On average, each loan is approximately six hundred US dollars—seven hundred and fifty thousand Malezi. Almost all are repaid in full and on time, and they are creating amazing small businesses everywhere!"

"And why don't we have these businesses in Maleziland?" asked Mateyo.

Kanzi smirked. "We likely would have them here if the lending people knew that the businesses they fund would not have their property seized by a greedy king or government."

"Of course," said Mateyo, wishing he had figured this out on his own.

"And of course you need solid and trustworthy legal and financial systems in place so that lenders aren't afraid to invest!" said Kanzi.

"And last on today's agenda," said Ms. Makiko, clapping her hands together, "foreign aid."

"Oh yes," said Mateyo, "we must seek *lots* of foreign aid! This new way of running our country will be expensive!"

"NO!" said Ms. Makiko so loudly that both Mateyo and Kanzi jumped in their chairs. "We must end all foreign aid to Maleziland. Immediately. And permanently."

"WHAT?" asked Mateyo, with Kanzi echoing him.

"I'm sure you meant 'pardon me,' but I shall nevertheless continue. Too many countries have become dependent on foreign aid. Whether it is to fight hunger or to build airports or roads, for decades, African nations have had their hands out every time there's an emergency or we need a huge amount of money for something. This practice *must* end and end now. Only when Maleziland and other countries like her can stand on their own two feet without being propped up and know that foreign aid is *not* an option will we ever get out of our cycle of dependence on foreign aid. Foreign aid is killing our people."

Both Mateyo and Kanzi sat in stunned silence.

Ms. Makiko continued. "For decades, Western countries have been sending billions of dollars—*hundreds* of billions of dollars, not Malezis—to African countries. Often very little, if any, of this money makes its way to the people who need it most." She narrowed her eyes and gestured around the room. "How do you think that this palace was built? The jets bought? Your coronation party paid for?"

Mateyo felt his cheeks grow hot. "But can this country survive without foreign aid?" he asked.

"Yes, it can. It can, and it will, because it must."

Mateyo winced but said nothing.

"I can tell that this concept will take some time to digest. Don't worry—time we have," said Ms. Makiko. She rose from her chair as Chumba entered through the heavy wooden door.

"With that, my two young friends," the schoolteacher said, "I am going to call it an evening. If you don't mind, I must get some badly needed sleep. Good night." And with that, Ms. Makiko turned sharply and was escorted from the room by Chumba.

Mateyo locked eyes with Kanzi. "Is it true? Did foreign aid pay for all of this?"

"Indeed, foreign aid made King Mabanda—and now you, Mateyo—a very wealthy man. By learned estimate, not public record, you are worth over a hundred billion US dollars."

"A hundred billion US dollars? What is that? The same as a hundred billion Malezi?"

"Yes and no. Yes, the US dollar is of course a currency, but that amount is actually worth about one hundred thirty-five *trillion* Malezi."

Mateyo blinked. "Mere months ago, I was among the poorest of the poor. Yet I was *happy*, very happy. Sure, my belly hurt from time to time when I was hungry, but now it hurts equally, if not more, when I've eaten too much!"

"Mateyo, although Ms. Makiko will certainly know more than me about this, there are two big problems with foreign aid. First, very little money gets to the people who need it. Second, if every time there is a crisis in Africa—be it drought, plague, or pestilence—and foreign countries send millions, even billions, of dollars to our aid, countries and people have very little, if any, reason to effect basic changes in order to plan for and avoid these problems in the future."

"I get it!" shouted Mateyo. "If people can always count on money from foreigners every time there's a crisis, why bother fixing the underlying problems? Why save some grain year after year? Eat it all, because if there's a drought, foreign people will send food our way in any event!"

Kanzi smiled, giving Mateyo the ultimate reward. Mateyo continued, "You are exactly right. Why bother to fix the problems if we are always saved by foreign aid? No, we *must* get used to surviving on our own. We must never expect foreigners to bail us out. We must proudly fend for ourselves. Indeed, as we learn to do this, there will be pain. And it might be very bad from time to time. But truly, we must become independent and look after our own peoples."

"I couldn't agree with you more," Kanzi said with excitement.

Several days later, Kanzi and Mateyo watched and waved as Ms. Makiko ascended the flip-out staircase of the Gulfstream. She paused at the top of the steps and turned back toward her hosts. She smiled, waved, and ducked into the plane, though she was nowhere near tall enough to hit her head on the doorframe.

"I can't believe how much she has helped us," said Mateyo. "Truly, we could never have come so far so fast without her. She is a truly incredible woman."

"Yes, she is," said Kanzi. "But now the real work begins. All of our plans—every last recommendation—must be fully planned out and ready to implement before we announce them."

After six weeks of working day and night, Mateyo finally believed he was ready to present their plan to the people of Maleziland.

"Kanzi, do you think the people will understand? Do you think they are going to believe that this will work?"

"I hope so. You know there is already talk among the people, wondering how you will change things," said Kanzi.

"Yes, I know," Mateyo said, sighing.

"The people have no idea what you are planning, and it makes them nervous," said Kanzi. They know you as a person of the people—their true 'People's Prince.' Now, we have disappeared for weeks, and they have begun to wonder. Some say that you will never do anything for them, despite having grown up among them. Others think you have become too used to power and the royal lifestyle and that you will never give it up!"

"I know, I know. But none of this belongs to me. This mountain-top palace was built with money given by governments and foreigners looking to help the everyday people. I could never turn my back on the people who raised me—and I will not."

"I know that," said Kanzi, looking deeply into his eyes. "It is what makes you the right person to lead your people out of poverty. It will be very important for us to do this right, though. Simply handing over the reins of power as was done years ago when the French left will not work. We need time to teach our people values that will support the permanent transition of power to the people. I hope that they understand."

"If they do not, our plan will be as doomed as our country's first, and last, democratic election," said Mateyo, his shoulders drooping as the adrenaline rush from the enormous task of planning finally subsided.

Mateyo had known this night would come, just as he knew the sun would rise each day. There was an absolute inevitability, even fate, to the consummation of their love. Neither he nor Kanzi had wanted to rush it, but both had wanted it badly.

Mateyo was nervous. The thought of making love with Kanzi both excited and frightened him. It wasn't sex itself that terrified him—in Maleziland, you saw sex everywhere: along the side of the road, behind a stall in the market, and through the doorway of a doorless shanty. No, the act itself seemed common and easy enough. It was simply that he was horrified at the prospect of disappointing Kanzi. He didn't ask, but he assumed that Kanzi was not a virgin—the odds of her being as beautiful as she was and still a virgin were impossibly low. That simply exacerbated Mateyo's fears. He had to measure up.

After a light rap on his door, Kanzi opened it slightly and slipped in, pausing a moment to lock the door. As she floated toward his bed, Mateyo noticed a look on her face that he had glimpsed only once before. She looked exceedingly calm, relaxed even. Her head was held high, exposing her long, beautiful neck. Her eyes were wider than he'd ever seen them, and they positively burned with desirous hunger.

Kanzi's lustrous dark skin shone in the dim light. She was wearing a beautiful white silk robe that hugged her every curve. Mateyo was shocked by how difficult it was for him to breathe. It was as if someone had somehow siphoned the oxygen out of his room—he was going through the motions of breathing, but his body seemed to come up short of sustaining air.

Mateyo's dream girl clambered onto the palatial-sized bed. She flung back the grand comforter and smiled at the sight of Mateyo, completely naked. Kanzi straddled him with her long, smooth legs.

Mateyo was shaking furiously. His mind simply could not process quickly enough what was happening. As he drew an enormous breath, hoping that he'd be able to speak a word of protest if he hyperinflated his lungs, Kanzi covered his mouth with her soft, sweet-smelling hand.

"No, Mateyo. We both know this must happen," she said. "If you can look me straight in the eyes and tell me that you do not want this, I will stop. If you cannot, please don't speak another word."

Mateyo summoned his strength. As his diaphragm, with great effort, forced air past his voice box and his mouth began to shape the air into the word *stop*, Kanzi slipped the white silk robe from her slender shoulders.

Mateyo gasped as though he had been punched in the gut. He had never seen a woman as exquisitely and perfectly formed as Kanzi, and though he had tried to vanquish the memory of her body from the night of Mabanda's attempted rape for so long, it all came flooding back. He focused on her long, slender, graceful neck. The dip in the skin above her collarbone fascinated him. Mateyo could not fathom the splendor of her shoulders, with each lithe and sinewy muscle responding as she moved. Kanzi's arms were sleek and defined yet feminine and erotically beautiful.

Kanzi's breasts defied any logic or laws of physics that Mateyo had seen apply to Malezi women. Kanzi's breasts were full, proud, and high-pointing—the result of a life of privilege and all its accompanying supportive undergarments. Yet now, Mateyo experienced a surge of desire when he saw this magnificence, a lusting that he couldn't understand or control.

The muscles on Kanzi's stomach flexed as she positioned herself atop Mateyo, and he was charged with excitement at the sight of her tiny round nub of a belly button—adorned with jewelry!

As his eyes lowered past her stomach, Mateyo's lust, nervousness, and confusion went into sheer overdrive. His jaw dropped, and as if she could read his mind, Kanzi stood up over him so he could get a better look at the object of his rapt attention. She was but a tongue's dart away from Mateyo's face. As her gaze met his, she reached for him. Placing one royal hand on each breast, Kanzi eased herself slowly— very slowly—onto Mateyo. The sensation was more than Mateyo could bear, and he was instantly overcome by fierce and frantic convulsions, roaring loudly.

As Mateyo lay back, recovering, his worst fear broke through into his consciousness. Kanzi was lying on top of him, sobbing softly. He had disappointed her as a lover, and he was angry at himself for doing so. "Kanzi, I'm so sorry! I promise to get better. I—"

Kanzi cut him off and began to giggle joyously through her tears. "Oh, Mateyo," she said, "that was the most beautiful thing I have ever experienced in my life!" He hugged her even more tightly and silently swore to improve for her.

CHAPTER 20

General Moto had told Shigeku he was surprised to hear from him when he respectfully but urgently requested a meeting. The general had acceded to the request, mostly, he said, to get a chance to visit with his friend from the Zambwanan war but also out of curiosity to hear why his young pup friend so urgently needed to see him.

The two men greeted each other in a heartfelt way that only two men who have faced a life-threatening situation can. Their embrace was warm, genuine, and strong.

"Well, young pup," boomed Moto, his golden shoulder epaulettes signifying his generalship reflecting sharply in the midday sun, "how are you enjoying life in the slums with your new 'brother'? I guess he's not a *new* brother per se, but I can tell you, after years of watching that imperious little prick Mandebala march around, give orders, and wreak havoc as if he were king, I certainly could never have shown him any kindness or mercy in the fashion you have, or so I'm told."

Shigeku smiled. He'd known the conversation would start out like this, for every senior Malezi military commander had borne the brunt of a verbal attack and tirade by Mandebala at one point in time or another in the past. It made the task he was looking to accomplish more challenging—but not insurmountable, he prayed.

"Bala isn't as bad today as he once was," said Shigeku, "but he sure was a handful. I think it's fair to say that a great deal of his attitude has been 'adjusted'—perhaps even wiped out entirely."

"Well," said the general, "that's probably a good thing if he wants to live to see his twentieth birthday. I understand he was close to death when you took him in. Why did you do it?"

"To tell the truth, Moto, I'm not entirely certain. It wasn't simply that he was my blood. If that were the only factor, I could never have fought with the Zambwanan army to try to remove him and his father from power, for surely Mabanda and Mandebala would have been executed had we been successful." Shigeku took note of the wince that registered on Moto's face at the mention of the Zambwanan army and made a mental note of the fact.

Shigeku continued. "At the time, I acted rather spontaneously, and without thinking, I took him in. Afterward, when I thought about it, I realized that I only hated him for what he had in his life of privilege and what we as a family did not have. After he was stripped of his cushy way of life, I no longer had any reason to hate him."

The general thought hard for several long seconds before responding. "Well, under that line of thinking, you must now hate your former 'brother,' Mateyo, for all that he has and is. And amusingly, someone from the slums has again risen to a position of power directly through your deeds. Is life not hilarious that way sometimes? Perhaps there are more like you who are not impressed with King Mateyo these days."

It was high-stakes poker now. Shigeku was uncertain if his read on the general was accurate. Had Moto just telegraphed his underlying thoughts to him? If Shigeku was right, then perhaps a necessary part of his plan would fall in line. If wrong, he could be shot for treason. Shigeku knew his life was on the line. *Fuck, here goes nothing.*

Shigeku tried to broach the subject. When he and Bala had practiced how the conversation would occur, Bala had told him to focus on getting one simple word out of his mouth, after which there could be no going back.

"Treason," blurted Shigeku.

"I beg your pardon, pup? Are you accusing *me* of treason?"

Shigeku thought he saw a twinkle in Moto's eyes, but he could not be sure. "No, friend, I most certainly am not. But you were there at the funeral for Mateyo's crazy speech. You were there at the reception afterward. You have seen with your own eyes and have witnessed with your other senses how nervous the people are. Certainly, they want change—economic change, though, not a change to the governing and societal fabric of this country."

"Are you going somewhere with this little lecture on Malezi society? Of course I know that the Malezi people are afraid of change. How do you think we got a king in the first place? Remember that King Mabanda's father was elected as head of the government, put there by the people for the people. He had no divine right to become king at first, but by carefully capitalizing on the people's fear of change, coercing and enlisting the support of the Church, consolidating support of the country's military leaders, and ruthlessly and savagely eliminating all political opponents, he and his son held on to power for over forty years without a single serious threat to his reign."

Shigeku smiled, as the conversation was unfolding perfectly, exactly as Bala had suggested it would. "Of course, General Moto, one has to have the support of the military and the Church, as well as that of the people, to secure one's position of power."

"Are you implying that Mateyo does not have the support of these institutions and that his regime might be unstable?" demanded Moto, a bit more dramatically, thought Shigeku, than the discussion warranted.

"Come on, Moto, you saw the faces of the people. You saw the face of Archbishop Sulamena—or you should have seen it. Two out of the three factors necessary to hold power in Maleziland have been destabilized. What of the military?" It was bluff time, and he needed to make his hand seem stronger than it was. "I personally know of at least one other general who is concerned about Mateyo's ability to govern and is prepared to act on that concern."

No shock registered on Moto's face; not even the slightest reaction was perceptible. Had he been speaking to other generals regarding this very subject? Did he know Shigeku was bluffing?

Then a broad smile began across Moto's face. "I always knew I liked you for a reason, Shigeku. You're always direct and to the point, if you speak at all." With that, he guffawed at his own joke. "And your judgment is sound. How you know the inner workings of this country's military, I'll never know, but of course, you are correct. The military sees Mateyo as a threat. Our lives of privilege—and there are few more privileged in this country, save for the king himself and I guess Sulamena—are threatened by Mateyo's promise of change.

"Mateyo has unsettled the people. He has destabilized the Church. And he has fundamentally undermined the military, such that we're nervous about his ability to lead his country's defense of its borders, as Mabanda did so successfully in the past. Yes, Shigeku, if that's the point of this discussion, and I believe it is, the military, too, is deeply concerned. That said, I am the least senior of the Malezi military's eight generals. I certainly don't speak for them, nor do I have the ability to make them listen. What would you propose that someone in my position might do?"

It was Shigeku's turn to smile. "We have to chat. Why don't you pour us some of that scotch, and we'll dig into this problem a bit more."

Moto smiled broadly.

Mateyo's world had never been brighter. He knew with certainty that he was absolutely in love with Kanzi, and she with him. She was his eyes to the outside world beyond Maleziland's borders. She was the formal education that he never had, or even contemplated, while growing up in the slums. She was the purveyor of love, affection, and attention that he so craved and never received as he and others tried to eke out an existence in the slums of the world's poorest nation.

The royal palace issued a press release announcing that King Mateyo would make a televised address to the nation. It was six weeks after the death of King Mabanda, and since the funeral, coronation, and reception, King Mateyo rarely had been seen in public—certainly not in any official capacity. The populace had been generally quite nervous about the disappearance of the king, particularly after his disturbing speech at the coronation. As a country, they gathered around whatever television sets could be found—if not, around radios—to hear what the king had to say. Unwittingly, the boy king's absence had played perfectly into the hands of those who opposed him.

Mateyo was nervous about the forthcoming press conference. It had turned into an international event, having been picked up on by major television stations around the world as a pivotal moment in the history of Maleziland, the world's poorest country, governed by the world's youngest head of state. As such, rather than speaking into the usual sum total of three microphones and having but one television and one video camera peering at his image, he was going to be speaking to the entire world. All the American cable networks were going to be there. The BBC, with its longtime outward focus on the world, would be there, as would Canadian, Russian, and European networks. Even Al Jazeera, the Arabic world's CNN, had been accredited by Mateyo for the event.

He'd practiced his speech a hundred times, but he couldn't keep himself or his voice from quivering. Finally, on the night before the speech,

Kanzi taught him a trick that she had learned from her public-speaking experiences at boarding school. "Just pretend," she coached, "that they're all naked!" Mateyo thought the idea was funny, but he failed to see how it would help with his voice or shaking. "It doesn't really, silly king boy, but if you imagine they're all naked, then you can laugh a little, and you'll forget to be nervous."

At 10:00 a.m. sharp the next day, Mateyo strode up to the podium at the Ministry of Communications, with Kanzi stoically by his side. Cameras flashed, people clapped, and forty-five video cameras' red lights began to blink.

"Thank you all for coming out here today," he started. "My name is Mateyo Mabanda, and I am the king of Maleziland. I've never done this before, and I am nervous, so please bear with me." Mateyo took a deep breath and began.

"Maleziland is an economic and political failure. We are, and shall remain, an international charity basket case unless we do something about it. We receive three times our domestic GDP in foreign aid each year. Expecting handouts from foreign governments and agencies, be it food or loans or other goods, has become a way of life for Malezis."

Mateyo paused to look around to see if people were paying attention. Every set of eyes in the hall was upon him, and nary a person so much as whispered.

"This is indeed a very sad state of affairs for a proud and formerly independent people. Most do not remember a time before handouts, and it has become a more or less accepted part of life here.

"As a colony under French rule, we were a prosperous little country. We were a net exporter of goods—tea, tobacco, bananas, maize, sweet potatoes, and ground nuts. All were exported throughout Africa and indeed to the rest of the world. Of course, Maleziland's native people owned none of the enterprise that produced these goods, and therefore the plight of the ordinary Malezi, though stable and fed, did not improve beyond that of the average paid employee—once, that is, the policy of 'free work,' or slavery, was forbidden." This time Mateyo saw people in the audience nodding.

"In the face of increasing internal and external pressure to reform, what did the French do to solve the problem? They left. First, however, in their great wisdom, they determined to allow Maleziland's native people to vote. With a government elected by the people to implement policies that favored her indigenous population and to, in effect, wrest control of the assets of capitalism away from the French, the fortunes of Maleziland's people would be enriched and improved. Or so the theory went.

"With hindsight we can see that democracy as a concept, and the institutions and infrastructure necessary to support it, failed in Maleziland after the French granted our independence in the 1960s, just as it has failed throughout much, if not all, of continental Africa. My father's father was duly elected in a free and fair election. Yet throughout Africa, country after country returned to dictatorship or one-man rule, with elections becoming little more than a facade designed to keep foreign aid from democratically inclined Western nations flowing."

Mateyo looked at Kanzi beside him, who smiled reassuringly. Thus fortified, he carried on.

"Stark examples of the failure of democracy abound. To the north, Zimbabwe, the former colony of Rhodesia, went from being the breadbasket of sub-Saharan Africa to being a road map for economic disaster, quickly succumbing to hyperinflation and suddenly becoming one of the poorest, and most foreign aid dependent, nations on the continent.

"I do not have an education or background that values democracy over dictatorship, and it might be difficult to accept my altruistic intention while I am a wealthy king living in royal palaces, but having grown up as one of the poorest individuals on the face of the planet, and having been thrust into a role where I can truly help my people with whom I grew up, I am determined to make a difference. I will hold this office, and the power that it wields, to successfully, and finally, create a nation that is economically prosperous.

"Today, Maleziland embarks on a brave new chapter in its history. The following is a brief outline of a plan we are implementing, effective today. A detailed report outlining the following six steps in our ten-year reform plan will be available from the Communication Ministry after this press conference.

"First, all foreign aid programs for Maleziland are immediately canceled, and no further payments to our country, in cash or in kind, will be accepted. And as of today, the value of the Malezi will be tied to the US dollar. New currency, called the New Malezi, or NKW, will be issued one month from today, with a value of one NKW to one US dollar. This rate shall not change.

"All international import taxes and tariffs are hereby suspended unilaterally, and Maleziland announces its intention to lead the formation of a Pan-African free-trade zone. Corporate taxes on profits are now reduced to a flat rate of 10 percent, and Maleziland is pleased to announce its agreement in principle to sign tax treaties with twenty-five nations around the world.

"Virtually all assets of the crown, including palaces, jets, and land, will immediately be sold." The audience gasped when they heard this pronouncement. "The proceeds from these sales will be used to fund infrastructure, such as roads, airports, trains, electricity transmission, and water and sewer systems.

"The crown's treasury will be used to fund the infrastructure program. And five hundred million NKW of this amount will be used to set up microlending businesses, allowing people who need capital to start up or grow a business, free from governmental bias or direction." Mateyo paused to take a drink of water, with every eye in the house watching him.

"All people of Maleziland will be granted legal title to the land they occupy, either as residents or farmers. This will give people assets upon which they can borrow or accumulate wealth.

"In consultation with the United Nations, I will lead the development and proclamation of a new constitution for the Malezi people. This will create a constitutional monarchy, entrenching the role of the king as the ultimate signatory of all laws and legislation. The constitution will also set forth principles of human rights, private ownership of property, the separation of church and state, and the formation of an independent judiciary. The constitution may not be overridden by any office, or institution, including that of the king. To be clear, the Church will no longer play any role in government, nor will it have any authority to appoint or manage any affairs other than its own.

"Finally, after these policies and programs have been in place for a period of five years in order for the principles and institutions to truly take root and gain acceptance, Maleziland will once again hold democratic elections to create a free, self-governed nation and, after five further years, abolish the monarchy in this country forever.

"Thank you for listening."

And with that, Mateyo and Kanzi walked away from the roar of questions, the flashes of camera strobes, and the countrywide upheaval and pandemonium Mateyo had just created.

CHAPTER 21

Shigeku and Bala's new home had been a beehive of activity. Shigeku had stood watch as it was built over the course of six weeks by a small army of carpenters on the royal payroll. Fabricated by concrete cinder blocks to construction standards for a benevolent climate, the process was relatively quick and simple. By the average Malezi's standards, it was palatial. It had a separate kitchen/eating/entertaining area; three small bedrooms, one of which had been converted into an office of sorts; and most importantly, a back door.

The brothers had chosen a location on the edge of the palace lands, the back of which was surrounded by trees that none dared cut down, through a forest thoroughly marked by game trails. Many a visitor whose presence would have otherwise been noted came and went clandestinely via the back entrance.

Together, Shigeku and Bala decided that it was time to initiate the second phase of their plot. They couldn't have scripted Mateyo's speech any better to suit their purposes. He was playing right into their hands.

In a country where mass media was a communication means available to few, Shigeku and Bala harnessed the single most effective communication device to their advantage—the Catholic pulpit. In a carefully crafted and simultaneously disseminated message delivered in Sunday sermons across the tiny, God-fearing nation, greater than 50 percent of the population of the country heard firsthand about the evils of King Mateyo's plan.

Although they were far from God-fearing or devout, Shigeku and Bala headed to church on the first Sunday morning after the speech to hear the message themselves. Shigeku smiled as he heard some of his own script being read from the lectern, as if it were the word of God Himself. King Mateyo was condemning the poor people of Maleziland to sure death by starvation by canceling foreign aid. Everything in Mateyo's speech was obviously designed to keep his royal hand on the seat of power. If Mateyo truly believed in democratic elections, he should resign as the king today and declare an election. After all, the people were able to vote, which was all that was necessary in a democracy. Priests railed from their pulpits against Mateyo's declaration that the Church didn't have the power to appoint a king. To deny this right would be to deny God's own will, as God spoke to His people through His bishopric, including, ultimately, the bishop of Rome. *This is good,* thought Shigeku. *Really good!*

It was all part of Bala's master plan, to which Archbishop Sulamena had readily agreed. Pulpit lectures across the country went on further to point out the inconsistency of Mateyo's earlier speech. If Mateyo rejected the right and ability of the Church to appoint him, how could he now propose a plan that would see him act as their divinely appointed king for the next decade? Clearly, thundered voice after voice from the pulpit, this was a carefully designed plan to maintain his power in a country that had been destabilized by his reign thus far, promising his people some sort of economic pie in the sky that would never materialize. It would come as no surprise, said the men of the cloth in a collective breath, that King Mateyo would likely have to stay on as king long after the ten-year plan expired—ostensibly, of course, to be a force still leading his as-yet-unready people toward democracy.

It was a well-crafted, synchronously delivered, and powerful message. Word of mouth transmitted the message to all who didn't hear it directly, and the continuous debate and discussion that it was sure to cause throughout the land formed the perfect factual backdrop for Bala and Shigeku. The entire plan was meant to cause Malezilanders to begin to think of King Mateyo as evil, ready to commit the worst atrocity the African continent had ever witnessed through forced mass starvation, certainly at least as horrific a fate as a genocidal bullet in the side of a head. As the sermon wound down, Bala and Shigeku looked at each other and smiled. The stage was perfectly set and lit, and the curtain was drawn open for Maleziland's next champion.

Each Sunday for several weeks, the clergy lectured from a thousand pulpits. And, as planned and on schedule, on the fifth Sunday following Mateyo's "change speech," Shigeku and Bala watched from a back pew as the priest began to hint about the coming of a new champion—a human savior, so to speak—for the Malezi people. Though neither the priest before them nor any other priest mentioned the new champion by name, individual parish priests countrywide began telling the good people of their flocks that a new political figure would soon emerge—one who wanted to turn back on the taps of foreign aid and hold immediate free and democratic elections.

After the service, Shigeku turned to Bala. "Do you really think these people are going to welcome you back? You grew up as a horrifically spoiled rich little tyrant. Why would they want you back?"

Bala gave Shigeku his most sly, all-knowing smile. "Now, Shigeku, I accept your question not as an indication of your lower intelligence but purely as one founded in naivete. For all of my faults, I am the closest thing they know to the great king Mabanda himself. They associate me with a ruler they loved and worshipped like a god. They know I was raised in his presence. They will trust me and love me as they did Mabanda, especially with the guaranteed support of the Church. Next weekend, my brother Archbishop Sulamena will announce me as this country's true and rightful heir."

The cathedral was the natural backdrop for the introduction of the new political savior. After the regular Mass, Archbishop Sulamena himself would take the lectern. As the service wore down, Shigeku looked around nervously from his front-row seat. *Wow, there are nearly as many people here as for the inauguration!*

Without introduction, Archbishop Sulamena glided onto the stage. Once again, he was resplendent in his finest white silk robe, and his bishop's hat made him appear larger than life. Gold jewelry once again bedecked his body and fingers, with the solid gold, fifteen-centimeter cross front and center. The great man of God held up one hand, and the murmur in the cathedral immediately ceased. Ever the showman, Sulamena waited for half a minute, inhaled deeply, and began to speak.

"In the name of the Father, and of the Son, and of the Holy Ghost," he said. "My faithful flock, we are here today not because of the will of man but at the direct behest of our Holy Father in Rome. As you all know, the pope speaks with, and for, our God. His word is God's word. His word is your *command.*"

Wow, this man is good! thought Shigeku. *It's a good thing that* he *doesn't want to be king.*

"Only a few short weeks ago, the so-called king of Maleziland outlined a plan to 'save' Maleziland. Perhaps I am naive, but I did not realize the king was in the business of saving people. One even might say that's my job," said the holy man of God with a twinkle in his eyes, and the crowd laughed politely. "As you all know, your king, Mateyo, has expressly rejected the Church's power to appoint any ruler or politician in the country. I tell you this, my flock. That assertion is nothing short of blasphemy. In earlier times, any person making such a pronouncement would have been stoned to death . . ." The archbishop paused and smiled ever so slightly. "Not that I am suggesting such a callous demise for the boy called Mateyo. And yes, he *is* a boy. He rejects outright the power of his Lord God's right and ability to appoint a king. If so, he rejects his own authority to govern. Maleziland can only be governed by someone in God's favor. Any who purport to govern without it—be that person elected or otherwise hereditarily appointed—lack God-given legitimacy and simply have no authority to rule.

"Yet today, God shines His favor upon us. God has indeed blessed the intentions of this man," said Archbishop Sulamena as he waved his arm toward the twin doors at the entrance.

Bala emerged through the doors, and an ominous and visible wave of shock hit the crowd as he walked past them up the center aisle.

As the ruckus died down, Bala made his way to the podium and began to speak. Shigeku was immediately impressed by his eloquence.

"My brothers and my people, I trust from your warm welcome," said Bala, his voice dripping with sarcasm, "that some of you may recognize me." The former prince paused for a full thirty seconds. "I am Bala—but most of you knew me as Mandebala. Mandebala was who I was, and Bala is who I now am and who I have become. I was, of course, the crown prince of all Maleziland until six long months ago.

"I grew up soft, leading a life of privilege in an environment where I was taught that I could do anything that I pleased, have anything that I wanted, and that no matter what I did, I had the right to do it! Who among you thinks that, given such an opportunity, you would have acted any differently? You might think yourself righteous, but believe me, the temptation is great—so great that the institution of the monarchy must be abolished. No, not even the so-called People's Prince, now King Mateyo, can resist the seduction of absolute power, for as you have seen, he is going to adopt a course of action that will lead to his absolute rule for at *least* another ten years, and likely more, if we let him. We will not.

"In fact, of course, I have not one drop of royal blood in my body. I am a product of the slums and the streets like you. Since being thrown out of the royal palace like a common criminal and losing most of three fingers on my right hand in the process—" Bala paused and held up his right hand high to show the missing digits. There was only silence as the people stared. "I have been beaten nearly to death, have drunk the same water, have eaten the same food, and have slept on the same dirt floors as the rest of you."

Shigeku snickered to himself. Bala conveniently hadn't mentioned the new house.

"We are the same, but different. We have shared some experiences, but I have had experiences that you have not had. I have led a life of privilege, and I know firsthand what King Mateyo now enjoys for himself. And I can tell you this sincerely: Unless it is forcibly wrested from his golden grip, he will never let it go. In his shoes, we would all do the same.

"But I tell you, my people, that since coming back to you, I am a changed man. I see how wrong it is for one to live so well while the rest of the people of a country starve. I see how important it is to welcome the beneficence of foreign nations who want to put maize into your sacks and meat on your plates. But most of all, I see the power of the people—a people who are proud and strong, who are intelligent and ready *now* to take control over their destinies *today* and to democratically elect a responsible government to guide them into the next decade as a powerful, independent, and prosperous nation, living in Western-level affluence.

"I am the person who can guide you there. I have the formal education and the international connections to make it happen. And happen it will, for you, my people."

And with that, Bala raised his right hand, meaning to make a victory V with his fingers. In his excitement, however, he clearly forgot that he was missing the necessary digits and had extended only his pinky and thumb.

Shigeku suppressed a grin as every man and woman in the room roared approval, folding their first three fingers and saluting him back. Seizing the moment, Shigeku also thrust his hand in the air, folding three fingers, and shouted above the tumult, "Salute the *true* People's Prince!"

The crowd erupted, shouting, "People's Prince! People's Prince! People's Prince!" as one voice.

Shigeku stepped back from the crowd to observe. It had gone well—better than they could have ever expected—and Shigeku was pleased. With the Church helping to pave the way, and with Mateyo himself causing the people to feel ill at ease and fearful, the country was well on its way, with a little luck, toward change in their favor.

Bala and Shigeku hit town after town, village after village, and the former prince's message was the same. Bala railed on against the cessation of foreign aid. He called Mateyo out for failing to hold immediate elections. He pointed out that he had the education and experience to lead the country and, having gone from riches to rags, knew how the impoverished people of the country lived. He had seen the error of his and his father's ways. He accused Mateyo of being a power- and luxury-hungry interloper who ruled without authority, as he had expressly rejected the Church's ability to appoint the king.

Over the next few weeks, as Shigeku and Bala personally delivered their message across the entire country, the Church continued its support. From the pulpit, priests called Bala the true People's Prince, noting that he alone would fight for more international aid; he alone would fight for a Church-sanctioned, democratically elected ruler; and he alone would fight for the people—the same humble, ordinary people that Mateyo, comfortably ensconced in his royal palace, had long forgotten.

Shigeku marveled at the influence of the Church. With God's help, Bala had emerged from his dead "father's" shadow as a well-spoken and changed young man. And with his formal, if selective, education, he slowly won over the people throughout the country. How quickly they forgot his former role as the junior terror of the royal palace, inflicting pain, suffering, and destruction on all who crossed him!

Shigeku was pleased to see the reception Bala was receiving across the country, delivering his powerful message to all who would listen, sometimes six or seven times a day. This nation was used to, and looked for, a strong, charismatic leader. And Bala's message of "Proper change *now*, not in ten years" began to win large numbers of adherents who were wary of the new king.

The brothers' master plan was falling into place.

Mateyo and Kanzi spent long days together working on the short-term action items required to implement the first steps of their plan. Although many of his plans were terrifyingly crazy to the general population, it was perfectly apparent to the young couple that their plan was absolutely necessary in order to bring Maleziland into her own as a strong, independent, and prosperous nation.

Although he and Kanzi were focused on his economic reforms, they began to hear troubling reports about the former prince. Bala was clearly attempting to mislead the Malezi people with respect to Mateyo's intention to give up power, and he had clearly gained momentum and supporters who were very much willing to listen to his message.

Mateyo was impatient to do something to respond. "Kanzi," he said, "we need to tell the people that Bala cannot be trusted. We all know that he is simply plotting to regain power! If he is reelected, it will be the last election this country sees for decades, if ever!"

Kanzi thought a bit before responding. "Of course, but we have to be careful here. Any attempt to publicly refute Bala will add fuel to his fire. It could result in the appearance that you are trying desperately to cling to power on the throne, rather than holding on to power with the beneficial intent of executing on a long-term plan of economic growth and independence for our country."

Mateyo stared blankly ahead, deep in thought.

"That said, the support for Bala grows stronger every day, Mateyo," said Kanzi, reading his mind. The two of them had become so inseparable that they often knew each other's thoughts without speaking.

"I know, I know!" said Mateyo. "And the damned Catholic Church isn't making it any easier! Every Sunday, the message is the same—*King Mateyo cares nothing for you. King Mateyo will never hold elections. Power to the people of Maleziland. Support Bala, the true People's Prince!* It is no wonder the people are growing impatient with our plans! But in order for them to work, I must have time!"

"Perhaps, then," said Kanzi, "we need to harness the voice of the Church and use it to our advantage."

"Do you really think that is possible? Archbishop Sulamena hates me. He will do everything in his power to undermine me."

"But he is first a man of God, and he must care about his people. Perhaps we can show him that your plan is the only way that the lot of the Malezi people can be permanently improved."

"I have my doubts he is indeed a man of God first, but I agree we must try anyway," said Mateyo.

<hr>

Sulamena entered Mateyo's office, robes of silk flowing gracefully as if he floated on air like an angel. He wasn't wearing his formal hat; nevertheless, he struck an intimidating image.

Mateyo didn't offer to shake Sulamena's hand, mostly because he didn't know if it was appropriate to shake the hand of a man of God. He then offered the archbishop a seat in the opposite chair, but the cleric curtly declined. Mateyo noticed that the archbishop was intently eyeing

Mateyo's desk, which was likely worth more than the collective annual salary of the archbishop's entire staff.

The archbishop took the offensive. "Thank you, my king," he said, dripping with sarcasm, "for inviting me into your resplendent abode. Pray tell, to what do I owe the great honor?"

Mateyo took it in stride and did his best to respond without emotion. "Your Worship, I need to understand something. It was only a few months ago that I was sworn in under your authority. In the time since that day, I have been working diligently to find a way to lead my people out of the cycle of poverty and despair. I understand that you may have been offended at my remarks at the ceremony, which I now very much regret, even if I do not take them back.

"For my offense to you, I apologize. But surely you must see, as an educated man, that what I am planning, and what I am going to do, will have positive, long-term beneficial effects for the people of your flock. The Church should be supporting, rather than undermining and outright attempting to block, my efforts."

Smiling dangerously, Sulamena spoke languidly, as a man of his position would. "King Mateyo, I cannot fathom of what you speak. Surely you are not suggesting that the Church, obviously an instrument of God and not the state, actually has been playing a role in shaping the will of the people, are you? Such an act would be beneath the Church. We are, of course, officially neutral in every country in which we spread God's words of redemption and salvation. Our only mission is to save souls and provide humanitarian assistance and relief to God's children."

Mateyo leapt out of his chair and leaned over his desk as far as gravity and physics would permit. "Cut the crap, Sulamena," he said, unleashing his tirade only centimeters from the archbishop's face. "I might be new at this game, but there's no fucking way that the same message could be preached from every pulpit in this country, simultaneously, without some form of coordination from *you*! No other 'man of God' is in a position to coordinate and dictate that such a message be delivered. And it is exactly the same message, everywhere, in every church, across the entire country! No, I know where this message has come from, and I demand, for the sake of your people, that it stop immediately!"

The gloves were off, Mateyo knew.

"Boy, you are but a pawn in a game played at levels that your prepubescent brain cannot even comprehend!" the archbishop spat out. "When the current pope dies—an event, as yet unknown to the general public, that has an extremely high degree of probability of occurring within the next year—I will become the pope. I will become, in effect, the world's most wealthy man, and most certainly one of its most powerful.

"Yes, my star has been rising for years, and it continues to rise, much on the strength of my track record and ability to deliver souls to the salvation of Christ. I'm sure you're not aware of this, but it is, indeed, fact. Maleziland has the highest percentage of declared and practicing Catholics in the world, currently well over 75 percent!"

"So this is about you becoming pope? What does that have to do with the price of tea in Britain?" asked Mateyo.

Sulamena ignored Mateyo. "Is it because I am a particularly good bishop? Is it because my clergy are that much better than their peers in other countries around the world? No. It is because Malezilanders are among the poorest fucking people on the face of the earth. These dregs of the earth are so poor that the Church, at least until you came along, offered them their only hope for a better life—in death. Oh yes, king boy, your plan indeed could work. In fact, it could turn Maleziland into the poster child of developing nations for the entire global community—but not on *my* fucking watch, and *not* at the expense of my journey toward the Vatican."

And with that, Sulamena spun on his heel, robes flowing, and strode toward the massive double doors. He then paused, turned, and raised his arm and hand in the "People's Prince's" thumb-and-pinky victory salute.

Mateyo sighed. One down and one to go. Hopefully his next meeting went better.

◆

Mateyo was beginning to get a clearer picture of the conspiratorial nature of the opposition to his plan. He'd presumed that the Church and Bala were operating independently of each other, but he was now beginning to suspect otherwise. Perhaps Shigeku would be able to help him understand what was happening. Indeed, Shigeku might even be willing and able to convince Bala that Mateyo's plan had a realistic chance of succeeding and to back off his constant public grandstanding against him.

Mateyo was worried sick about the growing opposition to his reforms. His government ministry advisors were telling him that Bala was inciting tremendous debate across the country, and wherever there was debate, it was quite a simple conclusion that he had won some converts to take up his side of the discussion. Mateyo knew that his advisors were painting a more positive picture than the actual reality and that Bala, with his efforts being actively supported and promoted by the Church, had managed to gain at least some level of widespread public support.

Although in recent weeks Shigeku was never seen in public with Bala, Mateyo knew he was still very much a presence. And Mateyo felt very much betrayed.

Shigeku, his father figure.

Shigeku, his brother in every sense other than blood.

Shigeku, his mentor.

Why could Shigeku not see what Mateyo was trying to do? Perhaps he simply didn't understand. Everything that Bala was doing threatened to undermine his efforts to effect real, meaningful, long-term change. And since Shigeku and Bala lived together and were in fact blood brothers, he must, at best, know and condone what Bala was doing. At worst, he was part of it. Perhaps, with Mateyo's explanation and his promise that he wasn't simply desperately trying to hold on to the throne, Shigeku could be convinced to call off Bala, if only for the good of the Malezi people.

Mateyo called the captain of his royal guard into his den and asked him to escort Shigeku to him. "Shall we use force, King, if he refuses to come?" the captain asked.

"Force? Are you kidding? Shigeku would never refuse to come if I asked him to meet with me. He is my brother." Mateyo's voice dropped. "Or at least he was for fourteen years." He thought for a moment. Had Shigeku turned against him? Would he betray him? "No, you are not authorized to use force."

"Very well," said the captain, looking not at all certain.

Several hours later, the captain returned, without Shigeku. "Were you unable to find him?" asked Mateyo, incredulously and slightly hopefully.

"No, sir, we found him. He refused to come."

Mateyo sat in his chair, motionless. *Refused?*

"Sir?" asked the captain, hoping for some direction or even a dismissal.

"Bring him to me—by whatever means necessary," came the monotone and flat reply.

When Mateyo's royal guard next returned, they had Shigeku in handcuffs. He was bleeding from one nostril, with angry welts and puffiness around his eyes. The king's guard, four in number, had not gone unscathed, with all but the captain bearing ripped and stained clothing and their own fair share of battle wounds, reflecting Shigeku's wiry strength and combat training.

"Unlock those cuffs immediately!" roared Mateyo. "I said bring him in, you idiots, not beat him senseless! What is wrong with you?"

"Sire, are you sure? He is dangerous—"

"He's my brother, you clowns!" Mateyo said. "Now leave us!"

"But, King—"

"Leave us NOW!"

And with that, the captain uncuffed Shigeku, and the four men fled the den.

"So, Mateyo, my *king* . . . ," Shigeku hissed from bloodied lips, "what could I have possibly done so that you needed to arrest me like a common criminal?"

"I'm sorry, but I needed to speak with you! And when they came back to me empty-handed the first time, I couldn't believe that you, my brother, wouldn't come. Why did you refuse my request?"

Smirking from one corner of his mouth, Shigeku replied flatly, "I guess I was busy."

Mateyo practically burst at his seams. "Busy? BUSY? Busy inciting the Malezi people against me, busy running the 'Bala Show,' busy doing anything but coming to the aid of your brother, the king, when he asks for your help?"

"We all have our priorities," stated Shigeku. "Apparently yours and mine are not the same."

"And what would you have me do?" asked Mateyo. "Give power to that son of a tyrant Bala? He would run this country into the ground worse than his father did, and it can't possibly get much worse than the worst on earth. Though I imagine he could find a way to make the poor even poorer and himself richer. No, I can't do that."

"Then let the people decide who should be king, or at least leader, of this country you claim to love so much," replied Shigeku.

Mateyo noticed an intensity and passion burning in Shigeku's eyes, and in a moment of epiphany, he recognized it as a lusting hunger for power. It took Mateyo aback, for he had never seen this look in Shigeku's eyes before, and it frightened him. It reminded him of the lust he had seen in Kanzi's eyes the first night that she came to him—and every night since—but different somehow. It was lust, but with extreme malice underlying it, not the underlying love that he saw when Kanzi wanted him. No, this was a lust of another sort, and Mateyo recognized it, at that instant, for the danger it presented. He called for his guard to escort Shigeku out.

"I'm sorry, Shigeku. I love you as a brother, and I always will."

Shigeku smirked again as the guard led him away.

And I hope it will not be my undoing, Mateyo thought.

CHAPTER 22

Across the eastern border of Maleziland, an elite force of the Zambwanan military, accompanied by their former combatant Shigeku, was on the move. It had taken some time—many months—for the Zambwanans to lick their wounds and rebuild a fighting force of any capability, but like a hyena pack sensing weakness in its prey, the scent of a kill brought many a predator forth. The mistakes of the previous military conflict would not, however, be repeated this time. A highly focused, highly mobile, and well-trained force of relatively small numbers would be used to strike deep, hard, and effectively into the heart of a confused and disorganized Malezi military that, for the first time in forty years, was looking more inwardly than outwardly.

When Shigeku had crossed the border and presented his plan to General Zumba, the Zambwanans had quickly understood both its merit and high probability of success. Within days, it had the support of the political overlords of the country and was made operational with haste.

The plan was quite simple and was entirely made possible by the uncertainty and confusion that King Mateyo had created internally within his country. Shigeku, with the help of Malezi sympathizers, had set up a series of hidden resupply depots, consisting primarily of fuel and water, for the use of the invading force along three alternative routes to the capital city. If the primary route depots were discovered or otherwise defended, the secondary and tertiary depots were available as backups. The men and equipment would continue toward the capital at maximum speed, stopping only to replenish their supplies.

Although Shigeku and the Zambwanans contemplated that it was inevitable the force would be spotted and reported at some point in time, the Zambwanan military command hoped that by the time the Malezi military was called into action, and with the help of a little bit of subterfuge, the Malezis would be too disorganized to coordinate an effective defense. The plan called for the seizure of the military headquarters; the Ministry of Communication, with its television and radio broadcast facilities; and finally the royal palace and King Mateyo.

The difference between success and failure in special military operations can often be measured in seconds and minutes. Shigeku and the Zambwanans knew that anything that could buy a few of these units of time could make that difference. In an attempt to delay the report of their attack, the Zambwanan military painted their RAVs (Rapid Attack Vehicles) in Malezi armed forces colors. All troops were issued genuine Maleziland military fatigues, purchased from the same factory in China, not surprisingly, where the Malezis purchased their own military clothing. The bribe had been expensive, due in part to the strength of the Yuan over any of its African counterpart currencies, but the Zambwanans hoped and expected that it would be worth every Zambo spent. As such, a casual observer would think the Malezi military was simply running yet another preparedness exercise.

On a starlit night exactly six months after the death of King Mabanda, the elite Zambwanan military unit blitzed the Malezi border, undetected and unchallenged.

Shigeku was pleased. *My plan is off to a good start.*

It seemed like an ordinary day at the Malezi Ministry of Defense, but that would imminently and drastically change. As the morning's intelligence reports came in, the duty general (the commanding general in charge for the day) skimmed through the printed pieces over a cup of Rwanda's finest. "Damn fine coffee," Moto mused to himself, partly aloud. "Too bad the rest of the country's output is not worth the price of invading." He chuckled at his private, generals'-level joke. He wasn't scheduled to be on duty this day, but he had swapped weekend daylight duty with one of his peers in order to get consecutive weekend days off a couple of months hence.

Moto flipped through the daily reports—a throwback to the Mabanda era of Big Brother–like observation of potential opposition to his regime. They seemed, collectively, to be painting a picture of a general population that was both uneasy and unsettled. Minor skirmishes, fights, and small-scale demonstrations were becoming more and more the norm throughout the country. It seemed obvious to Moto that the nation's people were growing increasingly uneasy with King Mateyo's rule, particularly as the message being delivered by the "People's Prince" Bala began to hit home with a burgeoning percentage of the population.

Chuckling silently, General Moto smiled inwardly at this news. *How quickly the population forgets who, and what, Mandebala was,* thought Moto. For fun, Moto practiced the thumb-and-pinky salute that Bala's supporters had adopted. "Ridiculous," he said aloud to no one.

He flipped through a cryptic report at the bottom of the daily reports, rated "Low" both on "Actionability" and "Reliability," regarding the suspected sighting of a foreign military force dressed as Malezi troops with vehicles painted in the fashion of the Malezi army 135 kilometers outside of Lalonga. There were in fact regular, random Malezi troop patrols around Lalonga, and as a result there were frequent reports of military "incursions." He was about to file the report in the trash bin when one small factoid in the report seemed to catch his eye, causing his military aide—always present—to focus in on his general. Leaping from his seat and sending scalding hot java flowing over his desk and lap, Moto thunderously roared, "Code 99! Code 99!"

The Malezi army didn't have any RAVs. The report, filed by a retired Malezi military veteran, clearly stated that there were RAVs painted in Malezi military colors. The country had been invaded. The reported sighting was at 6:30 a.m., and it was now 8:40 a.m. The enemy was literally banging at the gate, and it was highly unlikely that anything could be done about it.

Code 99 was the Malezi military's highest alert level, used only in the direst of emergencies. Its use ordered all hands to active duty and announced that an attack was imminent. Every general was instantly alerted, as were the king and the heads of government ministries. However, the Malezi military was structured in an internationally typical fashion, with a standing active-duty "regular" force, together with a larger body of lesser-trained part-time soldier reservists, or militia, available to be called up on forty-eight hours' notice.

The standing army typically saw duty spread out across the country, with more active duty and deployments closer to the borders when the threat from Zambwana was determined to be high—a state it had not been since the routing of its primary fighting force only a few months prior. None of the Malezi military was organized or trained to be rapidly scrambled and deployed—none, that is, other than General Moto's own Red Daggers.

Moto tried his best not to look concerned. It was going to be tight. As the invading force progressed toward the capital, multiple detailed reports relating to the invasion force were now pouring in, including one from a half-dead survivor from a routine military patrol that had the misfortune to be in the direct path of the Zambwanan force. As the patrolman called in the details of the attack, loud shots rang out, and his report abruptly stopped, presumably as he died. The enemy was less than twenty-five kilometers away, and only a handful of Mpini Ekundu had thus far arrived at Defense Headquarters, their muster point in case of imminent attack.

⁂

Chumba rousted Mateyo from a deep sleep at 8:41 a.m. Mateyo was quite annoyed by the disturbance and scrambled to pull the bedding over Kanzi's naked body.

"Chumba! What on earth?"

"King Mateyo, General Moto has issued a Code 99. Maleziland is under attack!"

"Under *attack*? How is that *possible*?" asked Mateyo.

"I don't have the details. General Moto is on Secure 1 in your office."

Mateyo was already out the doors of his bedroom, donning his robe as he shot down the hallway. It was 8:43 a.m. when he picked up Moto's call.

"General Moto! What is the situation? How can we be under attack? By whom? Is our army engaging?"

"King Mateyo," said the general as calmly as he could, "I'll quickly answer as many questions as I can, after which I must get back to the defense of our country. A small Zambwanan attack force has infiltrated our borders and has been reported to be en route to the capital. We do not yet know their number, but they are in vehicles painted as Malezi military vehicles and are also wearing Malezi military uniforms. We do not know their objectives as of yet, but primary targets are most likely to be you, the military headquarters, and the Ministry of Communication."

Mateyo could not bite his tongue any longer. "*Again*, General, how are we responding to the attack?"

"Sir, we are scrambling to put together as many active troops as we can. Local Red Daggers are arriving now. With a little bit of luck, and God's blessings, we may have enough men to counter the threat of these curs."

Mateyo nodded, even though he was on a call without video. "Please keep me informed, General Moto."

"Oh, I will, my king," said the general. And with that, Secure 1 went dead.

Mateyo looked up to see Kanzi standing in his office. He had no idea how long she had been there.

Mateyo ordered Chumba to hail his palace guards, but he knew that without significant help from outside forces, they would be of minimal deterrence once the Zambwanan army came calling. The palace had never faced any sort of military threat before, and as such its defenses were quite minimal. Mateyo knew that his only hope resided in the Red Daggers and perhaps some of his standing army—and in getting them to the palace quickly!

He began dialing each of his generals' cell phones to call them into action. To his utter shock and extreme dismay, not one of the seven remaining generals picked up! Never in his short reign had a single person ever not picked up one of his calls, yet now Mateyo couldn't reach any of his senior military men. It was as if they had vanished.

"Kanzi," said Mateyo, "you should leave the palace. I'll send for one of my cars, and you can take half the royal guards who are left. I'm sure the royal guards will probably be grateful for the opportunity to leave the palace on an official assignment and perhaps have their lives spared. With any luck, you'll be able to make it across the South African border and from there get to Europe somehow.

"Here. Take this," said Mateyo as he handed her a small black velvet satchel, with its silken black drawstring tightly cinched.

Kanzi looked perplexed. "What is this?" she said.

"Diamonds," stated Mateyo matter-of-factly. "Their value will be more than enough to get you across the border, on a flight to Europe, and into any university your heart should desire. I know that my father has Swiss bankers—I mean, I have Swiss bankers—who can help you."

"Don't be foolish," said Kanzi. "I'm not going anywhere without you. Why don't we *both l*eave—same plan—and go to Europe together, where we can live happily ever after without this treachery always at our gate?"

Mateyo hung his head. "I cannot go. The future of my people is at stake here. I would rather die trying to save their lives than save my own. But you do not have any duty to your country. *You* were not born into this. I was. There is a reason that I was put into the position of power that I now hold. I have a destiny, and that destiny cannot be fulfilled if I pick up and run."

"And why not?" said Kanzi. "The history books are filled with examples of regimes that were toppled by a leader in exile. Why can't we continue to fight from abroad—*alive*—rather than face certain death by trying to fight one last battle against impossible odds?"

Mateyo's face fell; he knew that he wasn't going to convince her to leave, and he knew that he had no choice but to stay. "But, Kanzi . . . my sweetheart . . . you *must* go. It is not safe for you here. If I am executed, you will be as well. Leave . . . now!"

"Mateyo, you might be 'king' to the rest of the country, but you can't order me to leave without you! I simply will not. Come with me."

With a sigh, Mateyo exhaled. "I cannot leave. I have a duty to lead my people out of this cycle of poverty. Someone must reform the government. It truly is my destiny. Perhaps, however, it is *our* destiny, as it was you who helped to show me the ways it can be done. Maybe it is only appropriate that the two of us face this challenge together."

Kanzi threw her arms around his neck and hugged him tightly, as if it might be their last embrace. "If there's a way to get through this, my love, we will—together."

The Zambwanan force reached the Ministry of Defense headquarters at 9:15 a.m. Five minutes later, General Zumba, Shigeku, and the entire Zambwanan military task force—some 2,500 men strong with seventy-five medium-armored and heavily armed RAVs—had rumbled into the square facing the building without a shot being fired. The Zambwanan force trained every weapon they had on the building and waited. After a minute went by, General Zumba picked up a megaphone to speak.

"Brothers, you have nothing to fear from us. As you can see, clearly we are Malezi soldiers that have come here on a mission of peace and fellowship." His troops roared with laughter at his joke. It was, apparently, easy to laugh when you had RPGs and light tanks on your side.

"I ask you to send out your commanding officer so we might avoid the bloodshed that will become inevitable as of precisely fifteen minutes from this point. I will not speak again, other than to whomever you send to us to plead for your lives."

Mateyo took the next report in his situation room, together with Kanzi and his loyal servant Chumba. This time they had video feed from the ministry situation room, although quickly Mateyo wished they did not. Moto was sweating profusely and appeared very distraught.

"My king," the general said, "only forty-seven Malezi Red Daggers have arrived. To a man, they are ready to die, but they are outgunned, outmanned, and completely without hope of organized, effective resistance. Their willingness to face certain death is exemplary. Each and every Mpini Ekundu has taken up defensive firing positions throughout the building."

"General Moto, what is your plan? Surely you cannot hold on to the headquarters with only forty-seven men," said Mateyo.

"That's forty-seven *excellent* men, my king. But indeed you are correct. We cannot. So, with your permission, I'd like to go talk to their general. After all, he and I have met before, as you'll likely recall. I see no alternative but to speak with this coward of a general who has not yet had the balls to walk up these steps to speak with me."

"But, General, you can't walk out there, exposed and without your Red Daggers as a shield! Surely they'll cut you down the moment that you step out the door!"

"Then either way I am a dead man—we all are, if we fight. This way, I will try to bargain with the cur."

⚬ ◆ ⚬

Shigeku watched in awe from the side of the square as Moto flung open the front doors of the grand building, looking proud and determined. Head held high, Moto marched down the several dozen steps leading from the entrance and then proceeded to close the one hundred or so meters across the parade square.

As Moto strode closer and closer to the Zambwanan soldiers in their Malezi kit, Shigeku watched as the Zambwanan force parted and melted away, exposing the one man among them who was not wearing Malezi combat gear—for he had replaced it with his official, gold-brocaded general's uniform of the Zambwanan armed forces.

Shigeku was close enough to see a flash of recognition light up General Moto's face.

"Zumba!" boomed Moto. "What fool put you in charge? After your last embarrassment on Malezi soil, I would have thought that you would never return, much less in a command position!"

"Ah, Moto—or I guess it's 'General Moto' now—my most sincere apologies. I learned much on our last little foray into what will soon be a Zambwanan protectorate."

"Indeed you did, my friend, indeed you did."

And with that, the two generals embraced, hugging each other mightily. Each then put one grizzled hand on General Zumba's sidearm—an AK-47, of course—and jointly raised it above their heads to the raucous cheering of the Zambwanan troops and the sheer and utter amazement, shock, and disbelief of the Mpini Ekundu within the ministry building.

— ◆ —

"No! No, no, no!" said Mateyo. One of the more senior Mpini Ekundu remaining in the military headquarters had reported the duplicity in the square. Somehow the Zambwanans had schemed with General Moto to effect a coup of sorts. As the Red Daggers within the building watched, more and more Mpini Ekundu arrived at the square and were faced with a choice.

"They're shooting Red Daggers who refuse to join!" reported the lieutenant. "They're piling the bodies of those who won't join them on the landing at the top of the stairs leading into the building!"

The last report Mateyo received by phone from the Defense Ministry headquarters estimated that the marauding force, as augmented by the elite ranks of Moto's Red Daggers, now numbered well over four thousand. It was a small but formidable force, especially given the fact that it was already within the heart of the country. With no further calls forthcoming, Mateyo presumed his source within the Defense Ministry to be dead—or worse, part of the enemy force too.

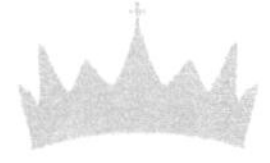

CHAPTER 23

Shigeku joined Moto and Zumba in the center of the square outside the Ministry of Defense. All three embraced, pleased with themselves. The Ministry of Communications had since fallen to a force of 250 men, without a single bullet having been fired. Shigeku turned to Moto and Zumba and said, "Perhaps it is time to pay a state visit to the royal palace, my friends. Have our distinguished guests arrived?"

"Indeed they have," said General Moto. "I have arranged for a military escort for the cars. No need to make it too large, but better safe than sorry. Do you not agree, Zumba?"

"Absolutely, Moto, please make the arrangements. We will meet on the front steps in ten minutes."

Shortly after noon, Mateyo spotted the single-file column of vehicles racing up the royal promenade at over one hundred kilometers an hour. The parade was led by a single RAV, which looked particularly menacing and overpowering, followed by two black Range Rovers and a second

RAV. Mateyo foolishly expected them to slow down at the gate and request permission to enter, but instead, the procession demolished the gatehouse and plowed through the barrier, pausing only slightly as the lead vehicle's wheels bumped over the now lifeless bodies of the two royal guards who had attempted in vain to stop the convoy.

Looking down from the window in his den, Mateyo blinked, astonished. Clearly, the insurrectionists were sending a message: They were ruthless and not afraid to show it by spilling blood.

Each RAV stopped on either side of the two Range Rovers, their main cannons pointing straight at the palace's main doors. A driver, dressed in the full gear of the Red Dagger unit, opened the back door of one of the Range Rovers. Generals Zumba and Moto climbed out of the back seat.

Moto! Mateyo had been very disappointed to learn of Moto's complicity in the event and realized at once that he hadn't done enough to secure the loyalty of the military and its leadership. His father would never have allowed the events of the day to occur.

His attention then turned toward the second black Range Rover, and he collapsed into a chair when he saw Shigeku exiting the vehicle.

"No," he whispered, "it cannot be."

And then Bala exited the vehicle, followed by Archbishop Sulamena. Mateyo's head began spinning wildly, and of course, it all began to make sense. The sermons from the pulpit; the cross-country stumping; the military invasion, unchecked and unarrested—all came together with this very objective in mind. That much was obvious to Mateyo—but his "brother" Shigeku? What role could he have to play here? Could he really be united against him with these traitorous men?

Perhaps Shigeku has come as some form of intermediary, a peace broker of sorts, to help reach some form of accommodation among us all? Of course, that had to be it. Shigeku was close to the power-hungry Bala—closer than anyone—and Shigeku knew Mateyo well, so he had probably come along as a mediator. Perhaps there was a way after all to negotiate a deal with the leaders of this coup and save the future of his country and people.

Mateyo hoped Shigeku was planning to help him find it.

With a renewed sense of optimism, and one last quick glance out the window, Mateyo headed toward the Grand Reception Hall, where his "guests" would arrive.

Thankfully, none of them seemed to be armed.

At that moment, Mateyo's cell phone began to vibrate.

A satellite call was coming through, and Mateyo's heart leapt. He answered, and General Nkamba, commander of Maleziland's Second Mechanized Division, spoke quietly and quickly.

"Sorry to disturb you, King Mateyo," he began, as if he needed to apologize for the most welcome intrusion ever, "but my entire division, loyal, at least in theory, to the crown, is amassed behind the back wall of the palace grounds. My scouts observed your guests and their puny escort arrive. They will be mere flies for us to swat. We number eight thousand men, with twenty-five tanks and mechanized transportation for all troops. I think, however, that you and I must come to some understanding, my king, before I am about to commit my men to battle."

"Understanding?" said Mateyo, gasping. "What do you mean? I am your king, and your country needs you to defend me!"

As Mateyo descended the enormous staircase into the reception hall, his guests opened the doors without knocking. Mateyo paused mid-step.

"There's not much time, General!" Mateyo said. "What is it you want?"

Mateyo could sense the man's sardonic grin on the other end of the phone. "Tut-tut, my king. I will become your minister of defense and your most senior military general. You will build me a palace that will be second only to yours in size and comfort, and I will be your number two in every way. Is that clear?"

Bastard. "And you? Will you support my reforms, even if that means your military control becomes subject to the will of the people in a free election ten years from now?" pushed back Mateyo urgently.

"I hardly think that you are in a position to make such demands," the general said with a laugh. "But considering that the likelihood of free elections in Maleziland is remote, then yes, I agree."

"Thank you!" said Mateyo, beaming. "Now . . . what are you going to do?"

"In what room will you receive your guests?" asked General Nkamba.

"Excuse me?" said Mateyo. "Are you really questioning me on protocol, General?"

Nkamba sighed. "Good King Mateyo, I suggest that you receive them in your den and that you then position yourself at least fifteen meters from the outside wall. When your guests have arrived and you are in place, dial this number. Let it ring once, hang up, and hit the ground."

⚜

Mateyo continued his descent down the staircase as the entire cabal filed in. No hands were shaken, no pleasantries exchanged, and for a tortuously long moment, awkward silence hung in the air.

"Come with me to my den where it is more private," Mateyo said, turning on his heel. The men followed. It was the first time for Sulamena in this part of the palace, and as Mateyo glanced over his shoulder, he saw the archbishop's eyes flitting enviously over various art pieces as they walked through the corridor to the den.

As he swung open the towering doors to the den, Mateyo let out a gasp. Kanzi stood in the room near a cluster of chairs, smiling at the men as if she were a socialite hostess greeting acquaintances for the thousandth time. She looked radiant, as always.

Mateyo noticed from the corner of his eye that even the archbishop—or perhaps especially the archbishop—seemed flustered at the sight of such a beautiful woman. Mateyo was in a bind. He couldn't protest her presence, for to do so would signal his affection for her. And if he gruffly ordered her out as if she were intruding, he knew she wouldn't leave. Mateyo decided it would be best for him to treat Kanzi as an unimportant servant girl who happened to be in the den busy with her chores. To do otherwise would only endanger her.

Everyone sat down, and Mateyo decided to be silent to see who spoke first, hoping it would tell him who among them considered himself in charge. It did not surprise Mateyo when Bala spoke up.

"Mateyo," Bala started, conspicuously and intentionally not using the word *king* and pausing for dramatic effect while he surveyed the room, as if making sure nothing had been changed in "his" palace, "your illegitimate reign is over."

Clearly, Bala intended to provoke him, but Mateyo was expecting this. With a crooked smirk, Mateyo said, "How amusing that you, above all people, would use the word *illegitimate,* Bala. I would have thought that you would be sympathetic to those who were illegitimately in positions of power. What makes my claim to power suddenly illegitimate? Clearly, I have been proven to be the fruit of my father's loins, a genetic ancestry that I resented at first but have come to view as my destiny. I believe that I can truly help alleviate the suffering and torment of the Malezi people."

Bala stood, sauntered over to Mateyo's chair, and slapped him hard across the face. Kanzi stifled a scream as Mateyo's head jerked backward.

"Your genetic makeup does nothing for you now, does it?" asked Bala, pressing his face into Mateyo's. "In fact, it may very well be your downfall. We all know very well what happens to the lion cubs born to the outgoing pride king once he loses to the new pride king."

"Don't fear death, Mateyo," said Archbishop Sulamena, sneering. "At least you won't have to summon a priest for last rites—I can do that myself . . . for a small fee, of course! Your legitimacy to rule was made impossible in the eyes of God and His Church when you rejected *my divine right* to anoint a new king. What you did that day was irresponsible and did much to undermine the stability in this country.

"Besides," the archbishop continued, the sneer returning to his face, "God's Church has already chosen the next divine-right ruler to lead his flock in Maleziland. If Bala will accept, I will swear him in privately at this moment, and we can do it all again for show at some future date . . . unless there are any objections." Sulamena made a grand show of theatrically looking around the room.

This was all happening too quickly for Mateyo.

"General Moto, by what treachery is the Zambwanan general by your side? What have you done?"

The commander of the Red Daggers smiled. "It was but a small price to pay. Maleziland is to become a protectorate of Zambwana. We will still be an independent country, with our own military and government structure, but our common people will be united as allies. Of course, I will lead Maleziland's armed forces."

Desperately, Mateyo turned to his brother. "Shigeku! Please explain to these men what Bala is truly like, what damage he would do to our country and its people! All Bala cares about is abusing privilege to suit his own interest! There's no way he means to ever hold elections, effect economic reform, or do anything to help his country or his people. This is all about power!"

Shigeku's face once again slowly broadened into his trademark full smile. "Indeed, it is about power, Mateyo. Indeed, it is."

And with that, Shigeku pulled out his assegai from the small of his back under his shirt and strode menacingly toward Mateyo with the traditional hunting knife. Mateyo reached deep into his pocket and pulled out his own weapon—a cell phone. He pushed a button, waited, pushed another button, and then fell to the floor, dragging Kanzi down with him.

"That is wise, Mateyo," said Shigeku, looming over him and Kanzi. "Once you accept your fate, it is easier for your soul to travel to the next world."

Shigeku raised the blade high and swung, and Mateyo's entire world went black.

A faint light began to filter through Mateyo's eyes. *Nkamba has come through!* A volley of shells from the first row of six tanks of the Malezi Second Mechanized Division had obliterated the walls of the den. As the dust and smoke began to clear, the occupants of the room began to recover from the trauma and shock they had suffered just in time to see tanks streaming in through the rubble. All but Mateyo appeared to be completely confused and baffled to see the Second Division's tanks rolling in, followed by heavily armed combat troops with AK-47s at the ready.

"Nkamba!" shouted Moto in his booming, thunderous voice. "By what treachery and deception have you managed to show up here? I order you to stand down immediately!"

"Tut-tut, Moto, simply because you are duty general today does not mean you have the right to command your more senior generals," said Nkamba calmly. "I also suspect that your small escort, despite being your own Mpini Ekundu, have laid down their arms in the face of eight thousand men of my heavily armored division, ready to move against the balance of your force."

"Eigh . . . eight thousand? B . . . bu . . . but how?"

"Tut-tut, Moto," said Nkamba again, with more than a touch of annoying condescension. "Despite being a rising star, you have much to learn. We truly valued your addition to the general's staff, and your

Mpini Ekundu are the class of the African continent. However, your political skills are indeed quite lacking. I and the other generals began noticing that you were the initiator of virtually all conversations—'general-speak,' as we like to call it—theorizing about whether or not we, as a military institution, should be supporting Mateyo or Bala."

Mateyo watched as Moto's face darkened and looked as if it would explode. Clearly, Nkamba had completely surprised him and foiled his heretofore flawless plan.

"Though I did not share my thoughts with the others, I became convinced that at some point in time, in some way, frustrated with your inability to effect a 'bloodless coup' by converting more generals to your cause, you would attempt to seize control of strategic internal targets with your Red Daggers. I have to admit, I didn't see the Zambwanans coming, and their numbers will make it a fairer fight than I expected, but the Zambwanans are *not* Mpini Ekundu, you have *not* trained together, and your resupply efforts have *not* yet been organized. As such, I see it as a fight that my troops will win, if it comes down to battle."

"But how did you get here? How did you manage to coordinate your troops?" said Moto, shaking his head in disbelief as if it couldn't be possible.

Nkamba grinned, seemingly happy to share his story and pat himself on the back in the process, especially in front of Mateyo. "Once I became convinced that you would at some point in time make an attempt against your government and King Mateyo," he said, nodding toward Mateyo and Kanzi, who were both dusting themselves off and listening intently, "I adopted measures designed to defend this palace, knowing that it would eventually be one of your military targets. We cleared the foliage and trees in the jungle on the far side of the palace walls. After years of seeing this happen time and time again, people probably just presumed it was yet another expansion of the royal palace's extensive grounds."

Impressive! thought Mateyo.

"I also adopted a special emergency protocol for my troops, handing each sub-commander a new micro–sat phone and making each one responsible for mustering his platoon at this new site within sixty minutes of my own Code 99 call. And if you bothered to check the logs, and I'm sure you did, this morning you took over from *me* as duty general. I had the report for over two hours before your weary eyes set upon it.

"Quickly, of course, I understood its importance and how it related to the plan I suspected you of trying to implement. I issued my divisional Code 99, put the report at the bottom of the New Reports folder, and signed off for the day. Suspecting that I would be seeing you later, I left the headquarters and had a nap while my troops came together—here, rather than at the Ministry of Defense, obviously your first target." General Nkamba looked around the room, obviously pleased with himself and relishing the moment he had taken to share his military prowess with all gathered on this most unlikely of stages.

"But why support Mateyo? You can still fall in line with our plan!" suggested Moto, hopefully.

"Because he is loyal to his king and country!" Mateyo nearly shouted.

Nkamba continued, ignoring the boy's outburst. "And be second-in-command to you, Moto? No, I would have to be forced into it, and right now I most certainly like my odds. Not only do I have numerical superiority and heavy armor on my side, I also have you and Zumba as my prisoners, together with, of course, your purported 'president'! We have surprise on our side now, as your troops think the battle is already won. No, Moto, I adopted the course of action that would most benefit *me*. My most sincere apologies."

The other members of the original party began stirring and shaking the rubble from their clothes, save for Archbishop Sulamena. The would-be pope's wide eyes remained open in an unblinking death stare, ironically with a rough cross-shaped piece of metal shrapnel—perhaps from a windowpane that had been turned into a jagged, molten projectile—wedged between his shoulder blades and spine, piercing and stopping His Holiness's heart. His campaign to become the next pope had taken a serious turn for the worse.

Mateyo noticed that Shigeku and Bala were also stirring, still very much alive but dazed and disoriented. The blast had leveled Shigeku near Mateyo and Kanzi.

The tense scene was interrupted by the loud sound of automatic weapon fire and RPG explosions. Suicidally, it appeared, the small protective detail of Mpini Ekundu were going to fight the Second Mechanized to the death.

Shigeku leapt to his feet and drove his assegai between Mateyo's lower ribs, plunging upward toward and deep into his brother's heart. Kanzi screamed and rushed to Mateyo's side. Mateyo felt nothing and was astonished to see the blood gushing from an open wound. He was even more astounded when his legs ceased to function and buckled under his weight.

My brother . . .

Mateyo registered the shock and fear in Kanzi's eyes and said to her, "It's okay, Kanzi. Everything's going to be okay."

CHAPTER 24

Shigeku watched with triumph as Bala was proclaimed head of state in an improvised ceremony attended by Archbishop Sulamena's second-in-command, deliberately crafted to be similar to that of the swearing in of a divine-right regent. Bala accepted the office graciously, with a pledge to the people of free, unfettered elections within six months.

With Mateyo dead on the floor of the royal palace and no logical ruler or regent to support, Generals Moto and Nkamba quickly negotiated a deal that would see Moto and Nkamba as joint commanders in chief of the Malezi armed forces. Although the coup was relatively bloodless, some of that which had been spilled was royal.

Shigeku and Bala had fed Mateyo's body to the crocodiles above a dam near the palace. The crocs were particularly well fed and were trained to recognize when food was coming their way, almost as hungry teenagers come quickly to the sounding of a dinner bell. As they watched the crocodiles close in and drag Mateyo's body under the surface, the water violently frothing around them, Shigeku had felt . . . nothing.

With Shigeku by his side, once again Bala was happily ensconced in the royal palace, there with the firm support of the people, the Church, and the entire military, albeit with the military presence of Maleziland's new sister country, Zambwana, forming an inconvenient impediment to his absolute power.

In a press release after the coup, President Bala vowed to effect democratic reform. This was, of course, popular with the West, and as quickly as Mateyo had turned off the taps of foreign aid, it was pouring back into the country as water flows over Victoria Falls in the rainy season. Civilized Western do-gooders wanted to be seen supporting the country's march toward democracy and Westernization. A legendary rock band even announced a worldwide tour in support of the poor, starving people of Maleziland. Construction resumed on the royal palace's new pool house in earnest.

Shigeku knew that Bala's first steps as leader were vitally important—to secure his position and squelch, stomp, and eradicate all opposition. Anyone seen to be opposing him in any way, shape, or form was executed publicly and violently.

Foreign news reporters were quickly expelled from the country. Bala, of course, controlled the state-owned media apparatuses, and the rest of the world either knew nothing of or conveniently ignored the "unconfirmed reports" about the violence and corruption leaking out of the little country.

King Mabanda had taught Bala well.

— ◆ —

One evening, Shigeku and Bala brought yet another young girl to their room. Hungrily, Bala tore off her clothes and tossed her onto the sofa. Shigeku protested. "Why do *you* always get to go first? I hate being second!"

"Fuck, Shigeku," said Bala, "why can't you ever figure this out? The president always comes first. And I am the president."

Bala heard a faint metallic sliding noise behind him and a few quiet words from the man who was his true brother and principal advisor.

"Not anymore you aren't," came the soft reply from Shigeku.

The gunshot sprayed gray, sticky brain matter from the exit wound in Bala's forehead all over the naked girl. Bala crumpled on top of her, lifeless. The girl squealed and ran naked from the room.

General Moto then strode through the doors into the den.

Shigeku turned to the general and smiled. The men gave each other great bear hugs, poured a couple of single malt scotches, fired up enormous cigars, and congratulated each other on a plan well conceived—and *executed*.

EPILOGUE

Paris, France, 2017

Kanzi smiled proudly as she helped her twelve-year-old son with his English lessons. Though small, the study in their flat where the two of them often worked was quite comfortable and had a cozy, warm feel. Books lined the shelves, and the hand-carved antique desk was large enough that they could both work online together at the same time. The boy's French and Malezi were perfect, and he was showing a remarkable knack for picking up the international language of commerce. Then again, she was not surprised, as all things seemed to come easily to her tall, lanky, handsome young boy. From time to time, when she gazed upon her son, her heart almost stopped. A spitting image of his father, her boy was but a couple of years younger than Mateyo when Kanzi first met him.

Out of the public eye, Kanzi and Mateyo Jr.—she called him "MJ" for short—had grown up together in a modest flat in the ever-fashionable and very international Latin Quarter of Paris. This truly multicultural section of Paris permitted the two of them to blend in with the general population unnoticed. Indeed, most of Kanzi's neighbors thought she must be the exotic mistress of a high-ranking politician or very wealthy businessman and, of course, that Mateyo was the fruit of that man's loins. No one had ever seen this man come or go, however, and so the speculation was that he had died and provided for the two of them in his will—not uncommon, or even remotely scandalous, in modern-day France.

Though there was some risk that Shigeku—former president and now king—might try to find them and eliminate the sole true heir to the Malezi throne, Shigeku did not share his dead brother Bala's fear of illegitimacy. Indeed, Shigeku knew that as long as he remained in control of the country's military and maintained a symbiotic relationship with the Church, he need not fear any opposition, either abroad or internal.

After working through his formal homework, MJ ran off to fetch the latest edition of the *Economist*, the truly global weekly tome on current events and right-wing economic rationale. Although in the earliest days of this ritual, MJ had balked at the relatively boring articles, Kanzi was very much inclined to expose him to economic principles and theory. She knew how much his father would have approved. Further, she believed the *Economist* to be the single best source of information on Africa generally, and Maleziland specifically. As such, she wanted to expose Mateyo to as much of the publication as possible.

Reading the *Economist* became an extension of MJ's English lesson that he truly enjoyed. The lad was obsessively interested in learning economic theory, and even more so in his homeland, Maleziland.

When he returned from the magazine stand on the street corner, MJ sat down and flipped quickly to the Africa section of the journal. His face lit up when he saw an article specifically on Maleziland. But Kanzi watched as his face suddenly fell, and her son looked as though he was gravely concerned. MJ shrieked in the soprano pitch of a lad who hadn't quite reached puberty.

"Maman! Maman! There might be civil war in Maleziland!"

"What's this?" said Kanzi, her interest immediately piqued. She took the magazine from his hands and read the headline: "A Civil War Looms?"

The boy was correct. According to the article, after twelve years of rule, and after successfully engineering Maleziland's break away from and reestablishment of hostile relationships with Zambwana, it looked as if Shigeku's reign was in peril. His military strongman, General Moto, had died ten days ago, his life quickly taken by a particularly aggressive form of cancer.

When Shigeku brutally massacred his brother and then-president Bala, he had done so with the strong arm of Moto at his side. Moto had been very much in tune with what was going on in the country and with the military, and the article theorized that President Shigeku would be quite lost without his combat friend. Shigeku's lack of understanding of such sophisticated matters did not weaken his reign while he was in control of the military but became quite important in the vacuum created by Moto's demise.

Kanzi saw the look of passion and determination in her son's eyes. It was a familiar look, and she had always known that someday her son's personality and conviction would bring the two of them back to Maleziland to fulfill Mateyo's destiny. She had no idea that day would come so soon.

"We must return to Maleziland, Maman. We must go *now*," said MJ with the strength of a man who could lead thousands and indeed millions of people. "And, Maman? We have to find Grand Mere!"

Kanzi sighed. MJ's obsession with Queen Carolanda was incessant. "MJ, I know it's important to you, and we will, of course, try to find her, but you have to know that we likely will not. It has been twelve years since the revolution, and they were very bad men who took over the country. We don't know what has become of her."

"Non, Maman. Grand Mere Carolanda is *alive*. I can feel her. I *will* find her," said the boy, putting his hands on his hips.

Kanzi gave a slight smile. "If anyone can find her, it is you, my son."

MJ grinned back at his mother, and the two began to pack their valises for the long journey home.

ABOUT THE AUTHOR

BRENT J. LUDWIG is a reformed lawyer who currently runs his own boutique headhunting firm in Calgary and Vancouver, Canada. Brent practiced mergers and acquisitions law in Toronto, Vancouver, and Calgary but did not let it stifle his love for storytelling and writing, first inspired while completing his undergraduate degree at St. Thomas University in Fredericton, New Brunswick. Growing up as a "mining brat" child, Brent moved with his family virtually every year to remote towns, nurturing his broad pan-Canadian outlook and an equally endearing and embarrassing small-town personality.

Brent currently lives in Calgary and spends his spare time cooking, drinking wine, and chasing soccer balls while coaching and shuttling three active children. He has a keen sense of interest in developing nations and trying to help as many people as possible by leveraging his writing and finance talents. Brent hopes that this book is the first of many.